Praise for the work

Full of Promise

This was a sweet young adult romance. This is a solid debut for Gavin with a very readable story. One of the mains is a lesbian where the other main is coming to terms with her bisexuality. This is a classic coming of age, coming out story, but with much more good feels than bad. I enjoyed the pace and feel of this book. Gavin's writing felt easy and smooth and didn't really have any of that choppiness that you sometimes find with new authors. If you are looking for a YA book that is a feel good romance, this would be a perfect pick.

-LezReview Books

Full of Promise was a very sweet young adult romance novel about discovering one's sexuality and the emotional turmoil involved…This was a very well written captivating read. I believe young adults will definitely embrace Cam's journey and hopefully realize that there are others like themselves who are also finding their way to their own true self.

Highly recommended!

-R. Swier, *NetGalley*

I have to say… I'm not normally a huge fan or reader of YA / NA novels, but this one really worked for me! Even better yet, it seems to be a debut novel for Gavin, so my hat's off to her!

This one was a very sweet YA read where our MCs Cam and Riley are both high school seniors. They meet when Riley moves to town and joins the soccer team that Cam and her best friend Claire are [illegible] th home life, taking on e[illegible] nger brothers while her r[illegible]. Riley is new to town, an[illegible] struggling to make frien[illegible] nds Riley, she begins to q[illegible] d realizes that she might not be as straight as she thought she was.

The relationship between Riley and her mom was beautiful, everyone deserves a mom like this, especially questioning LGBT teens. It was refreshing to see this POV. Best friend Claire's reaction was a bit over the top, but provided a bit of needed angst to the novel.

All in all, I enjoyed this one and was never tempted to skim ahead, which is my norm in a YA novel. It's a well written, low angst read, and I appreciated that Gavin didn't make the younger characters quite so… young. They were intelligent and had level heads instead of being over the top dramatic.

I really enjoyed this one, and think that many others will also. Recommended! I'm looking forward to Gavin's next novel! Solid 4 stars.

-Bethany K., *NetGalley*

We meet Cam at her summer job in the library, rolling her cart past the cute girl she's been sneaking peeks at and who she's been exchanging small smiles with. The hitch is that Cam has a boyfriend and is straight. Later, she meets this new girl, Riley, at school and gradually forms a friendship that has an underlying tension of something more, eventually building into an actual romance.

Full of Promise is a sweet story, smooth reading with all the heart tugs you'd expect from two young women falling in love. But rather than being a straight to gay tale, it was more about Cam recognizing and giving light to another part of herself. There were some emotional bumps but nothing harsh like other coming out books. Good, solid YA story.

-Jules P., *NetGalley*

TABLE *for* TWO

Other Bella Books by Kate Gavin

Full of Promise

About the Author

Kate Gavin is a native Midwesterner, currently living in Ohio. When not staring at a computer screen for her day job or this writing gig, she spends her time retrieving items from her thieving dog, playing video games, and bingeing TV shows with her wife.

TABLE *for* TWO

KATE GAVIN

2021

Bella Books, Inc.
P.O. Box 10543
Tallahassee, FL 32302

Printed in the United States of America on acid-free paper.

First Bella Books Edition 2021

Editor: Ann Roberts
Cover Designer: Kayla Mancuso

ISBN: 978-1-64247-187-8

Acknowledgments

First, I need to thank all of the folks at Bella, especially Jessica and Linda, for all of your support. You have given me the opportunity to tell the stories that float around in my head and I am forever grateful.

Ann – you have made the editing process even easier this time and I thank you for your patience and kind words.

Tagan – you have been the biggest cheerleader for this story and I can't thank you enough for that. You are truly one of a kind, my friend.

Em – I am thankful every day for your friendship and your guidance in all things writing. You challenged me with this one and it's a better book because of it. Thank you.

Dad Jobs – you are the best writing group a girl could ask for and I'm so thankful I get to be a part of it.

Andy – I still remember the morning I woke up next to you and told you about a dream I had where two women were forced to share the last table in a restaurant. We immediately began plotting and you told me to write it. So here it is. I could never have done any of this without your love and support. I am so lucky I can now call you my wife. I love you.

CHAPTER ONE

Soft lips trailed down Reagan Murphy's neck, and she tilted her head to give the other woman better access. Teeth scraped along her collarbone and the woman's hair fell forward and covered her face. She moved down Reagan's body, inch by agonizing inch. Reagan squirmed, desperate for her to pick up the pace and reach her obvious destination.

Her nails scratched underneath the waistband of Reagan's boxers, teasing her for a moment before sliding the boxers off and tossing them to the floor. Goose bumps erupted on Reagan's exposed skin. The woman's warm breath met the wetness of Reagan's center as she pushed her legs apart.

"Oh, f—"

A crash jerked her awake. Clutching her hand to her chest, she looked around for the sound that had pulled her from her dream. Her gaze landed on her father as he pushed the button on the remote to raise his bed, reaching out to clean up the glass of water he'd knocked over.

Reagan stood and rushed over to help. "Let me get that, Pops." She grabbed a hand towel from the hall bathroom and wiped up the water.

"Fuck. Give it to me," he said as held out his hand. "I'll do it."

"It's okay. I've got it."

"Reagan."

"All done. Nothing to worry about."

His drugs for pain management often made him clumsy, and accidents like these became more frequent with each passing day. Every incident reminded her that good days with him were numbered.

"Shit, I'm sorry. You shouldn't have to do that." His cheeks reddened and he avoided her gaze.

"It's fine. No worries." While he had wanted to live his last days at home, he'd struggled with accepting help from his only child. He had practically thrown a fit when she'd handed over most of her responsibilities at work to Gwen, her best friend and business partner, in order to move home and help her mom with his care.

Once she wiped up the last of the water, she tossed the towel on the bathroom counter, refilled his glass, and sat on the side of the bed, holding his hand. "How'd you sleep?"

"Meh. Better than the night before."

"That's good."

He raised one eyebrow and asked, "What about you? I've been up for a few minutes and it looked like you were having a nightmare. You were squirming around and making little noises."

Heat rushed to her cheeks. "Oh, um, it was nothing. Just a dream."

He chuckled. "By the look on your face, I'm guessing those little noises were from something a little more pleasurable than a nightmare."

"Dad, please stop talking." She covered her face with her hands.

"Never gonna happen." He squeezed her knee and she looked up. "So, tell me. When is the last time you went on a date?" he asked as he narrowed his eyes at her.

"Recently."

"How recent?"

"Um."

"Please don't tell me it was with that horrible Diane."

"I plead the fifth."

"Come on, sweetie. You two broke up, what, nine months ago?"

"Something like that," she mumbled, knowing it'd been over a year.

His face softened, and he looked into her eyes for a beat. "I'm worried about you, Reagan. I just want to see you happy. You need to live your life and not get bogged down with…" He lifted his arms, gesturing to all the medical equipment surrounding them in the spare bedroom, "…this."

The diagnosis of pancreatic cancer six months prior had come as a shock to the family, and while Reagan and her mom had fallen into worry, her dad had reacted the same as he had to any unexpected news in his life: with calm acceptance. He was her hero, and she wanted to spend as much time with him as she could—what little he had left anyway.

"I know. I will when—" She stopped and stared at him with wide eyes and the prick of tears forming.

"When I'm gone?"

"I'm so sorry, Dad. That's not…I mean…"

He reached for her hand and squeezed. "You shouldn't wait til I'm gone, kiddo. You gotta live your life every day. Look at me. I'm proof that we don't always get as much time as we want."

"Dad, I…I…" She looked down at her hands in his as words vanished and tears ran down her cheeks. She'd miss his perfect combination of strength and softness when he held her. She could still remember how it felt when he scooped her up into his arms when she had fallen off her skateboard at six years old. He had brought her inside to her mom so she could look at the scrapes covering her hands and knees. He stood next to her, cradling her head against his chest as she sat on the counter while her mom cleaned the wounds. His whispers of reassurance kept her calm and made her feel safe.

"It's okay. I know." He bumped her chin with his fingers and raised her head. "Hey. Why do you think I wanted to be here with my two favorite women instead of some damn hospital? You and your mom are the best things that ever happened to me. Even when she nags me about leaving socks everywhere."

"I heard that!" her mom yelled as she walked down the hallway.

They chuckled and rolled their eyes.

"God. The ears on that woman," he whispered. "Honey, I want the same for you. I want you to enjoy your life, love your work, and find a woman you look forward to waking up next to each morning. Okay?"

"Okay," she replied as she wiped the remaining tears from her cheeks.

"Knock, knock."

She turned to see one of her father's nurses, Angela, standing in the doorway. Aside from the help Reagan and her mom provided, he also accepted a little help from two home nurses. Angela and Betty checked in a couple days a week, giving Reagan and her mom much-needed breaks.

"Time to get you moving a bit and then get you cleaned up, Conor," Angela said cheerily.

"Oh, yay. Drill sergeant number two is here," he said under his breath as he sat up a little straighter in bed.

Angela came into the room and dropped her bag of supplies on Reagan's chair. "Excuse me. Why am I number two? What does Betty have that I don't?"

"For one thing, age," he said. "She's probably thirty years older than you. And with age comes intimidation factor. She can look at me with those narrowed eyes and I'll do whatever she says. No offense. This whole 'hands on your hips and head cocked to the side' routine needs a little work."

Reagan swatted at his arm. "You're such a dork, Dad." She scooted off the bed and kissed his cheek. "Love you. I'll see you later."

"Love you too, kiddo."

As Reagan passed Angela, she squeezed her arm and whispered, "Good luck." Angela snorted in reply.

After a quick shower, Reagan found her mother packing up food to freeze. With the unpredictability of their current situation, her mom had taken to freezing meals they could easily pop in the oven. Reagan suspected it gave her mom a sense of control to have several months' worth of homemade dinners ready to go.

"Morning, Mom."

"Morning," her mom said with a smile. "Fell asleep in there again, didn't you?"

Reagan shrugged. "Guess so."

"You don't have to do that. He'll be fine on his own. We each have a monitor to listen at night. You should sleep in your own bed."

"Sure, Mom. You know you'd be in there if I wasn't. You can't say any different."

"Well."

"Uh-huh. Pot, kettle," she said, pointing to herself then her mom.

Her mom chuckled. "Okay. You got me there. Do you have any plans for the day?"

"Probably check in at the office for a few minutes. What about you?"

"After I finish cleaning up, I'm going to take a walk and then come back for a nice long bath and a nap."

"I can clean up. You shouldn't have to do that."

"It's okay. I'm almost done." Her mom took a deep breath before setting down the towel in her hand and leaning on her elbows on the counter as she looked at Reagan. "I heard what your father told you. He's right, honey. Your life shouldn't stop because of everything that's going on."

"But what if something happens when I'm not here? I need to be here for him. The doctor said he didn't know the timetable. I couldn't live with myself if I wasn't here when, well, when it happens."

"You are, and he knows that. Something could happen at any moment, and we can't sit around holding our breath until it does. It'll just wear us down, and we won't be any good to him if that happens. Angela will be here until four. Take your time today. Go grab a bite to eat or take a walk. You deserve it."

Reagan slid off the stool and gave her mom a hug. "I might just do that."

Reagan unlocked the door to her apartment. She scrunched her nose at the staleness in the air. Sunlight streamed through a gap in the curtains, highlighting floating flecks of dust. Since she had moved back with her parents, she'd intended to stop by her apartment once a week, but after doing the math in her head, she realized she hadn't been here for almost a month. She missed this place dearly, and everything that used to come with it—independence, freedom from the now constant fear of losing her dad. But when she thought about it like that, she felt selfish, a mixture of emotions she tried to never let herself fully feel because if she did, she knew they had the power to overwhelm her.

Her gaze traveled around the large, open floor plan. The tall windows, exposed brick walls, and gleaming hardwood floors were a comfort and a source of pride. Her loft apartment took up the top floors of the building she bought a year after she and Gwen opened up their first restaurant together. They had formed a restaurant group eight years ago, fulfilling the dream they'd had since high school. After major renovations and finding an artist to lease the first floor as a gallery, they had established their office on the second floor. While Gwen handled everything food related, Reagan controlled the money and logistics. Their partnership had worked so well they'd opened three restaurants, and counting.

She tossed a stack of mail on her kitchen counter and opened the curtains covering the floor-to-ceiling windows. The

August sun warmed her face, and she took in a deep breath, only to remember how stuffy it felt. She propped open the door to her small balcony, stepping outside to stare down at the busy streets of downtown Indianapolis. She used to spend a lot of her evenings on this balcony with her feet up on the railing and a beer in her hand while listening to the sounds of the city. She closed her eyes at the memory she felt so far removed from now. Letting out a sigh, she went inside and upstairs to her loft bedroom and opened the windows. With any luck, the breeze would provide some freshness to the neglected space.

After about twenty minutes of organizing and cleaning, the mustiness disappeared, so she closed all the windows and locked the door behind her. She made her way down a flight of stairs and into the office through the back door. Past the conference room was a small open area with three chairs and a desk where her assistant answered a call.

"Taylor Murphy Group. This is Beth. How can I help you?"

She watched as Beth listened to the caller and made notes on a pad of paper, doodling along the edges as the call continued. "Okay, Rob. I have you down to meet with Gwen next Tuesday at three. Have a good day," Beth said as she hung up the phone.

"What did our wonderful real estate agent want? How many times did he bring up his cats?"

Beth grabbed her chest as she let out a gasp. "Jesus, Reagan. Maybe announce yourself next time."

She leaned against Beth's desk. "Why should I do that? You totally wanted to scream, didn't you?"

Beth slapped her thigh. "No. Well, okay, maybe. What are you doing here? No offense. I miss seeing you but I didn't expect you in today. I would've made a fresh pot of coffee."

"No worries. The nurse stopped by and my mom pushed me out of the house so I could have some time to myself."

The joy in Beth's eyes dimmed. "How's he holding up?"

She shrugged. "Good days and bad. You know."

"I do," Beth whispered. Her mom had died when she was fifteen.

She provided a tremendous amount of support to Reagan, in addition to being an amazing employee. She often went above and beyond by dropping off cookies or movies she thought Reagan's dad might like.

Reagan nodded toward the phone. "What did Rob want?"

"He has a new building to show Gwen. Just off Mass Ave. He said it's a prime spot and won't be on the market for long."

She bit the corner of her lip and nodded. Once she had stepped away from work almost two months ago, she had promised Gwen her focus would be on her family and not the company. But when big decisions like space for a new restaurant came into play, it was hard to sit on the sidelines. She pulled out her phone and looked at her calendar. "You said Tuesday at three?" Beth nodded. "Shit. I'm looking after my dad that day. Mom has her monthly get together with her friends. I can't ask her to skip it. I'll, um, talk to Gwen about it later." She clenched her phone and sighed before straightening up and putting it in her back pocket.

Beth squeezed her hand. "It's okay. She understands. I'll be going with her. We can handle it."

"Oh, I know you can. I wasn't implying that." Reagan trusted her opinion, but she struggled with needing it. She wanted to be there to look at new properties, help Gwen with menus, or even check emails daily. It was tough not to have enough time or energy to help with her dad and contribute at work. Reagan sighed. "It's just hard."

"I get it."

She smiled. "I'll be in my office for a little while and then I'll just head out the back. Might go to Gale's for a bite to eat."

"Sounds like a good idea." Beth stood, giving her a hug. "Tell your folks hi. And let your dad know I'll have another batch of oatmeal raisin for him soon."

"Thanks. See ya."

She returned to her office, sat at her desk, and looked at some invoices Beth had left in her tray. After checking their accounts online, she shut down her computer and headed for the door. Treating herself to a nice meal might be the thing she needed. Good food, a tall beer, and time just for her.

CHAPTER TWO

"You're fired."

"Excuse me?" The man's face drained of color and he sat with hunched shoulders, staring with glassy eyes. "But why?"

"Why do you think, Mr. Andrews?"

"I-I have no idea. I've worked my ass off for this company for eight years. And this is what I get?"

"And how many times in those eight years have you missed a deadline? Or taken sick days to go golfing with your buddies?" She didn't think his face could get even paler, but she was wrong. "Be careful what you put on social media, Mr. Andrews. Someone is always watching. Now, you have ten minutes to go back to your desk and pack your things. Security will escort you out."

He stormed out of the office muttering, "Bitch," loud enough for her to hear.

"How original," she said as she rubbed her face. Despite what people said, Jillian Jacobs hated firing people. Her boss passed this task on to her time and time again, which seemed to have given her a reputation around the company as a heartless bitch.

Jill shook her mouse, banging it on the desk to make it wake faster. As she scanned through the list of sixty new emails and flagged the most important ones, her assistant walked into her office. Jill held back a groan when she noticed them carrying several thick folders in their hands. "What is it, Ash?"

"Mr. Gibbons asked for you to meet him at eleven to talk about a new client. He wants you to look over the portfolio and business plan beforehand." Ash placed the folders on the desk in front of Jill.

"Eleven? That's in five minutes! Couldn't you have given these to me a little earlier?" Jill grabbed the first folder as she paced behind her desk, skimming the information.

Ash raised their hands. "His assistant dropped them off as soon as your meeting with Kevin started. I swear."

Jill stopped and looked at Ash. "Kevin?"

"Kevin Andrews? The guy you just let go?"

"Oh. Him. Fucking Harrison," Jill growled. "I need a cup of coffee." Jill watched as Ash adjusted their tie and flicked lint off the front of their pants. "Well? You're not moving."

"Oh, I'm sorry. Was that a request? Sounded more like a demand."

"Will you get me a cup of coffee?"

"You didn't say please."

"Please," Jill said through gritted teeth.

"Now, was that so hard?" Ash turned and walked out.

The amount of snark she tolerated from her assistant in private would surprise most people. But after five years of working together, Jill supposed Ash had earned a little latitude. She accepted it from them as long as it came with perfection in their work.

Jill opened a small closet and inspected herself in the mirror hanging on the inside of the door. She fixed a few stray hairs that had escaped her tight bun before hurrying out of the office. She reached for the cup of coffee in Ash's hands, but they pulled their hand away and raised an eyebrow.

"Thank you, Ash," Jill mumbled, ignoring the smirk on their face.

Jill needed all the coffee she could handle to deal with her boss, Harrison Gibbons, the vice president of marketing. After working as the director for five years, she longed for the day he would step down. Though his prowess had helped make their company the top advertising agency in Indianapolis, he came across as a person who hadn't worked very hard to get to his position. Most of his days were spent at the country club or taking long client lunches. She didn't envy that; it annoyed her. If working hard meant doing the dirty work that her boss didn't want to do, such as firing people, she would do whatever she could to advance her career.

Jill knocked on Harrison's open door and walked in the room.

"Jillian! I see you got the files. Sorry for the late notice, but I just wrapped up the deal with them last night at dinner. They didn't send all of this over until late morning."

"It's fine." Jill held back a sigh. She added yet another mental tally mark counting the times he had given her a last-minute assignment. *Dick*.

"Well, sit, sit. We have lots to go over."

Over the next hour, they discussed the client's portfolio, their vision for their partnership, and the dynamics Harrison had observed since he'd begun contact with them. While Jill loathed many aspects of his management style and personality, he knew advertising without question. They collaborated on the best approach for their campaign, and Jill made notes to schedule internal meetings with members from their design, finance, and production departments.

Jill gathered her notes. "I think I have what I need to get this rolling."

"Excellent," Harrison replied, shifting his attention to his phone. "We'll be presenting our full proposal to them on Monday."

Jill's stomach dropped. *He can't fucking be serious*. "But it's Thursday." She felt a headache coming on as she thought of all the work her team would have to do and how little he would contribute. "These take a full week to prepare. You want to have all of this put together by Monday?"

"I do. It's what I promised them." He shut his laptop and placed it in his bag before putting on his suit jacket. "But you'll get it done. You always do." He walked past her without looking at her.

She stood in the vacant office for several seconds fighting the urge to throw the folders at his retreating form. *Classic Harrison.* As she stepped out of his office and closed the door a little harder than necessary, her stomach grumbled. She looked at her watch to see it was almost two. Thinking back to the last time she ate, she realized she hadn't eaten anything since lunch yesterday. Unless two glasses of wine last night and three cups of coffee that morning counted.

She went back to her office and dropped the files on her desk before letting Ash know she was headed to lunch.

"Good luck," she heard as she walked away.

Why do I need luck?

As soon as she stepped out of the building, she understood. The streets of downtown Indianapolis were much busier than a typical weekday. Looking at the banners on all the street lamps, she saw advertisements for a large gaming convention.

"Fucking perfect." She straightened her shoulders, bracing herself for the crowds. She needed food, and she needed it now.

Reagan walked a few blocks to Gale's Tavern, her favorite spot when she needed to relax and enjoy herself. It helped that her good friend, Damien, owned it. She took in the variety of people walking the streets—old, young, in cosplay and not. Downtown held many conventions each year which always meant good people watching, and it always meant good business for her restaurants.

As she entered Gale's Tavern, a young woman at the host stand with the name Amy embroidered on her shirt greeted her. "Hi. Welcome to Gale's Tavern. Just one?" She smiled but the slight droop in her eyelids and fly-away hairs from her ponytail signaled she'd probably seen more customers today than she would've liked.

Reagan looked past her into the crowded dining room, wondering if going out for lunch was such a good idea. "Yes, please."

"We have one table left. It's a bit in the back near the kitchen, if that's okay?"

"Sounds perf—"

A slightly raspy voice from behind Reagan interrupted her. "Table for one."

Reagan turned and faced a woman with her hair pulled back into a tight bun, pursed and red painted lips, and designer clothes. They were the same height but only because the other woman wore four-inch heels. Reagan's first impression of her was that she was a woman who got what she wanted. The rasp in her voice alone made Reagan's stomach clench. Add in the sexy and serious look she had and that feeling increased tenfold. Too bad her demeanor screamed "stay away."

Reagan broke away from her gawking when Amy said, "I'm sorry, ma'am. We don't have any tables left. I can put you on the list, but a table won't be available for at least thirty to forty-five minutes."

"You're fucking kidding me," she mumbled as she pinched the bridge of her nose. "How are there no tables left? It's not even the lunch rush anymore."

"Well, there's a b-big convention in town and—"

"I know that. I'm not an idiot."

"Of course not, ma'am," Amy said, her eyes widening.

Reagan felt the frustration coming off the woman in droves. She'd dealt with customers like this often, especially when she and Gwen had opened their first restaurant, The Silo. She had to help run the front of the house often rather than staying in the office. Mitigating tense situations came easily because she genuinely liked people and wanted to see them happy. When they weren't happy, they tended to vent their frustrations publicly, whether that was a rant on Facebook or a bad review on Yelp. Knowing this was her friend's livelihood and deepest love, she stepped in.

"Excuse me?"

"What?" The woman turned toward her, eyes narrowing as her hands moved to her hips.

"I'm sorry. I was about to be seated at the last table. Would you like to share?" The woman opened her mouth, most likely about to protest, but Reagan continued. "I promise I won't bother you. Look at it out there. Downtown is packed. You're already eating late, so I'm guessing you're a busy woman. I bet you don't want to go try your luck again anywhere else."

The woman hesitated. Her eyes darted out the door and then back to the crowded dining room before settling on Reagan again. The furrowed brow softened, and the corner of her mouth quirked. Letting out a loud sigh, she turned to Amy and said, "That'll be fine."

The stiffness in Amy's shoulders released as she picked up two menus. "Follow me."

Reagan gestured for the woman to go first. She did it to be polite, but now that she was behind her she took the time to admire just how well this stranger wore her designer suit. Long legs, tight butt, and a jacket that strained a little at her athletic shoulders. She forced herself to focus on the woman's ugly attitude instead of her stunning looks, though it did little to cool her libido. Despite her earlier dream and the view in front of her at the moment making her a little turned on, this woman wasn't really her type. She typically went for women who seemed more laid back. Plus, with everything going on in her life, she just didn't have time for anyone.

Amy seated them and handed them their menus. "Your server will be right with you. Enjoy, ladies." She mouthed "thank you" to Reagan before heading back to the host station.

Reagan opened her menu before glancing up at the woman across from her, only to see her avert her gaze to her own menu. Knowing what she wanted to order, she set her menu aside in favor of conversation. "Hi, I'm Reagan." She reached her hand across the table. The woman hesitated before extending hers. Reagan took in the color of her eyes, brown with flecks of gold on the edges. Brief as the handshake was, Reagan couldn't ignore her soft skin and warmth of her touch.

"Jill."

"So," she dragged the word out, "what brings you to my lunch table?"

"Desperation," Jill muttered as she returned her gaze to her menu.

Reagan clutched her chest and gasped in mock outrage. "Ouch. You don't mince words, do you?"

"Not usually," Jill replied, looking up with a ghost of a smile.

She grinned. "Well, I hope you'll change your approach if you feel like commenting on my lunch. I really hope you don't hate people who eat meat. I don't want to order an amazing, juicy burger and then feel guilty eating it in front of you." She had gained a few extra pounds since moving back in with her parents while Jill looked as if she had never even been near a burger before.

Jill looked up, an eyebrow arched as if challenging Reagan. "Why would you think that?"

"Well, look at you. And then look at me. There's an obvious difference in our diets."

Jill's eyes swept up and down Reagan's torso. "You look just fine to me," she murmured and then cleared her throat. "I don't care what you order."

Reagan blushed and took in a quick breath. "Okay, decision made then. So, do you work around here?"

The woman rested the menu in her lap against the table. "Yes. I'm the director of marketing for—"

"Hey, Reagan!" their server interrupted. She'd known Trent since Damien had opened Gale's. "It's good to see you. Who do you have here? I didn't know you were dating anyone." Jill's eyebrows lifted at that last statement.

Jill spoke before Reagan had a chance to reply. "I'll have the garden salad with balsamic on the side and a glass of chardonnay."

Reagan narrowed her eyes at Jill, holding her gaze until Jill looked away. Focusing again on Trent, she said, "I'll have my usual burger and a pint of Wee Mac."

Trent nodded and then scurried away.

Reagan spread her napkin across her lap and sat back in her chair, frowning at Jill. "That was rude."

"No, it was rude and unprofessional of him to approach the table like he did. He should have introduced himself and told us the specials, if there are any in a place like this. Then he should have taken our order and rushed back to the kitchen. At least he got the rushing part right."

"I know him. He's a friend."

"Doesn't excuse anything." Jill took a sip of her water. "And what, may I ask, do you do?"

"I work in the restaurant industry."

"Ah."

"What 'ah'?" Reagan asked as she folded her arms.

"Nothing. It just would make sense that all you servers know each other."

The snobbishness dripped from Jill. Reagan opened her mouth to argue and defend her friend and her industry, but she couldn't find the strength. An oddity for her. She was proud of what she and all her friends in the industry did. *I'd like to see her work all day on a Sunday when the Colts were home*. Reagan rolled her eyes. "Little presumptuous, don't you think?"

"Maybe so, but I think it would just be better if we enjoyed our meals in silence."

"Fine by me."

Jill took out her phone and became mesmerized by whatever was on her screen.

Reagan sipped the beer Trent had placed on the table, contemplating the woman in front of her, who alternated between typing furiously on her phone and drinking her wine. Probably because of that morning's dream, Reagan's first thoughts about Jill had been sexual. Anyone could see that Jill was gorgeous, but, rudeness and conceit were the biggest turnoffs of all. *Pity*.

Trent returned with their meals and Reagan dug in. She enjoyed the silence from her lunch companion who focused more on her phone and her glass of wine than her meal. She had no desire to hear any more insulting comments from Jill, and

Reagan had gotten the impression that insults were Jill's forte. While Reagan spent her time eating and watching the bustle of the room, Jill looked at her several times, only to glance back at her phone when caught.

As Reagan finished her burger, Trent dropped off the bill in the middle of the table. "I'll take this whenever you're ready."

Jill snatched it before Reagan moved an inch.

"How much do I owe you?"

"It's nothing." Jill placed several bills in the book and stood up from the table.

Before she could reply, Jill was halfway across the restaurant. With an eye roll, Reagan settled into her seat to finish her beer in a more comfortable silence. *Glad I don't have to see her again.*

"Have a good lunch?"

Jill strode past Ash and into her office with no acknowledgment. She needed to forget about her awkward lunch, never mind the pleasing view across the table. Instead, she needed to focus on the pile of work waiting for her. Looking up from her phone, she came to a stop.

"Who the hell are you?" Jill found a woman sitting at her desk and doing god knows what with her computer.

"I'm C-Carly?"

"Is that a question?" Jill crossed her arms.

The woman cleared her throat. "No. I'm Carly. From IT. Just installing your new system."

"About damn time. I asked for a new computer months ago. What took so long?"

"I-I'm not sure. This is only my first day."

"That's just great." Jill pointed at Carly. "You better install everything correctly. I don't have time to deal with your incompetence. Ash, get in here."

Carly continued to do whatever nerdy thing she was doing while Jill plopped down in a chair at a small table on the other side of the office. Ash sat next to her, grabbing a pad of paper and a pen and making notes of everything Jill said. Meetings needed to be scheduled, research needed to be done, and proposals needed to be created. With every task she listed, the notion of getting to enjoy any part of her weekend faded away.

After an hour of conferring with Ash, Jill looked up to see that the woman from IT had left. Cathy? Carla? Whatever. Ash walked out of the office and Jill sat at her desk, silently thanking her for the new, speedy system. Maybe she'd be able to get things done sooner if she didn't have to fight with her computer.

By seven p.m., she began feeling good about the state of things. There was plenty to do, but it seemed a little less daunting. As she was packing up some papers to take home, her cell rang and she answered without looking at the screen.

"Jillian Jacobs."

"Jillian, it's your mother. Come to dinner tonight. Seven thirty sharp."

She held in a groan at the sound of her mother's voice. She had dinner with her mother and stepfather once a month and they rarely talked outside of that. *She must need something*. But learning what that was held zero appeal, especially with all the work she had to do. "Mother, I can't make it. I'm only leaving the office now."

"Early, isn't it? Anyway, I need to discuss something with you. Get here."

Before she could decline again, her mother had hung up. She sighed and rested her head in her hands. *Dinner with the folks. Joy*. Seemed all her meals were destined to be a disaster that day.

She raised her head to a knock at her door. "Need anything else, Ms. Jacobs?"

"No, Ash. I'm heading out now. My mother has demanded my presence at dinner." Ash's eyebrows lifted, but they remained silent. "I'll see you tomorrow at seven."

"Seven?"

Jill shoved papers in her bag and slung it over her shoulder. "Yes, seven. There's way too much to get done. Is that a problem, Ash? Do I need to find someone else to do the very basic task of showing up and doing their job?"

Ash straightened. "No. Seven sounds great."

Jill walked past Ash. "Lock up when you leave."

CHAPTER THREE

Driving through the gate of her parents' driveway always filled Jill with a sense of dread. Growing up, her parents pushed her to be the best, yet never praised her when she attained the top spot at a competition, test, or promotion. She had hoped things would have changed as she got older, but the chill she felt from her family only deepened.

Her mother's housekeeper answered the door within seconds of her knock. "Welcome, Ms. Jacobs. Your mother is waiting in the dining room."

Jill threw a stiff, "Thank you, Nadine," over her shoulder as she brushed past her and down the hallway into the dining room.

Her mother looked up from pouring herself three fingers of whiskey. "Jillian. Finally. I've been waiting forever."

"Mother, it's only ten til eight. I told you I was just leaving. As much as I wish I could, I can't magically appear somewhere when I snap my fingers."

"Enough of your attitude. Now sit." She looked over her shoulder at Nadine, who was waiting by the doorway to the kitchen. "Start serving." With a quick nod, she disappeared into the kitchen.

As Nadine returned and placed salads in front of them, Jill asked, "What's so important that I needed to be here tonight?" She took a brief look at the chair across from her mother. "Where's Douglas?"

"Your father—"

"Stepfather."

"Your father had to work late."

More like screw his new assistant, Jill thought.

"Plus, it's good that he's not here. What I need to discuss concerns him."

"Are you finally divorcing him?"

"Quiet! I don't know why you talk to me like that."

Jill suppressed an eye roll at her mother's denial of their marital issues.

"Now. As you know, he's turning sixty in November, and we're throwing him a party here at the house. I will take care of the guest list. You will work with the caterer."

"Me?" Jill almost choked on the sip of wine. "Why can't you do it?"

"I don't have time and because you're his daughter, you need to be involved."

"*Step*daughter. Make Ford do it. Where is he? Shouldn't he be helping as well?" While she had never been close with her younger half-brother, he'd always been a good deflection for her mother's judgment.

"Your brother is too busy. He just started his new job."

"And you don't think I'm busy? I actually work, and unlike him, I'm not on the golf course three days a week."

"Stop arguing. Networking is important. You *will* do this." Her mother stood and left the dining room. When she returned, she dropped a business card on the table next to Jill's plate. "You have a meeting there Tuesday at eight in the morning."

Jill didn't even bother looking at the card before snatching it up. She tossed her napkin on the table and stood. "I'm not hungry and I need to get home. Goodnight, Mother." She stormed out of the house and got in the car, tossing the business card into her work bag on the passenger seat. She drove home with a mixture of frustration and determination. If her mother wanted her to do most of the work, then at least it would get done right.

Entering her condo, Jill immediately went upstairs to her bedroom to change into thick socks, worn sweatpants, and a long-sleeve T-shirt to combat the chill of her air conditioner. She wiggled her toes as she poured herself a glass of pinot noir. Grabbing her bag, she collapsed on the couch and took a breath from her whirlwind day. She closed her eyes and took a sip of wine, feeling the day's stress drain away a little.

During moments like this, she typically ran through lists of things to do, but tonight her thoughts first drifted to her scramble for lunch and the woman who swooped in and saved the day. *And then I had to go and be myself, acting like an asshole.* Reagan was cute, with dark blond hair she'd pulled into a messy bun, a fair complexion with a hint of freckles across the bridge of her nose, and hazel eyes. Eyes that were kind but held a hint of something. Sadness? Exhaustion? Whatever it was, she hadn't let it affect the way she had interacted with Jill.

On the other hand, Jill had let the stress of her day tarnish any worthwhile conversation they could have had. Nothing new there, she thought. She'd had many first or second dates ruined because she could never fully let go once she left the office. Success was front and center in her mind and dating always seemed to get in the way. Dating also meant opening herself up to someone, and that was an even bigger struggle than letting go. Occasional loneliness prevailed when she compared it to showing emotions.

Before she could run through the entire list of her faults, she placed her glass on the coffee table and reached for her work bag. When she pulled out her laptop, the business card her mother had given her earlier fell onto the couch. The top corner had the initials TMG which stood for Taylor Murphy Group. The card was for Gwen Taylor, the co-owner and executive chef. She put a reminder in her phone for the meeting on Tuesday morning. Tossing the card back in the bag, she lifted her feet onto the coffee table and opened her laptop. It was time for a long night of work. And wine.

Reagan opened the door to the comforting scent of pot roast. After her late lunch, she thought she wouldn't be hungry for dinner, but her mother's cooking would make anyone's mouth water. Loud laughter came from her dad's room, and she set her wallet and keys on the counter before following the sound.

She found her dad out of bed, a rare sight these days, and sitting in the chair she or her mom normally occupied. Her mom sat in the chair opposite, smiling at him as they chatted and played rummy.

Reagan knocked on the door frame. "Need another?"

Her dad's eyes softened and he smiled. "Always. Grab a seat. Have a good lunch?"

She took the ottoman her mom wasn't using and slid in between the two chairs. "It sure was something. Deal me in and I'll tell you all about it."

Her mom shuffled the cards and dealt them out before settling in her seat and crossing one leg over the other. "What happened?"

As they played, Reagan recounted everything that had happened at lunch—the hostility, snide comments and eventual silence.

"Sounds like an ugly woman if you ask me," her mom said as she laid three sevens on the table.

"Not on the outside," Reagan mumbled.

"Excuse me?"

Reagan cleared her throat. "I mean, her personality and manners need a little work. Okay, a lot of work. But it wasn't a bad view from my side of the table, that's all I'm saying."

"Ahhh," her dad replied with a grin. "You liked her, didn't you?"

Reagan blushed. "I wouldn't go that far."

"Sure, dear," her mom said as she patted her knee. "Did you at least get her number?"

"Now why would I do that? Didn't you hear me say how horrible she was?"

"I did. Doesn't mean you couldn't have a night of fun." Her mom winked.

"What is with you two and trying to get me to hook up with people? First, Dad gave me the third degree this morning and now you. It's just wrong."

Her mom and dad looked at each other and laughed. "We want you to remember that you need to have fun."

"I do. I'm having fun right now. Well, except for this embarrassing interrogation."

"You need more than this. It wouldn't hurt to ask a woman out now and then."

"Geez, okay. I will. But not her. Got it?"

Both parents held their hands up and replied in unison, "Got it."

Reagan laid down a run and then her discard. "I'm out," she said with a smug smile.

"What? How'd that happen?" her dad asked.

"Guess you should pay a little more attention to the cards instead of my lack of a love life. Your deal, Pops."

He scoffed, saying something under his breath that sounded suspiciously like "cheater."

"What was that?" she asked, batting her eyelashes.

"Nothing. Just hand over the cards."

She laughed before stacking the cards and passing them to her dad.

"You two play. I'm gonna check on dinner," her mom said.

"Are you sure, Mom? I can do that." Reagan made a move to get up but her mother waved her back down.

"I'm sure. You two have fun."

Reagan watched as her dad tracked his wife the whole way, their deep love and connection evident in his eyes.

As she moved to take the seat her mom had just vacated, her dad said, "Take care of her."

She froze and then slowly sank into the chair. "Dad?"

He turned his tear-filled eyes. “When I’m gone, promise me you’ll take care of her. And you’ll take care of each other.”

“I promise,” her voice broke as she tried to hold back her own tears.

“And you need to tell her when you’re hurting, honey. She knows you try to bottle your emotions when you’re around her. She’s strong enough to deal with yours and hers. You need to make sure she doesn’t feel alone.”

“I don’t want her to have to worry about me. I can take care of myself.”

“I know you can, and I’m not questioning that. She’s your mother. She will always worry about you. Just because I’m dying doesn’t mean that stops. Let her worry about you.”

She looked toward the door as if she could see her mother through the walls. “Okay,” she whispered.

When she turned back, he was wiping the tears off his cheeks. Her father had never been shy about his emotions, which she’d been grateful for as she’d grown up. It had helped her feel as if having emotions was a normal part of life.

Before her dad could deal the cards, her mother yelled from the kitchen, “Dinner’s ready!”

“Think you’re able to make the trek to the dining room? Or do you want me to bring you a plate?”

Her dad raised an arm and flexed his bicep. “Are you saying I don’t look strong enough to make it?”

“Of course not. You look as strong as Thor.”

“You’re damn right I do,” he said with a wink.

“Goofball,” she replied before yelling, “Be right there!”

She helped her dad stand by grabbing onto his elbow and lifting as he pushed out of the chair. They shuffled to the kitchen, and Reagan looked up to find her mother smiling at them with the same look her father had earlier. Maybe one day she’d have someone look at her like that too.

CHAPTER FOUR

After a weekend filled with work, Jill, her team, and Harrison had presented their proposal to their new client, a sports drink company. Like always, Harrison had taken most of the credit when the client praised the work they'd seen. She'd had to smile and nod like it'd been the truth, only venting her frustrations when she was back in her office with Ash.

Now she sat waiting in the office of the Taylor Murphy Group when she should have been working. *Damn her mother for interrupting her life with this nonsense*. Not that it was surprising. Her mother liked to inconvenience herself the least, especially when it concerned her womanizing husband.

Jill was pulled from her musings by the sound of her name.

"Ms. Jacobs?" asked a woman with warm brown skin, short black hair buzzed on the sides, and a wide smile. She had the androgynous look nailed in vest, bow tie, and button-up shirt with the sleeves rolled up to her elbows.

"Jillian Jacobs," she replied, extending her hand for a firm shake.

"It's a pleasure to meet you. I'm Gwen Taylor, co-owner of TMG and executive chef at Wren. We'll head down the hall into the conference room so I can hear more about your ideas for this party. Birthday, right?"

Jill followed Gwen down the hall and into a room with a long table and about ten chairs around it. Several folders and papers were lined up in front of the chair at the end of the table closest to the door. "Yes, that's right. Sixtieth birthday party for my stepfather."

Gwen motioned for her to take the seat next to the one with the papers. "Great. Well, this will just be a preliminary meeting so you can tell me what you envision, and I'll tell you a little about how our process works. Any questions?"

"Yes. How available will you be to field questions should they arise? Are you one of those people that shuts their phone off at five or do you have enough decency to be available to your clients whenever they need you?"

Gwen's eyes widened before she schooled her features. "Well, I can't say I'll be available at all hours of the day. Like I mentioned earlier, I'm still the executive chef at Wren so there will be times when I can't answer. But if I can't take your call, I'll make sure to return it as soon as I can."

Jill held back a sigh. If her mother was going to spend an extravagant amount of money on this party, then Jill would make sure that everything was done right down to every last detail. It was unacceptable that the hired help would be unavailable at times, but that was a fight for a different day. "We can address that later. What can you tell me about menu options?"

Gwen's smile lit up her face and she jumped right in and went through all the options. Buffet, plated, or family style. Beef, chicken, fish, or vegetarian. As she droned on and on about side dishes and salads, Jill made a mental list of everything she'd need to do and how much input she'd still need from her mother. *Just what I want—more time with my mother.*

After going through every option, Jill realized Gwen really enjoyed talking about food and if she didn't stop her soon, she'd be there all day. When Gwen took a breath and reached for another folder, Jill interrupted her. "I need to get to work. Send me proposals for every combination you mentioned for a hundred and fifty people. Get them to me by the end of the week. I'll discuss everything with my mother so we can set up a tasting. You do provide complimentary tastings, correct?"

"Yes. But we should really talk over more options about linens and tables and chairs."

"Not now. I don't have time. This project was given to me only a few days ago. I'll have my assistant find time in my calendar and call you." Jill stood and slung her purse over her shoulder. She reached to shake Gwen's hand. "I expect to hear from you by the end of the week."

"You will. Have a nice day, Ms. Jacobs."

Jill murmured an acknowledgment and walked out of the conference room. Hearing Gwen release a sigh behind her, she smiled as she knew she'd given her a tight deadline that she probably wasn't used to. Would she make it or would Jill have to go on the hunt for a more capable caterer?

Reagan sat in her customary chair in her dad's room. She had kept him company by playing Yahtzee with him, but he had drifted off in the middle of their second game. She'd have to finish it with him later because she'd been doing well for once and had been hoping to break his ten-game winning streak. She stretched her legs out on the ottoman and opened a book she'd been meaning to read for over a year.

As she turned the page, she caught movement out of the corner of her eye. She looked up and found Gwen standing in the doorway, staring at her father with wide, wet eyes. Reagan glanced at him and tried to see him through Gwen's eyes. It had been a couple months since the last time she'd stopped by, and her dad had lost a considerable amount of weight since then. Probably didn't help that he hadn't wanted to shave much lately and was looking a little scraggly—a drastic change from the clean-cut look he used to sport.

Reagan closed her book and placed it on the ottoman. "Gwen?"

She snapped out of her trance and flinched. "Oh, hey." Her gaze drifted back to Reagan's dad for a moment. "Your mom said you'd be in here. How's he doing?" she whispered.

"He's okay. Tired all the time. We're just trying to control his pain. And no need to whisper. He's out." Reagan pointed to the other armchair next to her. "Have a seat. What brings you by?"

"I needed to talk to you for a few minutes about some things. Are you sure it's okay? I don't want to bother him. I can just call you about it later."

Reagan waved her off. "It's fine, I promise."

"Okay." Gwen took a deep breath and released it before reaching into the bag at her feet and pulling out a stack of papers that she placed on the small table between the two chairs. "I have two pressing things to talk to you about. Want the good news or semi-bad news first?"

"Let's go with good news. I could use some of that."

"Right." Gwen gave her a smile she had seen from a lot of people recently—understanding, pity, and love all rolled into one. "First, Beth and I met with Rob a little while ago and saw that building just off Mass Ave. He doesn't think it'll be on the market very long and told me that if we want it, we need to move on it quickly."

"What did you think of it?"

"Honestly, I loved it. Great location and I can really see potential in it. I brought over the comps for the area and took some pictures on my phone." She handed Reagan her phone and several papers that showed other commercial buildings which had recently sold in the area and their final sale prices.

Reagan scrolled through the pictures and liked what she saw. The wood floors were a little beat up, but they could be refinished to shine. She loved the open floor plan and tall front windows. It had a large back patio, and Reagan imagined it filled with customers enjoying their food and cocktails under some string lights on a warm summer evening.

"Think it's overpriced?"

"I don't think so. There's so much we could do with the space. I think it's worth it."

"Did you bring over our financials? I looked at them last week, but do you have the newest figures?"

"Yep, and I also talked to our contractor and got a very broad estimate for renovations." Gwen handed over another sheet of paper with a list of all their account balances and some hastily written numbers from their contractor.

Reagan scanned the numbers. "Let's do it."

"Just like that?"

"Yeah. Everything looks good. We've been looking for a place for almost a year now. I know we've been a little picky, but this seems like a great option for us."

"Don't want to see it first?"

Reagan shrugged. "I trust you. And I trust that little twinkle you've got in your eye. You're pretty jazzed about this place. I can tell. You're looking like you did when we finally found a spot for Over Easy."

"It's a great spot. I think we'll do well there."

"Then tell me where to sign," she said with a wink. "Did Rob write up an offer?"

"He did." She again reached into her bag for a new stack of papers. "He already marked every place we need to sign."

Reagan took the papers and began reading. Glancing briefly at Gwen, she said, "See, you never would've had him write up an offer if you had any doubts. Thanks for doing this."

Gwen smiled and they spent the next fifteen minutes reading through the papers and signing where necessary. Once done, Gwen put them back in her bag and fiddled with her pen.

"Get on with the bad news." She leaned her head back against the chair and turned so she could look at Gwen. "Or semi-bad news as you said."

"I've also taken a catering gig for us."

Reagan opened her mouth to protest, but Gwen raised her hand. "I know we said we'd stop doing them once we had three restaurants under our belt, but this was hard to pass up. It's a sixtieth birthday party for one of the best corporate lawyers in the city. His wife supposedly loves Wren, and when Beth talked to her, she said she'd pay any amount necessary for us. When Beth tried to tell her that we weren't in the catering business anymore, she threw out that she'd pay almost triple what we used to charge. I just couldn't say no, Reagan. We can get our name out there a little more, maybe schmooze the uppity people at the party and let them know about all our restaurants. This could be a big boost in business. Plus, it will give us a better financial footing for the new place."

Reagan sat up and rested her elbows on her knees, clasping her hands together. "Okay, so it's not an ideal situation with trying to get this fourth restaurant in motion, but I agree it could definitely help us in the long run. Why'd you say it's bad news then?"

Gwen cleared her throat and rubbed the back of her neck. "I think we should maybe broach the subject of temporarily hiring someone else to take the lead on it while you're still out. I also met with the daughter this morning and I can tell she'll be a handful. She basically asked if we'd be at her beck and call at all hours of the day if she had questions or demands." She rolled her eyes. "You could tell she had a huge stick up her ass and is probably not used to hearing the word 'no.'"

Reagan stared at her dad's pale face, watching him take each breath for several moments. "Who did you have in mind?" she whispered, her voice catching at the end.

"Myles."

Reagan sat up straight. "You've got to be kidding me."

Gwen held up her hands. "Look, I know you don't like him."

"That's an understatement."

"I know you have a history…"

"We don't have a history. He has a history with my ex before she was my ex."

"Yes, I know. It's not ideal, but I've heard he doesn't have anything going on right now."

"No? Too busy screwing other people's girlfriends to open his own restaurant? That's too bad."

"You've said yourself in the past that he knows how to get things done and manage people."

"He's a fucking asshole, Gwen." As her dad shifted in his bed, she winced. "I don't like him," she said quietly.

"I know that." Gwen's shoulders slumped and she stared at the floor. "I don't think I can do it all by myself. I hardly see Brett as it is aside from a quick breakfast every morning and my two nights off each week. I'm not blaming you at all. I know you need to be here for your dad and to help your mom. It's the best thing for your family. I just…I need a little help too."

"I'm sorry," she said. She turned her head, trying to breathe through the tightness in her chest.

Gwen reached for her hand and squeezed. "There is absolutely nothing to be sorry about. Your focus needs to be here. I haven't made up my mind on Myles, and I would never hire anyone without your full support. Just think about it, okay? If you have someone else in mind, let me know."

"Okay."

Gwen stood. "I should get going. Tell your dad I said hi when he wakes up." She leaned down and kissed her cheek.

"I will."

"We still meeting for drinks tomorrow night?"

"Yeah, that sounds great."

"Okay, see you then." She waved and left.

Reagan put her elbows on her knees again and held her head in her hands, her fingers clutching her hair every so often. She felt like she was being pulled in a thousand different directions. Knowing her best friend understood her current situation was one thing, accepting that understanding without feeling guilty was another.

"I can hear you thinking all the way over here."

Reagan snapped her head up, hastily wiping away the tears that had run down her cheeks. "Jesus, Dad. Did you really need to scare me like that?"

He chuckled. "Sorry." His eyes softened, and he waved her over. "She needs help, huh?"

"Shit. You heard all that? I thought you were out. We would've moved if I'd known otherwise."

"It's okay. I'm glad I heard what I did."

"What do you mean?"

"Because then I can tell you to go back to work."

"Dad, no. I'm not—"

He held up his hand. "Reagan, I appreciate you taking all this time off to help and to spend time with me, but I'm not the only one who needs you. And I'm not saying that to make you feel bad or to overwhelm you. It's just the truth. You going back to work doesn't mean you're abandoning me."

"But I need to be here for you and Mom. I can't just leave her to do all of this alone." She couldn't hold back the sob that bubbled from her throat, and her dad squeezed her knee.

"She's not alone. We still have Angela and Betty. So, we might have to ask them to come in more often. No big deal. I'm getting used to their drill sergeant tendencies. Don't tell your mother that. I don't want her getting any ideas."

She laughed and wiped her nose with the back of her hand.

"And maybe I'm being a little selfish in this request, but I want to see you thrive at work again before I go. One of the best things about being your dad is when you'd come over for dinner and update us on how the restaurants are doing. That smile would light up any room. I want to see that light again. Take on whatever Gwen needs you for."

"Are you sure?" Reagan asked, her bottom lip quivering.

"Positive. Now come here." He opened his arms wide and she fell into them without hesitation. She hugged and cried into his neck, taking care not to squeeze too hard and cause him any pain. The thought of how much she'd miss this when he was gone brought on a new round of tears. He squeezed her tighter, almost as if he knew this would be one of his last chances for a hug like this. She even felt tears seeping through her hair where his cheek rested on the crown of her head.

Once the tears ended, Reagan released the grip on her dad and sat back. He rubbed his hands together and a smile broke out across his face.

"Now, break out Yahtzee. I need to kick your ass again."

Reagan laughed and rolled her eyes. "Okay, Dad."

CHAPTER FIVE

Jill enjoyed getting shit done. The number of items on her to-do list had started at thirty-five in the morning, and now only contained seven tasks. Browsing the list, she picked the most pressing matter left and got to work. Thankfully, typing updates for her client and her team didn't require talking to anyone, which she'd done for most of the day. The silence felt superb.

Only a moment later, murmurs outside her open office door broke the silence, and Ash let out an uncharacteristically loud laugh. Jill grated her teeth at the interruption as her best friend, Samantha, sauntered into the room and claimed a chair in front of Jill's desk.

"Hey, stranger."

"Sure, have a seat, Samantha."

Sam grinned. "Don't mind if I do."

"What are you doing here?"

"Wow. Such a wonderful greeting. I'm great, thanks. How are you?"

Jill gestured to the papers strewn across her desk. "Busy. Now, what are you doing here?"

"I had a meeting with a client down the street and thought I'd stop by. And to tell you you're coming out with me tonight."

"No."

"Yes."

Jill pinched the bridge of her nose. "I'm sorry, but I can't. Look at all this. We just fully secured a new client and I'm neck deep in everything to get their campaign off the ground. I don't have time."

"You know what they say about all work and no play. So come on out and play. When's the last time you did? I'm sure there will be plenty of hotties at the bar. We can find you someone nice who might help get rid of your perpetual scowl."

"Since when do me and nice go together?"

"Fair point. But come on, it's been so long since we've let loose a bit. We're due."

"I get it, Sammy. But I can't tonight. Maybe another time."

Sam sighed, stood, and rested her hands on Jill's desk. "Stop letting work run your life."

"It's not running my life. I happen to like my job."

"You like succeeding at your job."

"Whatever," Jill mumbled.

"Instead of going out, just come over for a glass of wine on Friday. That better?"

"Sure," Jill replied, her focus on a schedule from her design department.

"Did you even hear what I asked?"

"Yes. Wine. Friday. I got it."

Sam sighed again. "See you then."

"Uh-huh." Sam left, and Jill heard another round of laughter coming from her assistant. Glaring at her doorway, her murderous thoughts were put on hold when her cell phone rang. "Jesus. What now?" She pressed the Accept button with a little more force than necessary. "Jillian Jacobs."

"Hi, Ms. Jacobs. This is Beth from the Taylor Murphy Group. I was calling to see if you'd be available for your next meeting on Monday at four."

Jill pulled up her calendar on her computer. She had a meeting at two that afternoon, but it should be over in plenty of time for her to get over to TMG's office. "Yes, that's fine."

"Great, thank you. Any questions?"

"No." Jill ended the call and tossed her phone on the stack of papers next to her. She pulled up her calendar and blocked off time for the meeting on Monday. She looked at her to-do list and then at her watch. Only six thirty. Plenty of time to knock out the rest of the list and reward herself with some takeout on her way home.

On Wednesday night, Reagan arrived at her friend Carly's house. She had gone to school with Carly and Gwen and they had been best friends ever since. Carly lived in an adorable blue house with a large front porch in the Fountain Square area.

After giving Carly a quick hug, Reagan toed off her shoes into the coat closet. "New glasses?" Reagan asked, pointing at the red, square frames. They went well with Carly's long, brown hair and bangs that hit just above the frames.

Carly nudged the glasses up. "Yep. Figured a new job meant new glasses," she said with a smile.

"Oh, shit. That's right. I'm so sorry I didn't check in with you more. You started last week, right?"

"Yeah, on Thursday."

The front door opened as Gwen walked into the house. "Hey!"

Carly clapped and headed to the fridge. "Yay, everyone's here. Now for the important question, who wants what? Standards?"

"Yep," Reagan and Gwen replied in unison.

Reagan nodded toward the living room and asked Gwen, "Can we chat for a second?"

"Sure. What's up?" Gwen asked, sitting on the arm of the couch.

Reagan took a deep breath. "I'll come back. I'll take the lead on planning that party."

Gwen quickly reached for Reagan's hand. "That's not what I was asking you to do at all. We can find somebody else. I know you don't want it to be Myles. I get that. We can go another route."

"That's not why I'm doing it. Okay, well maybe a little. He's just such a douche." She and Gwen chuckled. "My dad heard part of our conversation, the damn eavesdropper. He said he wanted to see me thrive one last time, so that's what I'll do." A small lump formed in her throat but she swallowed it down quickly. Shrugging, she continued, "Who knows. Maybe I'm just annoying him with all my hovering."

"Are you sure? I know how important it is for you to spend his…um…last days together."

"I'm sure. It's not like this will take up every waking hour of my day. I figured I'd come into the office two or three days a week. Kinda ease my way back into being involved in day-to-day things. Might make the transition a little easier when… Well, you know."

"If you're sure."

"I just said that I am. Are you constantly going to ask me once I officially get back to the office?"

"Of course. That's what friends are for." She pulled Reagan in for a hug.

"Thanks, Gwen."

"I should be thanking you. The next meeting is on the twelfth. I'll send you the details tomorrow."

"Why is there hugging?" Carly asked as she brought out a tray filled with their drinks and a plate of cheese and crackers.

Reagan pulled out of the hug and put her hands in her back pockets. "I'm easing back in to work a bit because of a catering client. Take some of the pressure off Gwen. And before you ask, yes I'm sure that this is what I want."

Carly handed Reagan a beer and Gwen a glass of wine then held up her gin and tonic. "Cheers to that."

Gwen and Carly sat on the couch while Reagan took the armchair. They were creatures of habit—same food, same seats, and same drinks. Reagan snagged a couple cheddar cubes and popped them in her mouth, washing them down with a swig of Upland Wheat Ale. "Now, Carly had started telling me about her new job when you got here. Time for more details. Where's it at again?"

"Touchpoint Media. It's an advertising agency. I'm one of three people in their IT department."

"Do you like the other two so far?" Gwen asked.

Carly shrugged. "Seem like nice guys so far. A bit quiet."

"You'll fit right in there," Reagan said with a wink.

Carly laughed. "Yeah, that's true. Oh! I never told you about my first run-in with the Ogre." She pulled her legs onto the couch and sat cross-legged, holding her glass in her lap.

"The what? Who's he?" Reagan asked.

"*She* is some head honcho in the marketing department."

"Is she ugly or something?" Gwen asked as she took a sip of her wine.

"Definitely not. She's got that prim-and-proper hotness, and she totally knows how to fill out a suit. But she seems a little intense. She came back after a late lunch on my first day while I was setting up her new computer. And let me tell you, she intimidated me so much I thought I was gonna pee my pants."

Reagan snorted. "What'd she do?"

"She didn't really do anything. Just stood there with her arms crossed, narrowed her eyes at me, and told me not to mess up. Then she barked at her assistant."

"Well, did you mess up?" Reagan asked, hiding her grin as she drank her beer.

Carly looked at her with wide eyes. "Of course not. What do you take me for?"

Reagan held up her hands. "I'm kidding, my friend. It's so easy to rile you up."

"Jerk," Carly muttered. "Just thinking about her scares me, though." She shuddered. "Thankfully, I shouldn't have much interaction with her."

"Cheers to that too," Reagan said as she held up her glass.

Gwen and Carly raised theirs in response. They spent the rest of the night catching each other up on the little things that had happened since their last get-together. Reagan sat back, listening to her friends and sipping her beer. She had missed this.

* * *

"Wow. You actually came," Sam said as she ushered Jill into her condo. Sam's place fit her well. It was modern, sleek, and ridiculously expensive, everything Sam was on the outside.

"I said I would. And you never specified a time so I came as soon as I finished up with work."

"You only just finished?" Sam asked as she walked into her kitchen, grabbing wineglasses from a corner cabinet. "Come on, Jill. It's eight thirty on a Friday night. Please don't tell me you kept anyone else with you that late."

Jill shed her suit jacket and draped it over the back of a barstool before claiming the one beside it. She accepted the glass of wine Sam had poured, taking a sip and savoring it. "I'm not that heartless. I let Ash leave at seven."

"Oh, how generous of you," Sam replied with a pointed stare. "Let's head over to the couch. I feel like I've been on my feet all day going from meeting to meeting."

Jill tucked herself into a corner of the couch. She slipped her heels off and pulled her knees to her chest. She took another sip of wine and closed her eyes. Even though she initially fought Sam on hanging out tonight, it was nice to relax with a friend.

Sam sat on the opposite end of the couch, extending her legs and crossing them at the ankle. "So, tell me what's been going on."

"Well, aside from all the bullshit at work, my mother decided to have a sixtieth birthday party for dear ol' Douglas. Get this, I get to do most of the planning."

"You're shitting me. Why you?"

"Because it's my mother. She wants to look like the dutiful wife and show off how much money she can blow on a party but not put in any of the actual work." Jill raised the glass of wine to her lips, but stopped just short of taking a sip. "That's not entirely true. She is making the guest list," she added with a scoff.

"Oh, goody. The same hundred rich assholes she has at every party."

"I'm sure your parents will make the list."

"Exactly my point."

Jill chuckled. "I'm sure you'll be on it too. Unless you want me to cross off your name when I make the dreaded seating charts."

"Oh, hell no. A night of free alcohol, people watching, and amazing food. I wouldn't miss it." Sam took a sip of wine before locking eyes with Jill. "Wait. There will be amazing food, right? The catering company she hired for Ford's last birthday was awful."

"Ugh. My stomach turns just thinking about that night. And yes. I think she's picked a better one this time. The Taylor Murphy Group? I met with the owner who is also the executive chef at Wren. Don't think I've ever been there."

"Yes, you have."

"When?"

"When I set you up with that woman from my office." Sam snapped her fingers several times before pointing at Jill. "Kirsten."

Jill pulled at the hair ties that held her bun in place, shaking her head as her hair fell to her shoulders. She ran a hand through the dark brown strands and groaned. "Oh, her. Another night I'd rather forget. Why did you ever think we would be a good match? She was barely out of college."

"So? She's hot. You aren't much for relationships so I figured you'd be fine with any gorgeous woman in your bed for a night or two."

"I have standards you know. And those don't include someone who spends their entire meal, an expensive one at that, on their phone. Sometimes I want a conversation with someone."

"Since when?"

"I have grown up a bit since college, you know."

"That's a pity. Those were some fun days, weren't they?" Sam tilted her head to the side, staring off to Jill's right, no doubt remembering the nights they spent partying and hooking up with whatever woman, or person in Jill's case, they deemed worthy. Jill hadn't had as many flings as Sam had, then or now.

She'd find someone when her hand tired of providing relief, but more often than not, she concentrated her focus on work instead of finding a quickie.

"Speaking of those days," Sam continued, "we need to go out soon. It's been too long, Jill. Don't get me wrong, I still enjoy spending time with you on a night in, but let's hit the bars."

"You just want to find someone new to hook up with. You don't need me along for that. Half the time you end up ditching me anyway."

"I won't next time. I'll put my charms into finding someone for you instead. What do you say?"

"I say I'll pass because I'm too busy."

"I will drag your ass out of that fucking office one of these days."

"Go ahead and try. Maybe I'll tell Ash never to let you in my office again."

Sam grinned. "Well, I like a challenge."

"Then tell me, who have been your challenges lately?"

Sam immediately dove into a story about a woman she'd met at a dinner party thrown by one of her coworkers. Supposedly they had spent all night flirting before sneaking outside and hooking up against the side of the house.

While Jill sometimes missed the spontaneity and overindulgence of that lifestyle, she had to admit it had left her feeling unfulfilled. A recurring thought also worried her—maybe she would end up just like her stepfather and spend her life working and having occasional meaningless or inappropriate sex. That life didn't appeal to her either and she certainly wanted to avoid being compared to him. Maybe one day she would look for someone to give her more, but today was definitely not that day.

CHAPTER SIX

Reagan stood in front of the floor-length mirror in her childhood bedroom. Her parents had taken down the movie posters and trophies that had lined the walls and shelves since high school and repainted the walls a light gray. Being in this room felt like home, someplace safe and comforting, a place to stay and be with two of her favorite people in the world. But it had held a different tone over the past couple months since she'd moved home, one of sadness, uncertainty, and finality.

Right now, though, the room held a tone of the future, of what life would be after her dad was gone. She looked at her reflection in the mirror, noting the circles under her eyes and the few pounds she had gained. The khaki chinos and the navy blazer fit, but she didn't dare button the blazer. Instead, she left it open, showing off her white button-up with navy polka dots. She only had one or two work-appropriate outfits with her, and she made a mental note to stop by her own place later in the week to grab a few more now that she'd be working several days a week.

She looked at herself one last time before going to the kitchen where her mom drank her coffee and read the paper. Reagan grabbed her keys off the counter and fiddled with them. "You sure it's okay I go, Mom?"

Her mom set down the paper and took off her glasses. "For the hundredth time, yes, sweetheart. Everything will be fine, and I'll call you if I need you."

Reagan let out a shaky breath and kissed her mom on the cheek. "Have a good day." She peeked into her dad's room quickly to see he was sleeping peacefully. With a final glance, she left.

Once at the office, she familiarized herself with the client's profile and lugged several boxes from their small storage room into the corner of the conference room. The table fit ten people, so she set the eight color options for linens on one side and the five styles of plates on the other. Before she could create any combinations, she needed to ask the client additional questions to get a better feel for the theme, if the client had one in mind.

Just as she glanced at her watch, she heard a knock on the door frame.

"Ms. Jacobs is here, Reagan. You ready?" Beth asked.

Reagan took a deep breath and looked around the room. Was she? Only one way to find out. "Yeah. Bring her on back, Beth."

With a quick smile, Beth turned down the hall. A moment later the client entered. It was *her*. *Oh, shit, it's the rude woman I had the hots for*. She really hoped her first impression would be wrong. Not about the hot part. She noticed that impression still held up as her eyes wandered down and then back up her body. "Jill."

Jill stuttered to a stop, her jaw clenched and nostrils flared. "It's you."

"Yeah, it's me." *Christ. Does she always have to look this good?* She wore skinny, black dress pants and a sleeveless, cream shell, showing off incredibly toned arms. Reagan shook her head of any wayward thoughts and walked around the table with her hand outstretched. "It's nice to see you again, Jill."

Jill shook her hand quickly before crossing her arms. "It's Jillian."

Reagan faltered briefly. "Oh, I'm sorry. In case you don't remember, I'm Reagan. Reagan Murphy."

"Murphy. As in Taylor Murphy Group? That's you?"

"Yes."

"This is unbelievable," Jillian mumbled under her breath.

"Excuse me?" When she had met Jillian at the restaurant, she had simply chalked up her bad attitude to her just having a bad day. Seeing her reaction now, Reagan understood this was who she was. God help me, she thought.

"Nothing." Jillian looked Reagan up and down. If she hadn't known any better, Reagan would have thought she was checking her out, but she knew she was really sizing her up.

Reagan held her gaze for a beat before relaxing her arms and gesturing to the table. "Shall we get started?"

"Yes. But please be quick about it. I'd like to get back to work soon."

As Jillian sat, Reagan took the seat next to her, pulling a couple of pages from her folder. "I spent my morning going over all the paperwork that Gwen left regarding the party for your father."

"*Step*father," Jillian gritted out, her hand clenched in a fist on the table.

"My apologies. Your stepfather." *That seems to be a touchy subject*. Reagan wouldn't make that mistake again. No wonder she didn't seem to want to be here. Why would she be the one planning a party for someone she clearly didn't like? Reagan took in a breath to calm the thoughts that were running away from her. "I'd like to go over some of it again to make sure I'm clear on all your initial requirements. Sound good?"

Jillian let out a small sigh. "Let's get on with it."

Reagan suppressed an eye roll. She was understanding what Gwen had meant about Jillian being a difficult client. Reagan went line by line through the initial paperwork, clarifying the location, day, and estimated guest count for the party.

"Now let's get to the details and I'll show you some options for the linens and plates. Do you or your mother have any theme in mind?"

"Money," Jillian muttered.

Reagan furrowed her brow and tilted her head. "Excuse me?"

Jillian cleared her throat and leaned forward with her forearms on the table. "She'll want everything to be the best. So show me the best."

"Right," Reagan drew the word out. "Does she prefer modern or a more classic look?"

"Classic."

"Okay. Colors—bright, pastel, rustic, dark?"

"Definitely not bright or pastel. Maybe navy or maroon."

"Okay. Again, going classic. No problem there. What about plates? Do you want ones with designs? Or plain?"

"No plain. That would be too simple. But too much of a design would look gaudy."

"Understood." Reagan sat back, glancing over the notes she had just made while holding her chin in her hand. After a quick moment, she stacked up her papers and set them to the side. "Okay. I think I've got a good idea. I'll set up some options on the other end of the table. It'll be a few minutes, so would you like me to get you something to drink? Coffee or water?"

"No, I'm fine," she replied before taking out her phone and giving all her attention to it.

Guess that's my cue to start. She moved around the table looking at plates first. She quickly nixed the solid white and floral options. Then she went to the other side and tossed any bright or pastel linens back in their box.

She opened a box from the corner and went about setting up place settings in front of empty chairs. Within a few minutes, she had set out three sample combinations of tablecloths, napkins, and china and silverware settings. She placed her hands on the table and leaned forward, reviewing her choices. She looked up to find Jillian staring at her. Well, not at *her* exactly, but at her chest. She glanced down and saw she was showing off a bit of cleavage with the top two buttons undone. Heat shot up her cheeks, and she stood up, clearing her throat to get Jillian's attention.

"I, um, I think these are our best choices after narrowing down everything from your mother's preferences. All are classic with just a hint of modern and colors that aren't too flashy. They're bold, but just the right amount. What do you think?"

Reagan's question snapped Jill out of a trance she hadn't realized she'd been in. Either Reagan had sped through setting up the options or Jill had gotten lost in her perusal of Reagan's body. Judging by Reagan's blush, she was pretty sure Reagan had caught her staring at her breasts.

"Are these not okay? Or do you want me to find something else?"

"No," Jill replied, a tad louder and more high-pitched than she wanted. "Sorry. No. These are great. I have a feeling my mother will want this navy combo with the gold-rimmed plates, but I'll take some pictures and show her the next time I'm summoned for dinner."

"Summoned, huh?" Reagan asked with a soft chuckle. "Does she vanquish all humor and joy when she enters the room, too?"

Jill snorted. "So you've met her?"

"Actually, no. She's only been in contact with Beth and Gwen."

"I was kidding," Jill replied with a grin.

"Right." A cute blush blossomed on her cheeks. She looked up with wide eyes. "Oh, shit! I am so sorry. That was rude of me to say. I'm sure your mother is a lovely woman."

"No, she's not. You got her exactly right."

Reagan's horrified look softened to one of empathy. "I'm sorry," she whispered.

Jill gave her a half smile. "Thanks."

Reagan returned the smile and Jill's breath hitched as she stared at Reagan's lips. After a second, she shook her head and straightened. "I'm going to take some pictures and then I should get back to work."

"Oh, um, sure. Take as many as you'd like."

Jill went around the table and took a picture of each of the three samples. She took a minute to study them all one more time. "Show me more. My mother is the pickiest woman on the planet, and I know she'll demand to see more."

Reagan walked around the table, stopping a couple feet in front of her. "I have to disagree. I've been at this a long time, Ms. Jacobs. The more choices people have, the more difficult it is to make that choice. If by some chance you show her these and she's still not satisfied, then we can discuss more options. But after chatting with you today and reading the profile your mother filled out, I'm confident that I've given you at least one option she will love."

Jill crossed her arms. "How can you be so sure?"

"Like I said, this is my job and I know what I'm doing. Trust me."

"Hmm. I trust no one."

"Well, I think by the end of all this, you'll have at least a little trust in me."

"We'll see."

"Now, have you picked other vendors? Bartender, florist, music?"

"Contracts are in the process of being signed. My mother has several that she typically uses for parties."

"Makes sense. Are we the newbies on the list?" Reagan grinned.

"Yes, Ms. Murphy. The last caterer was a disaster, so the pressure's on."

"Right. Well, we're ready. Would you be able to get me a list of the vendors? I like to have their contact information in case we need to coordinate on anything. Also, our pastry chef has almost finalized a few drawings for the cake, which I'll have for you soon. Would you prefer email or face-to-face? I can come to your office. Same time in two weeks?"

Another chance to see her. The thought popped in Jill's head before she had a chance to stop it. She clenched her jaw at the unsettling reaction and replied, "Fine." Without looking back, she walked out the door.

As soon as she stepped out of the building, her shoulders dropped and she let out a sigh. It wasn't every day she got caught ogling another woman. She couldn't even think of the last time she'd done anything like that. What was it about Reagan that drew her in so easily? It wasn't just her looks. Reagan was obviously beautiful, but it had to be more than that because that alone had never been enough to draw Jill to any person. Maybe it was her humor or her perceptiveness when Jill had told her she'd been right about her mother. Something captivated her, but she was having hard time identifying what it was.

As if her mother could read minds, her phone rang. "Hello, mother. I just met with the caterer." Figuring out Reagan's appeal would be a question for another day.

CHAPTER SEVEN

It had taken a couple of weeks, but Reagan had found a good balance between working and helping her mom at home. Working had the added benefit of giving her mom time alone with her dad. But as the days passed, her father began sleeping more and more so most of the time Reagan had spent with him was just sitting with him as he slept.

While Betty, today's nurse, attended to his needs, Reagan went into the kitchen for coffee.

"So, how does it feel to be back at work?" her mom asked.

Reagan released a slow breath. "Honestly? It's been great."

"Good," her mom said with a smile. "Are you still working on that catering gig or is that already finished?"

She groaned before taking a sip. "I wish it was over. Oh, crap. I didn't tell you, did I?"

"Tell me what?"

"Remember that lunch I had with that one woman a few weeks ago?"

"The one you had the hots for?"

"Oh, my word. Yes. Wait, no. I definitely did not have the hots for her." Her mother laughed loudly and Reagan threw up her hands, glaring. "Are you done?"

Her mom coughed and wiped at the corner of her eye. "For now."

"Okay, so I think she's attractive."

"Think?" her mom raised an eyebrow.

"Thought! That day. I *thought* she was attractive."

"Mm-hmm."

"God, you're impossible."

"So I've been told. But I promise to be good. Yes, I remember you mentioning the hot woman."

Reagan glared again. "*Anyway*. She's the catering gig. Well, her mother is really the client. Or her husband. It's for his birthday."

"Wait. The mom's husband or the daughter's?"

"The mom's husband. Daughter's stepfather, I guess," Reagan replied with a shrug. "But the daughter, Jillian, is basically in charge of it."

"How's that been? Is she as snobby and jerkish as she was the first time?"

Reagan tilted her head. "A little. We've only had one meeting so far and she definitely had her moments. You should've seen her surprise when I laid out perfect options for her for table settings and linens. I know she assumed I was a server when we had lunch. Then I showed her I know my shit. I think I almost made her head explode."

Her mom chuckled. "When do—"

"Kathy," Betty called as she entered the room, "I'm not trying to panic you, but I've just called an ambulance for Conor. His breathing is labored and—"

Her mom jumped off her stool and rushed down the hallway.

Reagan made her way around the counter when Betty gripped her arm. She wanted to pull away, but Betty's voice stopped her.

"Reagan, honey. Please wait outside for the ambulance. Can you do that for me?"

"No. I need to see him." She fought against Betty's firm grasp, but she hadn't moved an inch.

"Reagan."

She stopped and looked at Betty, already feeling hot tears streaming down her cheeks.

"Please. I need to go check on him. They'll be here soon. Can you do that for me?"

Reagan mutely nodded. When Betty was out of sight, she wept silently against the counter. "Not yet. Not yet," she whispered. She lifted her head when she heard the faint sounds of sirens. She stepped outside, hugging herself tightly and begging the universe to just let her dad be all right.

Two paramedics stepped out of the ambulance and hurried into the house with large bags slung over their shoulders. Silently, she led them down the hallway and into her father's room. They immediately began to work on her dad, asking him questions he couldn't answer, putting an oxygen mask on him, wrapping a blood pressure cuff around his arm. While Reagan sensed their movements, the only thing that registered was that this could be the last time she saw her father alive.

Her mom moved to her side and clung to her arm. All the years as a nurse still hadn't prepared her to watch her husband's body fail in front of her. Reagan pried her arm from her mother's grip and wrapped it around her shoulders, pulling her mom into an embrace. Before she understood what was happening, the paramedics transferred her father to a gurney, and they rushed out of the room. Her mom followed them, but Reagan stood rooted to the spot, staring at the now empty bed.

"Reagan."

Her breathing quickened and she continued to stare at the crumpled sheets and discarded tubing strewn across the bed. She rushed over and stuffed it all into the garbage can. "He'll be home soon. I need to get it back in order. He'll be home soon," she muttered to herself.

"Reagan."

She fluffed the pillow and tried to pull the sheets up when Betty turned her away from the bed.

"Reagan!"

She lifted her eyes to meet Betty's concerned gaze. "Your mom is going in the ambulance with your father. You need to follow them in your own car."

As she started to turn toward the bed again, Betty gripped her chin and held her in place.

"Reagan, do you understand?"

"Y-yeah."

"Do you need me to drive you?"

Reagan shook her head.

"I'll straighten up around here. You don't need to worry about this. I'll meet you at the hospital as soon as I can, okay?"

"O-okay."

With a gentle push from Betty, Reagan went back into the kitchen and grabbed her phone, keys, and wallet. As she made her way outside, the ambulance was just pulling away so she hurried to her car. In the back of her mind, she knew she shouldn't be driving, but if she stayed close enough to the ambulance, she'd have something to focus on and would be safe as she drove.

Ten minutes later, she pulled into the emergency room parking lot behind the ambulance. While it continued to the unloading area, she quickly found a parking spot and hurried into the building. She watched as her father's gurney was wheeled through two large doors. When they closed, she stood there and stared at them, willing them to open and let her through. She knew her mother stood next to her, but she couldn't find the strength to acknowledge her.

She didn't know how long she stayed there, but her phone chimed in her back pocket and she jumped at the noise. Pulling it out, she read an alert reminding her she had a meeting with Jill in thirty minutes.

"Shit," she muttered before typing out a message to Gwen. She gave her the rundown of the situation and asked if she could cover for her at the meeting at Jill's office.

It'll all be taken care of. Anything you need? Gwen replied.

My dad, Reagan thought. *I'll let you know.*

She pocketed her phone, glancing again at the closed doors leading to the emergency room. She turned and found her mother sitting in a chair, staring blankly at the floor. Reagan plopped down in the chair next to her, cradling her mom's hand in her lap. All they could do now was wait.

Jill stared at her computer screen, going through email after email. She was looking forward to her four o'clock meeting with Reagan, definitely not because she'd be seeing Reagan. *Nope. Not one little bit.* She just wanted a break from the monotony of dealing with Harrison and his constant emails. Normally he didn't check in much during the planning phase of projects. She didn't understand what it was about this project that made him become so involved.

As she finished a reply to her design team, a knock on her door drew her attention away from her screen. She looked up to find Ash standing there and Gwen a few feet behind them. She glanced at the corner of her screen just as the clock changed to four on the dot.

"Ms. Taylor is here to see you."

Taylor? Why's Gwen here? Where's Reagan? A sense of disappointment hit her square in the chest. So much for looking forward to the meeting. Jill stood and nodded to Ash. They stepped aside to let Gwen walk through the door—and she didn't look good. Her eyes seemed a little wild and red, and her breathing was too fast for attending a meeting about table settings. If she didn't know any better, Jill would have assumed Gwen had run up the five flights of stairs to her office.

"Ms. Taylor. Have a seat," Jill said as she gestured to a chair in front of her desk.

"Thank you." Gwen sat and rubbed her hands on her pants. She took several deep breaths which calmed her breathing some.

"May I ask why you're here? I'm supposed to be meeting with R…Ms. Murphy."

"She had a last-minute conflict and asked me to cover for her."

Jill sighed. "Fine. What do we need to go over today?"

Gwen wiped her hands on her pants again. "To be honest, Ms. Jacobs, I'm not exactly sure where Reagan was in the planning. I felt it'd be better to come here in person and apologize for the late notice. I know th—"

"This is entirely unprofessional, Ms. Taylor. My mother is paying you a lot of money to make this damn party be whatever it is she wishes it to be. When I hire someone to do a job, I expect them to meet the deadlines they have set for themselves. Like I did. I've prepared the list of other vendors we will be using like Reagan asked." She handed Gwen a sheet of paper. "She was supposed to bring cake ideas from your pastry chef. Since you don't seem to have those, will this put us behind schedule? If so, it won't be me relaying that message to my mother. It will be you," Jill said as she pointed at Gwen.

"I understand completely. We have no intention in this causing a delay. It's just a little hiccup."

"We'll see about that. And what was so important that Ms. Murphy needed to cancel on me without giving me proper notification?"

"That's really not relevant at the moment."

"I think it is. So?"

Gwen tightly clasped her hands in her lap. "Her fa—" she cleared her throat and continued, "father had a medical emergency. I'd deem that as pretty important."

Inside, Jill deflated a little. Outwardly, she didn't react at all. "I see. So, you don't have any planning updates for me then?" She crossed her arms and stared down at Gwen.

"No."

"Then you can see yourself out." Jill sat in her chair and pulled it up to her desk, focusing on her computer screen.

"Very well. We will be in touch soon to reschedule. I'm sorry for the inconvenience this has caused you. It won't happen again."

"You're damn right," she replied as she leveled a glare at Gwen.

Gwen looked as if she wanted to reply with words that were a little less conciliatory, but she muttered, "Have a good day," instead and walked out the door.

Well, that seemed a little bitchy, even for me. She reached for her phone and brought up Reagan's contact info, hitting the icon for a new text message. She stared at the blank screen and reassessed her actions. It wasn't her place to check in with her. She and Reagan weren't friends. Or anything really. Vendor and client, that's all. And while concern for Reagan hovered in the recesses of her mind, she didn't have time to dwell on the situation. She had her own deadlines, and she wouldn't stop until she met them.

CHAPTER EIGHT

For the first few days after her dad had come home from the hospital, Reagan spent most of her waking and sleeping hours at her father's bedside. Every noise her dad made and the constant beeping of the new monitors kept her on edge. She only left his side when her mom forced her. He hadn't had any more terrifying episodes, but that hadn't stopped Reagan from holding her breath every day.

Once he started to improve and he spent a few more hours awake each day, Reagan had let herself work from home when she needed to. She'd even been able to sleep more than a few hours a night.

As she sat in a chair with her feet propped up on her dad's bed, she looked over bank statements and made notes in the margins for areas where she wanted to cut back. Her phone buzzed in her lap, and she unlocked the screen to read the latest message in her group chat with Gwen and Carly.

Gwen wrote, *Drinks and a little dancing on Saturday?*

Not this time.

Carly joined with, *Reagan, he's been home for almost a week now. Let yourself have a moment away. You can't care for him if you're burned out. We promise not to keep you out long.*

Gwen added, *Pleeeeeeeeeeease?*

Reagan sighed, dropping the phone into her lap and covering her face with her hands.

"What's wrong?" her mom asked as she walked into the room.

Reagan sat up, watching as her mom put some of her dad's clothes into the dresser. "It's nothing."

"Didn't sound like nothing with that long sigh I heard."

Her phone buzzed again, the notification reading *??* from Gwen. "The girls want to meet up for drinks on Saturday night. Told them maybe another time."

Her mom switched the laundry basket to her other hip. "Nope. Give them a better answer."

"But, Mom…"

"Don't 'Mom' me. You've been at his bedside basically every minute since he's been home. You need a break. You're not good to me if you're burned out."

"That's what Carly said," she mumbled.

"I've always liked her."

"What if you need me?"

"Then I promise to call you. Is that good enough?"

"I guess," Reagan muttered as her eyes flicked to her dad's frail body.

"Reagan, the doctor said he has at least a few weeks left. Enjoy yourself for one night. That's all I ask."

Reagan took a deep breath and stared at the phone in her hand. Simultaneously, she typed and said, "Okay."

With a nod her mom left the room. Her friends responded with heart emojis. She turned her phone off and laid it on the side table. She softly took her dad's hand and let her tears fall.

* * *

On Saturday night, Reagan walked into the bar feeling excited and guilty. She hadn't gotten together with Gwen and Carly since the night at Carly's house, and she'd missed being in the company of her best friends. But she felt she had no right to be there, not when she had such little time left with her father.

So, here she was in a bar that was already crowded even though it was only eight. Most tables and almost every stool at the bar had been claimed. A few couples moved together on the dance floor on the far side of the room, and Reagan knew it would be full in just a couple hours. Music pumped through the speakers and would only get louder as the night progressed. She looked around for her friends, finally spotting Carly waving from a high-top table along the far wall.

"Hey, guys," Reagan said as she approached. She gave each of them a quick hug before taking her seat. Reagan found a beer in front of hers, raised the glass, and took a sip. "Thanks for this."

"No problem," Carly replied. "You get the next round."

"You got it," Reagan said with a smile.

"How's your dad? I felt bad pestering you about coming out. I just thought you might need to relax and let loose for a second."

"He's doing okay. Happy to be home. And you don't have to feel bad. You should thank my mom, though. She's the one who really guilt-tripped me into coming out."

"I should send her some flowers then."

Reagan laughed. "I'm sure she'd get a kick out of that. Speaking of flowers...Get any more from your new guy, Carly?"

She sighed. "He is definitely not my new guy. And thankfully, no. After the second date, I politely told him there wouldn't be a third and to save his money."

"What was wrong with him? I thought he was nice," Gwen said.

"He was. Very nice, in fact. But he's a nerd."

Reagan set down her beer and reached for Carly's hand. "I hate to break it to you, sweetie, but you're a nerd."

Carly pulled her hand back and adjusted her glasses. "I know that. He's Tolkien and I'm Trekkie. He's MMORPG but I like FPS. I got the vibe he won't stray from what he knows."

Gwen folded her arms on the table. "Okay, I know first person shooter, but what's the other one?"

"Massively multiplayer online role-playing game. Duh."

"Ah, right, of course." Gwen shrugged. "His loss. Should we be looking for someone tonight? Anyone catching your eye?"

Carly glanced around the bar, taking her time and assessing each person. "Nah. Not tonight. I'd rather focus on…Holy shit!"

"What?" Reagan and Gwen replied in unison.

Carly nodded her head over her shoulder. "That's the Ogre."

"The what?" Gwen asked.

"Remember when I was telling you about the woman that I met on my first day? She's at the bar. The one with the dark hair and leather jacket."

All three turned toward the bar. Reagan caught a glimpse of Jillian leaning against the bar with one foot on the rail. *God, she looked good in leather.* The way she stood allowed her skinny jeans to stretch rather nicely across her ass. Reagan raised the back of her hand to her forehead, checking to see if her face was as warm as she thought. Yep, definitely was. *Can I blame it on the one beer?* Reagan stopped her gawking when Gwen groaned.

"Shit. That's our client," Gwen said.

"Wait. What?" Carly asked.

"She's the catering gig. It's a party for her stepfather."

"No way," Carly replied as she stared at Jillian. "Well, I feel sorry for you two. She's awful."

"She could definitely be better," Gwen muttered. "Fuck. Should we say hi?"

Reagan wanted to say yes for selfish reasons, but she didn't think that was appropriate. "I don't know." She shrugged. "Might not be necessary. Plus, I think she's still pissed about the last meeting. I sent an email to check in with her a few days ago, and her response was a little terse. Maybe we can avoid it." *Not that I want to avoid it.*

But just as she said that, Jillian turned away from the bar and locked eyes with Reagan, who waved awkwardly. Jillian offered a surprised smile, and Reagan's chest clenched. Though the pleasantness disappeared as Jillian's smile was replaced with a slight scowl as she turned back toward the bar.

"Well, shit," Reagan murmured. "Looks like she is still pissed. I'll go. I should probably apologize again."

"Are you sure? I can come too," Gwen said.

"No, I've got it. Looks like we're ready for another round anyway. Same thing for you guys?"

Both nodded in reply.

Reagan made her way next to Jillian. She gave her order to the male bartender, and once he stepped away to make the drinks, she turned and leaned an elbow on the bar. "Hello, Jillian."

Her scowl was still firmly in place. "I'm surprised to see you, Ms. Murphy. Shouldn't you be at home with your father? You can miss an important meeting but you can leave him to get drunk at a bar?"

Reagan straightened, the comment hitting her as if she'd been slapped, and tears pooled in her eyes. Steeling her voice, she replied, "Look, I'm sorry for missing our meeting. But I don't have to explain myself to you, and I won't. Have a good night, Ms. Jacobs." She turned away, forgetting about the drinks, until Jillian gently gripped her wrist.

"Wait. I'm sorry. That was completely uncalled for." She glanced away and took a deep breath. "I just don't know how to turn it off."

Reagan pulled away from her hold and crossed her arms. "Turn what off?"

"Being me," she replied with a self-deprecating laugh.

Reagan dropped her arms to her sides. "Well, at least you recognized it this time and apologized. I'd say that's a step up from our other encounters."

"I really am sorry, Ms. M…um, Reagan. I wish I could blame it on my bad mood, but it's just who I am. Sad as that is." She looked away and turned her glass on the bar. She cleared her throat and asked, "Is your dad okay?"

Reagan stared for a beat, wondering if Jillian was just being polite or if she was really interested in the answer. Her scowl had faded and her eyes had softened, leaving a hesitant curiosity in its wake. Reagan didn't know what Gwen had told her, and she also didn't want to get into any details at the moment so she said, "Yeah, he's okay. Thanks for asking."

Jillian nodded and took a sip of her drink. "Sure."

The bartender placed Reagan's drink order on the bar, and Reagan reached for them but stopped herself from picking them up. Instead, she studied Jillian for a moment. She was staring at a TV above the bar but she didn't seem to be paying attention to what was on the screen. Her slightly slouched posture made her seem sad, and Reagan was curious as what had made her that way. "Why are you in a bad mood?"

"My friend, Samantha, made me come out tonight."

Reagan looked around in the immediate vicinity, but they were surrounded by a couple different groups of guys. "Where is she?"

Jill nodded over her shoulder toward the end of the bar. "She's down there chatting up the short-haired woman."

Reagan looked behind Jill and immediately saw the couple. With all the closeness and the touching, they seemed to be one minute away from making out. "Ah. She ditched you, huh?"

Jill snorted. "Oh, yeah. Somewhat typical of her."

Rubbing the back of her neck, Reagan glanced at her table before returning her gaze to Jill. "Well, I'm here with Gwen and our other friend, Carly. You're more than welcome to join us."

"No, that's okay. I wouldn't want to impose. I'm just going to finish my drink and head out."

Reagan schooled her features, hoping her disappointment didn't show. It was probably for the best. She and Gwen typically didn't socialize with clients. "If you change your mind, we'll be over there," she said as she reached for the drinks and nodded to her table across the room. "Enjoy your night, Jillian."

"Wait. Reagan?" Jillian said, lightly brushing her fingers against Reagan's elbow.

"Yeah?" she asked over her shoulder.

"Um, you can call me Jill. If you want."

"Is that what you want?"

Jill shoved her hands in her front pockets, making her look like a combination of sexy and vulnerable. She took a moment to answer, which Reagan found odd seeing as she didn't think it was a difficult question. Finally, Jillian took a deep breath and answered, "Yes."

Reagan smiled. "Then I'll do that. Have a good night, Jill." She walked back to her table, glancing back once to see Jill was watching her, regret obvious in her eyes.

Jill turned back to the bar, downed the last few sips of her vodka soda, and gestured to the bartender for another round. As he stepped away to make it, Jill found the short-haired woman grabbing Sam's ass and pulling her in between her legs. So much for hanging out, she thought. She should've just gone home after her first drink like she had told Reagan she had planned to do. But something told her she should stay, at least for a little longer.

When the bartender placed Jill's drink in front of her, she felt a hand wrap around her forearm. For a tiny moment, she hoped Reagan had returned. Instead, she found a young woman in her mid-twenties. Cute and shorter than Jill with tight black curls, she smiled as if she'd found exactly what she'd been looking for that night.

"I'm Mira. How about you buy me a drink?"

Jill hesitated. She could easily say no and Mira would be on her way. But in the back of her mind, Sam's voice nagged at her. Hooking up with random strangers used to be a semi-regular occurrence for her because it was always so much easier than full-blown relationships. Admittedly, it had been a while since she'd hooked up with anyone. For some reason, even a no-strings hook up had started leaving her unsatisfied, though maybe it was what she needed tonight. Maybe it was why she'd been feeling unsettled lately so she decided to give Mira a little time. If she couldn't stand her, then she'd head home. "What would you like?"

"Jack and diet."

Jill grabbed the attention of the female bartender and ordered Mira's drink. "So, come here often?"

Mira choked on her drink. A smirk forming as she replied, "That's overdone, don't you think?"

Jill shrugged. "I get the feeling you don't really care what I have to say. Unless it's in the bedroom."

Mira's eyes darkened and she knocked back the rest of her drink. She closed the space between them, brushing her hips against Jill's as she stood on her tiptoes to whisper in her ear. "You're absolutely right."

Suddenly the music changed from current rock to dance music. Whitney Houston's "I Wanna Dance with Somebody" blared through the speakers. People in various states of intoxication rushed to the dance floor. Mira grabbed her hand, pulling her toward the crowd as she shouted, "Let's go!" over her shoulder.

Finding an open space in the crowd, Mira threw her arms above her head and danced with abandon. Normally, Jill never saw herself as a dancer. But after two strong drinks, the beat seeped into her body and she reached for Mira's hips to match her movements. If she hadn't understood Mira's intentions before, she now had a good idea of what she wanted. Her hands roamed freely across Jill's torso. After dancing through two songs, Jill stepped back, craving space.

As she did, she bumped into someone behind her. Reagan's annoyance transformed into a smile wide enough to crinkle the corners of her hazel eyes. "We meet again, Ms. Murphy." Jill felt a tiny shudder beneath her lips as they grazed Reagan's ear. "Where's Gwen and your other friend?"

"Gwen headed home to her husband. Carly's dancing with that redhead over there." She pointed off to her left where a pretty brunette with bangs was dancing with another woman.

"Got dragged out here, huh?"

Reagan shrugged. "Kinda, but I don't mind dancing. It's been a while. What about you? You don't seem like the dancing type."

Jill found Mira behind her hitting on another woman. She threw a thumb over her shoulder and leaned forward again so Reagan could hear her. "I'm not. It was her idea."

Reagan stepped back and waved her away. "I'm sorry. I'll leave you to it then."

"Wait." Jill gripped Reagan's wrist and stepped forward until their bodies touched. "Don't go. I just met her tonight. It's nothing. I swear." Looking down at the grip she still had on Reagan's wrist, she let go. "I'm sorry. I seem to be manhandling you tonight."

Reagan placed Jill's hand on her hip. "I don't mind."

The corner of Jill's mouth turned up, and she stepped into Reagan's space once again. They moved to the beat of the song, and Jill melted into Reagan's warmth. She never imagined she'd enjoy dancing but being in Reagan's arms felt right.

As they swayed, Reagan gripped the back of Jill's neck and pulled her close. Reagan's hot breath washed over her skin and she stifled a groan. She dipped her head, lightly brushing her lips below Reagan's ear. Jill pulled back and met Reagan's fiery gaze, sending a shot of heat straight to her core. She licked her lips in anticipation, but before she could lean in, a firm grip on her shoulder pulled her away.

"Jill! I've been looking all over for you." Sam rested her hand on her hip. "Never thought I'd find you on the dance floor. Want a dr—"

Jill's attention moved to Reagan, who muttered, "Excuse me," before walking away.

Sam shook her arm, but Jill pulled away and shouted to Sam, "I'll be back in a minute."

She moved through the crowd, nudging people out of her way. Once the crowd thinned, she looked toward the bar but didn't see Reagan anywhere. She turned to her right and walked to the back hallway where the bathrooms were located.

The hallway was abandoned and Jill groaned to herself. "Where the hell is she?" As she reached for the restroom door handle, the door opened and Reagan stepped out.

She looked up as she clutched her chest. "Jill. You just keep bumping into me, don't you?"

"Seems that way."

Reagan pushed open the door and held it open for Jill. "Here you go."

Jill stepped back and away from the entrance. "Oh, I don't need to go."

"Then what are you doing here?" Reagan let the door close and stepped to the side, wrapping her arms across her torso.

"I wanted to make sure you were okay. You rushed off and I thought you might be upset." Jill bit the corner of her lip and stuffed her hands in the back pockets of her jeans. "I want to apologize if I took our dancing too far."

"It's fine."

"Are you sure? Because you seem a lit—"

Reagan's lips crashed into hers, lips she found to be just as soft and hot as she imagined. Jill closed her eyes as she melted into them. Reagan gripped the lapels of her jacket and pushed her against the wall. Jill groaned. Her mind went blank except for one thought—she needed more. So much more. She tightly gripped Reagan's hips and pulled her closer. She begged for entrance with a sweep of her tongue across Reagan's lower lip, and Reagan let her in with a whimper.

Jill slipped her hands under the hem of Reagan's shirt, but the moment Jill's fingers brushed against her skin, Reagan backed into the opposite wall. Her eyes were wide and unfocused, her breathing fast and ragged. Just as Jill reached for her, Reagan scurried away.

Jill stared at her retreating form as her breath returned to normal. She ran her hands through her hair, replaying what had just happened. She hadn't initiated the kiss so it wasn't like Reagan didn't want it, right? Why did she run away? Had Jill done something wrong? Taken it too far? She fought the urge to follow Reagan and ask her all those questions. She sighed as she thought about all the unknowns.

She stepped back against the wall, closing her eyes, her body still vibrating with arousal. She could look for Mira so she could take her home and take care of the throbbing between her legs, but it wasn't Mira she wanted. What she wanted had just run away from her.

Reagan rushed back to the dance floor and found Carly. She gripped her wrist and pulled her around. "I need to go!" She headed for the bar and closed her tab as quickly as she could before heading for the door.

"Wait up!"

She stood just outside the door and hugged herself around the waist. She needed to walk but it would be a dick move to pretend she hadn't heard Carly and ditch her.

A few seconds later, Carly pushed through the door, frantically searching for Reagan. Her shoulders relaxed as she met Reagan's gaze. "What's wrong? Are you okay?"

Reagan shook her head.

"Want to talk about it?"

Another shake.

"Let's go."

Reagan nodded and turned in the direction of her car.

What in the world had she been thinking? Why did she kiss Jill? She wasn't even a nice person. Maybe Reagan could blame it on the alcohol or wanting to feel something more than the sadness and heartache over the past several months. But why did she have to find comfort with Jill? Any other available woman in the bar probably would have been a smarter choice than Jill.

Reagan groaned inwardly as she pictured Jill waiting for her in the hallway. She looked so fucking good. And she kissed even better. So what if they had fit perfectly together on the dance floor? So what if Jill's lips looked so soft and tempting, so much so that she was half-tempted to turn around and finish what she started. But that would be an awful idea. Jill was snobby. And abrupt. And a client!

"Stupid," she mumbled to herself.

"What's wrong, Reagan? What was with the sudden exit? You can tell me."

"Not right now." She continued her slow jaunt to her car, parked a couple blocks away.

"Okay. No problem."

They walked in silence for the final block until Reagan whispered, "I kissed her."

Carly pulled her to a stop with a grip on her elbow. "Who?"

Reagan rubbed the back of her neck, staring at the ground. "Jill."

"The Ogre?"

Reagan covered Carly's mouth with her hand. She had no idea if Jill was still in the bar or not, but she never wanted Jill to hear that nickname. She stepped back and slammed her hands on her hips. "Keep your voice down. I know she was awful when you guys met, but don't call her that, especially around me."

"Whoa. Calm down." Carly raised her hands. "Did this just happen?"

"Maybe." Reagan kept walking.

"So?"

"So, what?"

"How'd it happen? Why'd you run afterward? And most importantly, how was it?"

They reached the car and Reagan leaned against the trunk, running a hand through her hair. "It was so good. Like toe curling good."

"Yeah?" Carly asked with a grin.

"Oh yeah," Reagan breathed out.

"And then you ran."

"And then I ran."

"Why?"

Reagan pushed off the car and paced. "Because it was so stupid. And impulsive. And yes, I'll admit that she isn't always the nicest person, which I'm assuming is the thought running through your mind right now."

"Maybe a little." Carly shrugged. "But I only have that one interaction and the office rumor mill to go on. You're the one who's been working with her. How is she with you?"

Reagan stopped pacing and stood with her hands in her front pockets. She shook her head. "I don't know. I'm guessing that what you saw in her office is what she's like most of the time. She's definitely been like that with me. I actually met her last month and we had lunch."

Carly's eyes went wide, but Reagan waved her off. "Don't worry. I'll tell you about it another time. She wasn't very nice to say the least." Reagan took a deep breath and released it. "But there's still something there. Humor seems to always be in the shadows, hovering there for just the right moment. Then it's like as soon as she realizes she's not acting like this buttoned-up, cold person, she wipes away any glimpse into who she really is. My gut keeps telling me that's how she wants people to see her."

Carly blinked. "Wow. It sounds like you're reading her pretty well."

"I doubt that."

"Don't you think it'd be worth it to find out?"

"No, it's not a good idea."

"Why not?"

"Well, aside from everything going on in my life right now, she's a client."

"Oh, right."

"Yeah. And while Gwen and I don't have any written rules about dating a client, it's just not smart."

"What if it wasn't dating? It wouldn't hurt you to have a bit of fun. Might help take your mind off things."

Reagan hugged herself and shook her head, a sad smile lifting the corner of her mouth. "No. The biggest thing I've learned from being home with my parents over these past few months is that I want a love like they have. I won't settle for anything less."

"So, that's it then?" Carly asked.

"That's it," Reagan replied with a sigh.

"Sorry, Reagan."

She shrugged. "No biggie. Other fish in the sea and all that, right? Plus, it's just better off this way." She held back another sigh and grabbed her car keys out of her back pocket. "Want me to drive you to your car?"

"No need. I'm only a few cars down. Tell your folks I say hi, okay?"

"Will do."

They parted with a hug, and Reagan got into her car. Leaning against the headrest, disappointment lingered in the back of her mind. Examining it would only extinguish the last bit of excitement still surging throughout her body. Knowing a kiss like that wouldn't be happening again, she wanted the feeling to last a bit longer. It was all she had for now, and that would have to be enough.

CHAPTER NINE

"So, she liked the place setting I suggested, didn't she?" Reagan asked, her lips curled in a grin.

Jill didn't expect gloating to be Reagan's response when she told her which place setting her mother had chosen. But she had to admit, gloating looked damn sexy on Reagan. She could tell Reagan had a small amount of swagger she could probably dole out any time she wanted. Maybe if Jill was lucky, she'd be able to see that again. In a more private setting.

"If you must know, yes she did. I didn't even have to show her the others," she muttered. "Happy?"

Reagan shrugged. "Maybe. Does it show?"

Jill scoffed. "You can get off your high horse there, Ms. Murphy."

Reagan chuckled. "I guess I can do that."

Her smile made Jill's breath hitch. Something that hadn't happened since the night at the bar. Jill met Reagan's gaze. Probably staring too long as the next noise she heard was the clearing of Reagan's throat, making her look up to see hesitancy in Reagan's eyes.

"So, next step will be for us to nail down the menu and organize the tasting. I know you've seen our general meal options, but Gwen's informed me she has a few additional choices for you. I'll have those plus photos of their platings so we get a better idea of how everything will be presented. How about we have a quick meeting on October seventh? Say, two o'clock?"

Jill looked at the calendar on her phone. "That'll work. At my office?"

"Sure. After that, we'll set up a meeting so Gwen and I can have a small tour of your mother's house. We need to see the room we'll have available and what the kitchen space is like. Would you like to talk with your mother and find times that work best? Or would you like me to call her?"

"I'll talk with her." The less exposure Reagan had to her mother, the better. Jill didn't even want to talk to her, but the party planning was adding more contact between them than she preferred. Soon it would all be over and she could go back to only suffering during their monthly dinners.

"Great. If you know of options before the seventh, then call me. If not, you can just let me know the dates and times then," Reagan said as she turned to collect her notes from the table.

Jill made a mental note to do that, but her thoughts drifted to the night at the bar. The softness and heat of Reagan's lips and mouth. She wanted to feel them again. Over the past two weeks, Jill had found every excuse she could to text Reagan. Each time she'd started the conversation by asking inane questions about the party before segueing into whether Reagan would want to get together. Each time Jill had been met with refusal or silence.

Now that she had Reagan in front of her, she wanted an actual explanation. Jill took a couple slow, deep breaths, trying to calm an unusual amount of nerves. "Reagan?"

"Hmm," she replied, her gaze focused on the papers in her hands.

"Are we ever going to have a real conversation about that night at the bar?"

Reagan sighed and turned toward Jill, lifting one leg to half-sit on the table. "It's not a good idea."

"Talking about it? Or what might happen once we do talk about it?"

"Both."

"Care to explain your reasoning?" Jill asked as she stepped forward until only a foot of space separated them.

"It's just not a good time right now, Jill." Reagan ran her hand through her hair and looked away briefly. "Plus, if I was looking for something, it'd be something more than a hookup. And I don't think that's something you can give me."

Jill stepped back, immediately feeling as if Reagan had poured a bucket of cold water on her head. She cleared her throat, trying to keep her features neutral and hold back any sign of disappointment. "And why would you say that?"

"Because when you only text late at night, that's the conclusion I come to. I'm not a booty call."

"Reagan, I wasn't looking for one." Jill took Reagan's hand, gently brushing her thumb over her soft skin. "What if I said that I might be looking for something more than that? Something real."

Reagan squeezed her hand and then let go. She grabbed her notes and held them against her chest as if they were a shield. "I'm not saying this to hurt you, but I don't see you being interested in that."

"Why not?"

"Because you've been unpleasant and rude more often than not. And I don't know if that's who you are or just how you choose to present yourself. But relationships need compassion and vulnerability and communication. I see it every day between my parents, and I want that too. Someday."

"I see." Jill grabbed her phone off the table and shoved it into her pocket. "Since that seems to be it, then I'll be going. I'm glad we were able to nail down most of the details. Soon this will be over and I'll be out of your hair." She nodded and walked out of the room.

As she stepped onto the sidewalk, her shoulders drooped. Never before had another person called her out so thoroughly. She expected anger to bloom in her chest, but she mostly just felt sad that Reagan saw her that way. Jill knew she hadn't projected her best self when she was around Reagan, but she wanted to, and that was something completely new for her.

Jill sighed and glanced at her watch. It was early enough that she should head back to work but that had zero appeal. Instead, she wanted to make a quick stop before heading home.

As Jill walked into the lobby of Happy Tails Animal Shelter, its sounds and smells inundated her senses. Strangely, the cacophony of barking and the smell of dogs and cats comforted her. While she didn't have time for much outside of work, she had made it a priority to stop by the shelter at least once a month to volunteer. She made regular contributions as well and increased those on months when work made it impossible to stop and help. These extra contributions also helped her skirt around the shelter's volunteer requirements of spending a set number of hours volunteering each month. She never liked to use her money to her advantage because she had seen too much of that growing up, but this was the one time she allowed her money to open doors for her.

With a nod to Stacey, the intake coordinator at the front desk, Jill headed to the staff locker room. She quickly discarded her work clothes for jeans, long-sleeve T-shirt, and a pair of hiking boots. After stuffing her bag away and locking it up, she went back to the front desk to look at the list of things still left to do for the day. Knowing she didn't want to interact with others, she picked the most isolated job. Moving a large quantity of dog and cat food from a truck into a storage room sounded like the perfect way to keep her body busy and her mind occupied. Jill had never shied away from physical labor, which was frowned upon by her affluent upbringing.

The high volume of food the shelter went through each week always amazed Jill, but knowing the shelter stayed at or close to full capacity every day, it made sense. After she dropped the last bag of dog food onto the waist-high pile, she stretched her back. The dull ache signaled that she'd done a fair amount of work in the hour since she'd arrived and that she wasn't getting any younger. *Another thought for another day.*

She lifted the front of her shirt and wiped her forehead, taking a couple of slow, deep breaths to calm her heart rate and her breathing. She grabbed a drink of water at the fountain before returning to Stacey. "Who can I walk today? I've only got time for one."

"Well, hello to you, too," Stacey replied with a huff. She looked at a paper taped to the wall behind her desk, dragging her finger down the list of dogs in the back and the last time they had been walked. "Take Haley. Cage eleven. She's a small pit and lab mix. Just arrived this morning."

"Got it."

She could hear them as she approached the kennels, and as soon as she opened the door, the sound increased tenfold. Dozens of distinct barks reverberated against the walls. She moved along the aisle between the cages. She frowned as she noticed that Star and Korie were still here. She had walked both of them the last time she had volunteered.

Jill stopped in front of number eleven. Kneeling down, the sight in front of her made her take in a quick breath. It wasn't a surprising sight, but a heartbreaking one.

Haley was black with small patches of white on her paws and a larger patch down the center of her chest. She sat in the back corner of the cage, quiet and scared. She looked at Jill but she didn't move.

Jill flattened her hand against the front of the cage. "Hey there, pretty girl. Want to take a walk?"

Haley's ears perked up but she stayed in the same spot.

Jill unlatched the door, kneeling at the entrance and holding out her overturned hand for Haley to sniff. "I'm not gonna hurt you," she said in a calm, low voice as she kept her eyes averted.

The tip of Haley's tail beat against the tile floor once and then a second time. Out of her periphery, Reagan noticed Haley's nostrils flare with tentative sniffs. Haley stood and took two small steps forward, which was enough to cover the distance between her and Jill. She continued to sniff her hand and then nudged it.

"Yeah, that's a good girl. It's okay," Jill whispered. She knelt again, and Haley sat in front of her. "Let's get you outside and away from all this noise." Jill took the leash that was tucked away in a small pouch attached to the front of the cage. She hooked the leash on Haley's red collar, and they walked out the back door.

They took a dozen steps in relative silence, as one could still hear muffled barks from the shelter. They also weren't the only pair out walking the grounds. A few other volunteers had their own trusty sidekicks as they meandered around the dirt paths.

Haley sniffed her surroundings but stayed close to Jill's side. She was calm but hesitant. Every few feet, she looked up at Jill making sure she was still there. She didn't seem to mind the other dogs and their handlers.

Jill enjoyed time like this. She often used it to decompress from a difficult week at work, particularly if Harrison had been grating on her nerves. Typically, she left the shelter with a clear mind for the days ahead.

But today would not be a day that she'd leave with a clear head. She just knew it. She knew it because now that her brain had a chance to slow down after lugging around dog food, thoughts of Reagan and the tough words she'd spoken rushed to the front of Jill's mind. Reagan probably hadn't meant for her words to hurt, but they did. And that scared Jill a little.

She'd never given much thought to relationships before because she'd never felt any type of connection to anyone in the past. She knew her intense focus on her job was partly to blame for that. She needed to prove to Harrison that he should promote her into his role once he retired. And she'd do whatever she needed to make that happen.

So, why now? Why Reagan? She'd been wrong by assuming that Jill's late-night texts were only so they could hookup. "Haley, they were late at night because I get home late at night. Do you think I should have clarified that?"

Haley looked up with her head cocked to the side. Her amber eyes looked insightful, but she offered no answers.

Not that Jill expected them. If she had, that would lead to a whole other set of problems she'd have to think about. And she already had enough on her plate as it was.

"What if I want a relationship? Is that crazy?"

Haley sniffed the ground in response.

"It is, isn't it? Like Reagan said, I don't open up. She's better off without me." Jill groaned. "But why did she have to kiss like that, Haley? That kiss would stop anyone in their tracks and they'd count down each and every second until she gave you another. It's just not fair."

The vibration of her phone against her butt distracted Jill from her thoughts. After making sure she had a good grip on the leash with one hand, she pulled the phone from her pocket with the other. Catching the name of the caller as she raised it to her ear, she answered, "Yes, Ash?"

"Hi, Ms. Jacobs. Are you not coming back to the office?"

Jill heard the hint of annoyance in their voice. "No. I had an appointment come up."

Haley barked at a squirrel on the other side of the fence.

Jill turned the phone away from her mouth, and said, "Hush."

"Ah. Judging by the noise, it's a furry friend appointment."

"Mm-hmm."

"Would've been nice to know," Ash mumbled.

Haley chose the perfect moment to quiet down, because Jill heard every word Ash spoke, even though it was probably not what they intended.

"What was that?"

Ash cleared their throat. "Nothing, Ms. Jacobs. Do you need me to do anything before I head out?"

"No. I'll see you tomorrow."

"Sounds good. Don't pull a Cruella while you're there."

Before Jill could call out Ash for that comment, they had hung up. She pulled the phone away from her ear and stared at the screen. "Smartass," she muttered.

Haley looked up at Jill, her ears flattened and head cocked to one side.

Jill knelt down and scratched Haley behind the ears. "Not you. I'd never say that about you."

Haley responded with a swipe of her tongue on Jill's chin.

"Ugh." Jill wiped away the wetness with the back of her hand. "I like you, but don't push it. Maybe I will pull a Cruella."

Haley barked twice.

"Okay, okay. I'm lying." Jill glanced at her watch and then to the backdoor of the shelter. "Sorry, girl, it's getting late. I need to get you back inside."

Once Jill got Haley inside her cage, she knelt down and kissed the top of her head. "Be good. And show all these people how beautiful you are. You'll find your forever home in no time."

She replied with another bark.

Jill smiled, one mixed with sadness and hope. She'd love to take any of these dogs home with her, but it wouldn't be fair. They deserved more than her. *Just like Reagan*. With that sobering thought, she stood up, closed the cage, and walked away with one last wave for Haley, hoping that had been the first and only time she'd see her.

CHAPTER TEN

Ash walked into Jill's office with Gwen trailing behind her. "Ms. Taylor is here to see you."

Jill nodded and Ash walked out. "Where's Ms. Murphy? I wasn't notified that I'd be meeting with you instead." Jill crossed her arms and stood tall behind her desk. "Is she avoiding me or something?"

"Why would she be avoiding you?"

Fuck. Would Reagan have told Gwen they kissed? Gwen would have asked her something different if she knew. "I thought I might have done…um, said something to offend her."

"How surprising," Gwen mumbled.

Jill bristled at that. Gwen didn't know her or her relationship with Reagan. Not that there really was one. "Did you have something to say?" Jill snapped and didn't let Gwen answer. Instead, she came back with more anger since that seemed to be what everyone expected out of her. "This is the second occurrence of a switch. I just think it would be a little more professional for Reagan to show up when she said she would. If this is the level of—"

"Her dad just died."

Jill's arms dropped to her sides instantly and her shoulders deflated. "When?"

Gwen visibly swallowed before clearing her throat. "A few days ago."

Poor Reagan. A barrage of questions flooded Jill's brain. What happened? Was she okay? Should she call or text to check in on her? But Jill didn't let herself ask a single one. She didn't know Gwen, and it seemed clear that Gwen didn't know about anything between her and Reagan. Gwen would probably think it was weird or creepy for her to ask any of that, especially if Gwen had the image of her as a bitch. Gwen also seemed to be upset and she didn't want to make that worse either. So, all she said was, "Oh."

"Yeah, oh." Gwen took a breath and slowly released it. "Now if you wouldn't mind, I'd like to go over the menu one more time so we can set up the options you and your mother will want to taste."

"Yes, of course." Jill gestured to the conference table. "Please have a seat. Did Ash offer you something to drink?"

"They did. I'm fine." They sat at the table and Gwen pulled out a stack of papers. "It's a nice touch having their pronouns on their nameplate. I didn't notice that last time. Was that their doing or yours?"

"Mine. I respect my employees. I'm not a complete asshole."

Quietly, but not quietly enough, Gwen mumbled, "Could've fooled me."

"Excuse me?" Jill asked.

Gwen stared for a moment. "Nothing, Ms. Jacobs. Shall we look at the options?"

Jill waited a beat, taking her time to size Gwen up more than she had the first time they met. Jill sat back in her chair and replied, "Very well. Show me what you've got."

Gwen laid out the menu options and a small photo album. "There will be some passed hors d'oeuvres during the cocktail hour. Then we will have a four-course meal. You will need to choose three salads and soups, four entrees and sides, and two desserts." Gwen opened the photo album. "Here are some examples of how the various options have been plated in the past. Does that sound okay?"

"Yes, please continue."

Gwen began describing each option with a passion that Jill found rare nowadays when people were talking about their work. With each new dish, Jill's thoughts turned further away from food and more toward Reagan and how she was handling her father's death. From their short interactions, Jill knew Reagan cared for people deeply, and when it came to caring for a father, she figured it would be off the charts, which meant that Reagan probably wasn't doing very well. She wanted to call or text, do something and check in with her. But she didn't feel like she had a right to do that. Reagan clearly didn't want Jill in her life as more than a client. Maybe it would be best if Jill didn't cross any sort of line. But she also couldn't ignore the nagging feeling that that was the wrong choice.

"Ms. Jacobs, are you listening?"

Jill jumped ever so slightly and cleared her throat. "Sorry. Thinking about all the things I'd rather be doing than this."

"Right," Gwen replied, dragging the word out longer than necessary. "Well, I think we've covered everything, so I'll just get out of your hair." Gwen stacked the menu lists and plating examples, placing them in front of Jill. "Take these and look them over. Let me know what you'd like to try. I'll need the photos back when you're done. Thank you again for meeting with me, Ms. Jacobs. Would you and your mother be available for a tasting at Wren next Monday, the fourteenth at two o'clock? The restaurant is closed that day, so that's the best option for me."

"Fine. I'll let my mother know."

Jill strode behind her desk, absently straightening a few papers before sitting down. Gwen gathered her things together and eventually made her way to the door.

"Is she okay?" Jill whispered.

Gwen turned, her brow furrowed. "What was that?"

"Reagan. Is she okay?"

Gwen clenched her jaw. "No. She's not." Then she left.

Shit, Jill thought. She reached for her keyboard and searched for the last name Murphy in the obituaries of the *Star*.

* * *

Numb. That was how Reagan felt. She stood at the front of the room, between her mother and her father's casket. The wake had only started thirty minutes ago, and she had four hours left. Her dad would be cremated in the morning with no funeral, so this was the final chance for his friends and family to say goodbye. The line of people paying their respects never seemed to end. She knew her father was loved, but if she had to hear, "I'm sorry for your loss" one more time, she might scream.

She understood what her role was today, and she had tried to prepare herself for it over the past few weeks, but this was the worst day of her life. *Excuse me if I want to grieve alone*. But she didn't tell anyone that. Didn't share those feelings with her mother either. Her mother had just lost her husband and best friend. Reagan would do anything to make sure her mom was okay. And if that meant putting on a brave face for every mourner, then so be it. She'd have her time to grieve.

An hour before the end of the wake, the funeral home director stood in front of the room. "Can I have everyone's attention, please?" He waited a beat as people stopped their conversations and took their seats. "As many of you know, Conor was never very religious, so instead of a typical prayer service with a minister, he wanted part of the wake set aside for anyone to come up and say a few words if they so choose. The floor is yours." He gestured to the front of the room and then stepped off to the side.

The first person to step up was Reagan's Uncle Mike, her dad's younger brother. He stopped at the casket, bowed his head for a beat and then faced the room. "Conor…Conor was a great older brother. And a typical one at that. If anyone messed with me, he dealt with it. But, if I ever stole his comic books, he would chase me around the house until I coughed them up. Mom never liked that too much."

Reagan and her mom chuckled.

"Speaking of Mom, she always recruited Conor every St. Patrick's Day to dye Dad's hair in the middle of the night. You'd think he would've woken up from that each year, but he never did. Once he was out, he was out. Except if Conor or I tried sneaking into the house after curfew. You better believe he woke up for that. Of course, it was Conor that did that more than me. I was the good kid."

"Yeah, right," Reagan's mom interjected.

He gasped and held his chest. "You know it's the truth, Kathy."

Her mom laughed and shook her head.

Uncle Mike laughed too before clearing his throat and glancing back at the casket again. "But Conor, you weren't just my big brother, you were my best friend. And I…I'll miss you, brother."

Reagan's bottom lip quivered as she tried to maintain control of her emotions. She reached for her mother's hand and used the other to wipe away a few tears from the corners of her eyes. Her mom quietly cried beside her and Reagan wrapped her arm around her mom's shoulders.

Several more people came up and told stories about her dad, but Reagan tuned most of their words out. She knew how great her dad was, but she couldn't take hearing about it anymore. One of her dad's cousins was the last to speak, and as she went to sit down after her speech, soft music began playing again through recessed speakers in the ceiling.

Reagan stood and stretched from side to side. She glanced toward the main door to see if people were still trickling into the room. A couple people entered, but Reagan didn't pay them any mind. Her focus stopped on Jill standing just inside the door. She leaned against the wall with her hands in her pockets, her eyes skipping around the room. When their eyes met, Jill looked back at Reagan with obvious relief, and Reagan gave her a small smile in return.

Before she could excuse herself, another pair of mourners stopped in front of her and told her once again how very sorry they were. Reagan thanked the unknown women and smiled politely until they moved along. When Reagan looked back toward the door, Jill was gone.

Reagan knelt down in front of her mother. "I'm going to step outside for a minute, okay?"

"That's fine, sweetie. Take all the time you need."

Reagan kissed her mother on the cheek and then turned toward the door. As she passed Gwen, she whispered in her ear, "Can you look after her for a bit?"

"No problem," Gwen replied. She moved next to her on the couch.

Satisfied that her mom was taken care of, Reagan went on a search.

Jill walked out to the parking lot, pulling her coat tighter around her waist. The first day of fall had brought chilly temps along with it. But knowing Midwestern seasons, it'd probably be in the eighties tomorrow. She heard the familiar chimes as she unlocked her car with her key fob. As she reached for the door handle, she heard a voice quietly call out behind her.

"Thank you for coming." Reagan stood a few feet away, her arms crossed and her eyes puffy and red, but dry.

"You're welcome. I'm sorry I didn't come say hi. I, um, I'm not great at the whole comforting thing. I just wanted you to know that I'm so sorry for your loss."

"Thanks." Reagan stared off to the side, her eyes tracking the cars driving down the street in front of the funeral home.

"Do you need a break from all that? I'm sure it's…a lot."

Reagan took in a quick breath and released it. "You're right. Not for long, though. I don't want my mom to be alone too much."

Jill led Reagan to the front of her car, where they sat against the hood. "Well, judging by that crowd, your mom isn't alone."

"That's not what I meant."

Jill squeezed Reagan's hand. "I'm sorry. I know. But to have all those people in there, it seems your dad was a popular guy."

Reagan smiled. "Definitely. Always had a story to tell or an ear for listening. He was the best." Her voice cracked on the last word.

Jill interlaced their fingers and squeezed again, receiving an even stronger squeeze in reply. And then her shoulders shook with her cries. She turned away to hide her emotion.

At first, Jill hesitated. She wasn't good at this. Her mother had always told her that emotion should be kept private. But a fierce need to protect Reagan overwhelmed her. She reached for her chin, gently turning her head, and she was met with watery eyes. Jill cupped Reagan's cheek with her hand, wiping away a few tears with her thumb.

"It's okay," she whispered. "I'm here." Reagan leaned into her and Jill pulled her close until her head rested on her shoulder.

They sat there without saying a word. The only sounds were Reagan's sniffles as she let the tears fall. Jill hadn't known exactly what she was doing when she'd pulled into the parking lot of the funeral home. It had taken her over five minutes to get out of her car and into the building, second-guessing herself the whole way. Any doubts she'd had earlier had been washed away as Reagan let herself breakdown. As she sat there with her arm wrapped around Reagan, she couldn't imagine not being here for her. She may not know what words to say or exactly how to act, and that made her feel inadequate, but she understood that sometimes being present for another person was enough.

When Reagan's tears ebbed, she lifted her head and stared into Jill's eyes. A connection Jill didn't want to break. "Thank you."

Jill shrugged. "No need to thank me. I didn't do anything."

"You did. More than you know," Reagan whispered. She looked behind her to the entrance of the building. "I should get back in there."

Jill straightened. "Of course. Please reach out if you need anything."

"Okay, thanks."

Jill brushed her lips against Reagan's warm cheek, lingering for a beat longer than was probably appropriate. "Again, I'm very sorry."

Reagan gave her a sad smile and a squeeze of her forearm before turning around and walking inside. Jill let out a breath, staring at the door until she could no longer see Reagan through the glass. The emotion of those few moments had left her feeling a little awkward and unsure of herself. It seemed like she'd done the right thing judging by the warmth Jill felt from Reagan despite the extreme sadness of the day.

Her phone buzzed in her coat pocket. Pulling it out, she checked the alert reminding her she had dinner with her mother and stepfather. She went from warm to cold in an instant.

"You're late," were the first words out of her mother's mouth as Jillian entered the dining room.

She bent down for an expected kiss to her mother's cheek. "Nice to see you too, Mother." She nodded at her stepfather. "Douglas."

"Jillian."

They sat in silence as Nadine served their salads. Jill gave her a small smile as she placed one in front of her. After swallowing her first bite, Jill heard a commotion in the hallway and then her half-brother, Ford, walked into the dining room.

"Hey, guys." Ford kissed their mother's cheek and then he gave his father a hug when Douglas stood to greet him. He sat across from Jill and said, "It's nice to see you, Jill. I feel like it's been a while."

Jill wiped her mouth with her napkin. "It has. Good to see you too, Ford." She and her half-brother acted friendly with each other, but they'd never been close. He was ten years younger than her, and because he was an actual offspring of Douglas, he had been treated much differently than Jill as they grew up.

The obvious difference in Douglas's attitude toward the two of them was on full display as dinner continued. "How's the new job, son? Get promoted yet?"

"Not yet, Dad," Ford replied with a chuckle. "It's only been a few months."

"Don't worry. You'll be head of sales in no time. Have you been able to get a round in with George yet?" Douglas asked. George was one of his oldest friends and the owner of the company where Ford worked.

Wonder how you got that job, little bro. Jill knew her brother was smart, but he had always used the family name to get ahead, something that irked Jill as she had preferred to use her knowledge and skill to get where she wanted to be.

For the rest of dinner, Douglas talked with Ford about networking and the investment opportunities at his new job. Not once did he address Jill, which didn't come as a surprise to her. Dear ol' Doug had always preferred to ignore Jill ever since she was a kid. The only interaction they had was if her mother forced them to spend time together or to get a lecture about always being the best. She wanted to believe she'd gotten over his favoritism for Ford, but sitting here in silence made her stomach turn sour.

As Nadine cleared away the last of the dishes, Jill's mother finished off her glass of wine before speaking. "Jillian, join me in the den for a drink."

Jill knew better than to argue. She tossed her napkin on the table and followed her mother out of the dining room and into the den.

Her mother closed the door behind them and then moved to the drink cart to pour Jill and herself glasses of whiskey before diving in with questions. "Now, how is the planning going?"

Jill held back a sigh. Not surprising that her mother hadn't asked a personal question all night and didn't seem to be starting now either. "It's fine. I met with Gwen earlier and she left me with the menu options. I've starred the ones I think will be best and left the papers with Nadine. She said she'd be sure to give them to you tomorrow while Douglas is at work."

"Why did you meet with her? Just because it was the menu? I thought Ms. Murphy was taking the lead on everything."

"She is. Or was. I'm really not sure." Jill turned to the bookshelf, absently scanning the titles. "Her father passed away, so I met with Gwen instead."

"Hope that won't delay any of our planning."

Jill snapped her head around to glare at her mother. "How could you say that? Her father just died. Show some damn respect."

Her mother slammed her glass on a side table and pointed at Jill. "You watch your tone with me, Jillian. I raised you better than that."

"To be like you, you mean? Cold? Hiding every emotion? Even when your husband is fucking every young thing that walks into his office."

The sting of her mother's slap registered slightly behind the warmth that now spread across her cheek. She reached up and covered her cheek with her hand, her mouth slightly agape. Several emotions streaked across her mother's face—anger, sadness, surprise, and maybe even a hint of regret.

"Jillian, I—"

"Let me know what you'd like to try at the tasting. It's on the fourteenth at two." Jill set her glass on the table next to her mother's. "I assume you can make it?" Her mother nodded, seemingly struggling to find words and when she didn't respond, Jill said, "Goodnight, Mother."

She strode out of the room, grabbing her jacket and purse from the front closet. After quietly closing the door behind her, she slumped against it and took in a ragged breath. Never in her life had her mother, or anyone, hit her. The sensation was painful and confusing and infuriating. So maybe it had been a little out of line to say what she did, but did that really warrant a slap? Although if she had to be married to Douglas, she'd probably lash out too. Jill had never seen an ounce of love between the two of them. She must have hit a nerve with her comment, though it wasn't a very well-guarded secret that he hired women just out college as his assistants and usually ended up sleeping with them.

As she felt the uncomfortable sensation of tears burning her eyes, she stepped away from the door and looked up at the house. And that was what it was to her. A house. It had never felt like a home, not when she felt such indifference from everyone who was supposed to love her. She shook her head at the melancholy thoughts invading her brain. It had been a long, emotional day, and she just wanted to sleep.

CHAPTER ELEVEN

Within a week of her father's wake, Reagan went back to work because she desperately needed some normalcy. Staying at home meant being surrounded by the memories of her father. She couldn't bring herself to enter the spare room where his medical bed sat in the corner, stripped of linens but not his presence. It was suffocating. Reagan planned to talk with her mom about moving back to her place soon, but she wasn't ready for that conversation yet.

Working was another story. Reagan needed to feel productive again. She needed to move. If she didn't, she'd spend her day crying. As the tasting for Jill's party was scheduled to start in an hour, Reagan figured today would be the best day to get back into the swing of things. Walking through the back door of Wren, she tossed her jacket in the tiny office and made her way into the kitchen. She found the large workstation covered in several types of plates and bowls. Gwen stood at the stove stirring a pot of soup.

"Hey there."

Gwen spun around so fast that soup fell off the spoon she was holding and onto the floor. "Reagan! What are you doing here?"

"It was time to come back. You have enough on your plate as it is. With me here, today will go a little more smoothly. You deal with cooking back here and I'll present the dishes to Jill and her mother."

"But, Reagan, I can take care of everything. It hasn't even been a week since—"

"Please, Gwen, stop. I need this," Reagan replied, her voice cracking and tears stinging her eyes. Gwen turned down the burner and opened her arms when Reagan held up her hands. "Don't. If you hug me, I might cry and never stop."

Gwen stopped mid-step and gripped the edge of the counter. "Okay. I get it." She held Reagan's gaze for a beat before taking a deep breath and turning back to the stove. "I have the menu choices written there," she said, gesturing with her chin to the far end of the workstation. "You know what's in everything, but if you need a refresher, I can write all that down too."

Reagan waved her away and then dabbed the corner of her eyes. "No, I remember. Are you going to bring each choice out one by one? Or are you going to bring out all of the choices for each course at the same time?"

"I'll bring out each course all at once. Then they can go back and forth with each choice if they need to. Sound good?"

"Sure. You're the boss today."

Gwen laughed as she added a pinch of salt to another pot. "Okay. They should be here in five minutes. Do you mind waiting out in the dining room? Soups are ready to be poured and then I'll start getting the salads together."

"No problem. I'll give my spiel then come and get them."

Reagan ran her hand through her hair as she pushed through the doors into the dining room. She double-checked that silverware and water glasses were set on the table and found everything in order. Not that she had any doubts. Gwen was the best.

Two minutes before the scheduled time, Reagan heard a knock on the front door. She pushed it open with a smile and ushered them inside. "Hi. Welcome to Wren."

Jill stopped short. "Reagan." She quickly glanced at her mother. "I mean, Ms. Murphy. I…I didn't expect to see you." She opened and closed her mouth as if to say something else, but instead cleared her throat. "I don't believe you've met my mother, Maureen."

With a quick glance, Reagan saw the clear resemblance between them. Their brown hair and eyes were almost the same color, but Reagan figured Mrs. Jacobs's hair color came from a regularly scheduled color job.

Reagan extended her hand with a wide smile. "It's a pleasure to meet you, Mrs. Jacobs. I'm Reagan Murphy."

Maureen returned the handshake. Delicately.

"May I take your coats?"

Maureen and Jill took off their coats and handed them to Reagan. Maureen continued into the dining room, but Jill reached for Reagan's hand before she could turn away.

"Are you okay? I didn't think you'd be here."

"I'm fine. Now head on in. I'll hang these up and be right with you."

Jill hesitated, skepticism in her eyes.

"It's okay, Jill. I needed to come back," Reagan said as she squeezed her hand.

Jill nodded and followed her mother.

Reagan released a sigh and quickly hung up their coats. As she walked into the dining room, Jill held out a chair for her mother before sitting in her own. Maureen took her napkin and placed it across her lap and then leaned back in her chair, resting a hand on the table and tapping her fingers against the tablecloth. Reagan stood across from them, holding her hands behind her back.

"Again, I'd like to welcome both of you to Wren. Gwen is in the kitchen preparing the tasting options you chose. I will bring out all the choices for each course so you can go back and forth between them if you have any trouble deciding. Does that sound okay?"

"Per—" Jill started to say before being interrupted by her mother.

"Will we be getting any wine with our meal? I would have assumed it would be part of this complimentary tasting."

Jill cut a sharp look at her mother before settling her gaze on Reagan, the hint of apology apparent as her eyes softened.

"Well, that's not normally included, but I'd be happy to open a bottle for you. What would you like?"

"Your finest cabernet."

Reagan nodded and grabbed a bottle of Stags' Leap Estate cabernet sauvignon and two glasses from behind the bar. She placed the glasses on the table and quickly opened the bottle. After pouring one for Maureen, Jill held up her hand.

"None for me, thank you. I have an important meeting after this."

Maureen scoffed under her breath and picked up her glass for a sip. "Very nice."

Reagan kept her expression in check as Jill closed her eyes and inhaled slowly as if to calm herself. Did Maureen not care about Jill's job or just not care about Jill in general? Either way, Reagan didn't have to wonder anymore where Jill's rudeness came from. Reagan cleared her throat, trying to get her mind back on track. "Now, I'll go back and get the first course, okay?"

"Do get on with it."

Out of the corner of her eye, Reagan saw Jill scowl. She nodded again and said, "Be right back." As the door to the kitchen closed behind her, she let out a small groan.

"Going that well out there, huh?"

"Now I'm starting to see why Jill is a bit pompous at times. Just opened a three-hundred-dollar bottle of wine for her mother, if that's any indication. Because it was her assumption that it would be part of the complimentary tasting," Reagan said, mimicking Maureen's voice.

Gwen winced. "Yeah, that's not ideal. But I guess for as much money as they're spending, we can give them that."

"Bit too generous if you ask me." Reagan helped Gwen put six bowls of soup on a tray. She squatted down a bit to lift the tray and grunted. "Ugh, haven't done this in a while. Wish me luck."

Reagan made her way back to the dining room and placed the tray on the table, distributing three bowls of soup to each woman. "Here we have tomato basil bisque, morel mushroom, and lobster bisque. Please taste each and let me know what you think." She watched as they each took small spoonfuls.

"No. This one will not do," Maureen said with a bit of disgust as she pushed away the bowl of morel mushroom soup.

"Okay, that's off the list," Reagan replied as she took the bowl from Maureen and put it back on her tray. She reached for Jill's untouched bowl, and as Jill pushed it toward her, their fingers brushed, calming Reagan instantly. She smiled at Jill before focusing again on Maureen. "What do you think of the others?"

They took a couple more spoonfuls of the last two soups. "Lobster bisque. I want the best of everything at this party."

Reagan cleared her throat. "Duly noted. Let me take these dishes back and then I'll bring out the salads." She gathered the remaining bowls and carried the tray to the kitchen, setting it down on the counter next to the dishwasher.

"So?"

"Lobster bisque is the winner. Presumably because of the higher price tag. Sorry, but she did not like the mushroom soup."

"Well, the customer isn't always right," Gwen grumbled as she tasted a spoonful from the pot still on the stove. "Mmm, still just as good as when I poured it."

"Of course it is. I think she was set on the lobster from the beginning. Her loss."

"How is it out there?" Gwen asked as she slid plates of salad on a tray.

"I think it'd be more fun to get my eyes gouged out with an ice pick than deal with this woman."

Gwen chuckled as Reagan picked up the tray and left the kitchen. With each of the next two courses, Maureen quickly discarded the options she didn't like with a barely veiled level of disdain, and the tasting was over within an hour. Maureen poured the last of the wine into her glass as Reagan piled the dessert plates onto the tray.

Reagan took out her phone and pulled up her calendar. "We still need to schedule the tour of your home, Mrs. Jacobs."

"That has already occurred. Do you two not talk to each other?"

"My apologies. I've been out for a few days and I haven't gotten caught up on everything yet." Reagan cleared her throat. "Then all that's left is a final meeting to make sure we have everything in order. It should be rather quick and we'll want to do it about a week before the party. How about the thirtieth?"

Jill looked at her phone and said, "That works for me. Mother?"

Maureen waved her away. "You do it. You're more than capable of handling such a simple task."

"Fine," Jill replied through clenched teeth.

"I am just going to take these back to the kitchen. Please stay and enjoy the rest of your wine."

"Where's the restroom?" Jill asked.

Reagan pointed toward the back. "It's just down the hallway in front of the kitchen. You can follow me."

"Thanks. Excuse me, Mother."

"Hurry. I'd like to leave as soon as I'm done with my wine."

"Of course."

Reagan picked up the tray and headed in the direction of the kitchen. "It's just down this hallway. I'll be out in a couple minutes to say goodbye." Without waiting for an acknowledgment from Jill, she pushed open the kitchen door and set the tray down on the counter. "Hey, I heard you already had the tour of the house with our lovely clients."

"Ah, yeah. Sorry, I thought I'd let you know once you were back. But now that you are, I can catch you up. Okay?"

"That'd be great. Let me go say goodbye to them and see if they have any other questions."

"Sure thing."

As Reagan left the kitchen, she stopped when Jill called out to her.

"Hey, Reagan. Can we talk?"

"Yeah. What's up?" Reagan asked as she met Jill in the middle of the hallway.

Jill reached out to hold Reagan's hand. "I just wanted to check if you were okay."

Each sweep of Jill's thumb across her knuckles comforted Reagan and gave her the strength to be honest with her. "Not really, no."

"Do you think you should have come back already?"

"I needed to, Jill. I couldn't take just sitting around at their house and crying all the time. I needed something to occupy my mind."

Jill caressed her cheek and wiped away a few tears. "Makes sense. You're sure then?"

"I am. What better way than to deal with a demanding party that needs planning?"

Jill groaned. "Now you've gotten to meet her and I'm truly sorry about that."

"I'm just glad I got to see you," Reagan said as she gazed at Jill's lips.

"Is that right?" Jill whispered.

"Mm-hmm." Just as Reagan was about to close the distance between them, the kitchen door opened and Jill abruptly stepped back.

Reagan looked at Gwen walking through the doorway, her eyes wide as she glanced between her and Jill. Then confusion took hold before she schooled her features and nodded to Jill. "Ms. Jacobs, it's nice to see you. I hope the tasting went well."

"Yes, it did. Reagan was very helpful."

"I'm sure," Gwen replied with a tight-lipped smile. "I wanted to come out and say hello to you and your mother."

"Let's head into the dining room," Reagan said as she walked in that direction. "I'll get your coats." She quickly retrieved their coats and brought them back, all the while thinking about the upcoming conversation with her best friend. *Shit*. After helping

Maureen into her coat, she did the same for Jill but added a soft squeeze of her hand as she stepped away.

"Thank you for coming today. I hope you enjoyed the food. If you have questions, don't hesitate to reach out," Gwen said.

"We'll be sure to do that," Maureen replied. "Let's go."

"Thanks again," Jill said before following her mother out of the restaurant.

"So. I guess we have some things to catch up on."

Reagan sighed. "We do. Let's head into the kitchen." She walked out without waiting for Gwen to reply, knowing she'd follow.

Reagan headed for the stacks of dirty bowls and plates near the dishwasher. She sprayed down leftover bits of soup, salad, and steak into the sink and loaded up the tray before sliding it in and shutting the door. As she dried her hands on a towel, Gwen settled on a stool by the workstation, two well-poured glasses of wine in front of her. Reagan held in a sigh and took a healthy sip. She watched Gwen study her, a mixture of confusion, hurt, and disappointment on her face.

"Ready to talk?"

"Not really."

"Tough." Gwen sighed. "What was that, Reagan?"

"It's noth…ugh, honestly I'm not sure yet." Reagan took another sip, licking her lips as a drop threatened to escape. "We're not dating or anything. Or even having sex. But sometimes there feels like there's something there."

"How long has it been going on?"

"Not long. Our one and only kiss was that night we saw her in the bar."

Gwen's eyes widened. "That was over a month ago! Didn't you think you should fill me in?"

"Look, I'm sorry if I've had other things going on and I didn't rush over to tell you."

"Shit, I'm sorry. That was uncalled for. It was just a knee-jerk reaction." Gwen pinched the bridge of her nose as if she was battling a headache. "She's a client, Reagan."

Reagan closed her eyes briefly. "I know."

"I mean, I know we don't have any hard-and-fast rules, but I always thought it was an unspoken boundary."

"I get it," Reagan replied as she held up her hands. "It's kinda why I told her I didn't think we were a good idea."

"Kinda? What were the other reasons?"

Reagan shrugged. "Told her I wanted something like…my parents had. And I wasn't sure she could give me that."

"Maybe a tad harsh, but I can see where you're coming from. I always pictured you with someone, um, a little warmer."

"Fair point," Reagan said with a slight chuckle. "But if it helps, I think that warmth is there. I just don't think she could ever show it. Her mom wasn't a ray of sunshine herself."

"Oh yeah. I got that vibe during the tour of her house."

Reagan grimaced. "About that…I'm sor—"

Gwen waved her off. "Nothing to apologize for. Ever. You were where you needed to be. As for the tour, it was fine. Typical high-end party. Nice kitchen setup. Me and the team will do most of the prep here, but we'll arrive at their house at three for final prep. I have the size of the room and how she wants the tables arranged. I'll email it to you later. I also took some pictures."

"Any surprises coming our way?"

"Doesn't seem like it. Of course, they're going to be picky and on us all night to make sure it's perfect. But I'm guessing you already figured that out."

"Definitely," Reagan replied as she drank the last of her wine, twirling the glass for a moment once she set it on the counter.

"She cares about you."

"Who?"

"Jill."

"I don't know about that."

"I saw how she looked at you in the hallway. Ya know, before she stepped back and wiped every emotion off her face."

"Yeah, I think that's her M.O."

"A little unnerving if you ask me."

Reagan chuckled. "After meeting her mother, I just think that was how she was raised. But in the time I've spent with her, she's not as cold as she wants you to think she is."

Gwen nodded and took a deep breath. "Just be careful."

"I'm fine. I told you, I've already let her know that we're a terrible idea."

"Then what was that in the hallway?"

"I-I'm not sure," Reagan replied as she looked away briefly.

"You care for her too. It was clear as day, Reagan." Gwen studied her for a moment and blew out a breath. "Go for it."

"But what about her being a client?"

"I don't love the idea; I trust that it won't cause any issues. Plus, she won't be our client much longer. If you think there's more to her than we see, take a chance on her. You deserve every happiness in the world."

"What if it doesn't work out?"

"Don't you risk that no matter who you date?"

Reagan shrugged. "I guess."

"You just won't know until you try. And since you've already tried a little and seemed to enjoy it…"

"Oh yeah," Reagan replied as she let out a shaky breath.

"Then there ya go. Something's obviously there. Explore it."

"Maybe you're right."

"I always am," Gwen said as she hopped off her stool. "Now help me clean up this place and we can get out of here."

Reagan stood and bumped hips with Gwen as they made their way around the workstation. She'd have to give some thought to Gwen's words later. Any relationship was a risk, but a relationship with Jill could be much riskier. But high risk meant high reward, right?

CHAPTER TWELVE

"Reagan Murphy," she answered just as she was packing up for the afternoon. She had been back at work for almost two weeks and she was happy to be getting into the swing of things. Finalizing details for the Jacobs party and making plans for the new restaurant kept her busy and for that, she was grateful.

"Ms. Murphy, this is Maureen Jacobs. I wanted to let you know that we will have an additional fifteen people on our guest list. I'm sure that won't be a problem. Right?"

Okay, maybe not that grateful, she thought as she held back a groan. "Mrs. Jacobs, I'm sorry, but it's too late in the game to add that many people. We've already put our orders in for the food and everything—"

"You will get this done, Ms. Murphy. I have paid a lot of money for this party and I expect you to meet all my requirements. Will that be a problem?"

"No, ma'am," she said through gritted teeth. "If you'll email me their names, meal choices, and where you'd like them to sit, I will add them to the list. I'll get an invoice together for the additional guests."

"Fine. Give it to Jillian. She'll write you a check."

"I will. Is there anything else I can help you with, Mrs. Jacobs?"

"No."

With that, she hung up. Reagan dropped her phone on her desk and held her head in her hands. *I so don't need this.* Instead of heading home for a quiet night of reading a book and enjoying a couple beers, she sat down and opened her laptop again. An email from Maureen was waiting in her inbox, which contained all the information she had asked for. *At least she finally did some work on this.* Jill had taken the lead on planning a party for a man she obviously had issues with, even though she had her own job to balance as well. Reagan couldn't imagine the stress Jill was under to make this party perfect. Now Reagan would be giving her one more thing to deal with and she didn't picture it going well.

Within an hour, Reagan had everything recorded where it needed to be and a new invoice printed out. She picked up her phone and was about to call Jill's office, but thought better of that. She needed the payment for the invoice anyway. What better way than to give it to her in person? Seeing Jill again would be an added bonus.

After being directed to Touchpoint Media's offices on the fifth floor, Reagan stepped out of the elevator. She stopped a woman rushing past with a stack of folders in her arms. "Can you tell me where I can find Jillian Jacobs's office?"

Her eyes widened briefly, and she pointed in the direction she had come from. "Down that way. Her office is at the end of the hall."

"Thanks." She found the main door opened into a small waiting area. She stepped in front of the desk on her left, occupied by someone who was bent over an open drawer. She looked down at the nameplate, happily taking note of their pronouns listed on it. "Hi."

"Hi. Can I help you?"

Reagan held out her hand. "I'm Reagan Murphy from the Taylor Murphy Group. I was hoping to speak with Jill."

"I'm Ash, Jill's assistant," they replied, shaking Reagan's hand. "I'm sorry, but she didn't come into the office today. Is it something I can help you with? Did you need to schedule a meeting?"

Reagan glanced at Jill's closed door and noticed the lights were out. "No, I need an invoice paid."

"I know she was working from home today. If you want, I can give you her address."

"Um, I don't want to bother her at home."

"It's no bother. She would want to get it taken care of. I'm sure you know how she is by now."

Reagan cleared her throat. "Well…"

Ash laughed. "I'll take that as a yes." They ripped a small sheet of paper from a notebook and started scribbling. "Here you go."

"Thanks, Ash. Have a good one."

"You too."

Reagan headed down to her car. Nerves threatened to overtake her as she made her way to Jillian's. *Maybe I should just email her*. But she discarded the thought as curiosity won out. Maybe she could get a better glimpse of the real Jill.

Reagan pulled up to a beautiful building that was a mixture of old and new. The bottom half had large columns, ornate windows and housed a lawyer's office. The top half held condos with tall windows and large balconies. It was more modern and looked as if it was added several years ago.

She pulled open the heavy doors into a marble-floored lobby. To her right was the door to the lawyer's office and just ahead to her left were elevators. Within seconds of pressing the button, the first set of elevator doors opened, and she stepped in, hitting the button for the eighth floor. *Of course she lives on the top floor*. Stepping into the hallway, she realized there were only doors to two condos on this floor and Jill's was at the end of the hall.

Taking a deep breath, she knocked twice. She adjusted her messenger bag on her shoulder after several seconds passed and there was still no sign of Jill. Just as she raised her hand to knock again, the door opened to a slightly disheveled but adorable Jill. Her hair was up in a loose bun, and she wore leggings, an oversize sweatshirt, and wire-framed glasses.

"Reagan," Jill said, her voice a hoarse whisper. She cleared her throat, stood a little straighter, and spoke again. "What are you doing here?"

She pulled out the invoice from her bag. "Your mother added a few more guests to the list. She told me to give you the invoice. When I stopped by your office, Ash said I should drop by and give it to you."

Jill muttered what sounded like, "I'm sure they did."

"What was that?"

"Nothing. I'll take it," Jill replied as she reached for the paper.

Reagan snatched it back as she studied her more. "Wait. Are you sick?"

"I'm fine. I…I…" Her words ended as she loudly sneezed into the crook of her elbow.

"Shit. You are sick. Do you need anything? Tissues? Soup?"

"Ms. Murphy, I—"

Reagan held up her hand. "It's Reagan."

Jill sighed. "Reagan, I don't need anything."

She used the back of her hand to feel Jill's forehead, and Jill closed her eyes and leaned into the touch. "You're burning up. Get inside and I'll check you out."

"This is really not necess…" Jill replied, but she began coughing hard and turned away to cover her mouth.

"Okay, okay. Step back." Reagan let herself in and closed the door behind her. Looking around, she saw Jill's condo had a beautiful open floor plan, a kitchen with a large island on the left and the living room to her right. Before she got lost in her inspection, she wrapped an arm around Jill's waist as she led her to the dark gray couch. Reagan expected Jill to squirm out of her grasp but instead she settled her arm around Reagan's shoulders. Papers were spread across the coffee table along with new and used tissues while the TV played quietly in the background.

She lowered Jill to the couch and sat next to her. She felt Jill's weakness as she held on to her and she didn't want to let go, but knew she should. So she scooted back a bit and turned toward her. "Nice glasses," she said as she tapped the frames.

"Girl's gotta see, ya know," Jill replied with a shrug.

Reagan smiled at the slight blush on Jill's cheeks, as if she was a little embarrassed to be seen in glasses. "True." Reagan surveyed the papers on the coffee table. "To do work? Jill, you're not feeling well. Don't you know how to take it easy?"

"No," she said as she fiddled with some papers.

"Well, how about you try today? Let me make you some soup."

Jill let out a small laugh. "It's nice of you to think I actually have ingredients to make things."

"How silly of me. Do you have tea?" Jill nodded. "Then I'll make you some and order delivery. Allergies?"

"No, but again, it's not ne—"

Reagan stopped her with a hand to her cheek. "I know it's not. But I want to help. You helped me at my dad's wake, remember? I'd like to do this for you. Okay?" Another nod from Jill. "Now clean all this up. You're not allowed to work anymore."

"You can't be serious. I have so much to do."

"And it will all be there waiting for you after you've gotten some rest. I'll go make you some tea. You watch TV."

"Fine," Jill grumbled, looking adorably sullen.

Satisfied she was listening, Reagan went into the kitchen and admired the beauty of it. Dark blue cabinets with white marble countertops. Stainless steel appliances. When she peeked into the fridge, she saw there were absolutely no ingredients for anything, unless white wine, ketchup, and mayo counted as a meal. She really hoped Jill didn't count that combination as a meal.

Reagan found a kettle and filled it. While she waited for it to heat up, she checked on Jill and found her with her head back and her mouth slightly open as she slept not so peacefully. Reagan quietly ambled across the spacious living room to sneak a peek at Jill's books. Lots of marketing and advertising books.

Second shelf was all thrillers and memoirs. But what caught Reagan's attention the most was the only personal item on the shelf.

A large candle hid a wooden picture frame. It held a picture of what she assumed was a young Jill, judging by the big brown eyes and small scar on her chin. She was maybe six or seven, wearing a Pacers hat that was two sizes too big. She sported a wide smile that showed a missing front tooth, and ketchup stained the corner of her mouth. She looked happy—an emotion Reagan didn't think she had seen yet from Jill. And she wasn't sure if Jill was even capable of it anymore.

The kettle whistled, and Reagan fumbled to put the picture back as Jill let out a loud snore and sat up, looking around with a furrowed brow.

"What's going on?" she asked groggily.

"It's just the teakettle. Let me go get that." Reagan rushed to the kitchen and pulled it off the burner. She snatched a tea bag from a jar on the counter, placed it in a mug, and poured the hot water over it. As it steeped, she pulled out her phone and ordered some chicken noodle soup for delivery from a local diner. Taking the mug to living room, she joined Jill on the couch. "Here you go."

"Thanks. You know you don't need to stay. I've been able to take care of myself since I was a kid," Jill replied with a bite to her voice.

Need to unpack that statement sometime, maybe when she isn't sick. "I'm sure you can, but since I'm here, I might as well help you."

"Suit yourself," Jill mumbled. She settled further into the couch and leaned into Reagan.

She hid a smile as Jill got more comfortable. "Some soup will be here in about fifteen minutes. What are we watching?"

"Oh, um, *RuPaul's Drag Race*," she replied quietly, as if she didn't want to admit it.

"Which season?"

"Eleven."

"Awesome. I love Nina West. I can't believe she—"

Jill cut her off by covering Reagan's mouth with her hand. "No spoilers. I'm only on the second episode."

Reagan smiled behind Jill's hand and gently pulled it away. "My apologies. I promise, no spoilers," Reagan replied as she lifted her feet up on the coffee table and crossed her legs at the ankle.

"Sure. Make yourself at home, Ms. Murphy."

"Don't mind if I do, Ms. Jacobs."

Jill scoffed but didn't say anything more. As a comfortable silence settled over them, Reagan noticed Jill had interlaced their fingers. A warmth enveloped her and she fought against the giddy smile that wanted to break free. She didn't want to make a big deal about it, especially if Jill didn't realize she had done it.

A knock at the door sounded, and Reagan regretfully withdrew her hand from Jill's. She answered the door and took hold of Jill's soup. "Let me just get a bowl."

Jill waved her off. "No need. I usually just eat out of the container."

Reagan chuckled and sat on the couch, handing Jill the container of soup. "Duly noted."

Jill took the lid off and sniffed before frowning. "Well, I'm guessing it smells good," she mumbled.

Reagan sniffed near the bowl. "Yep. Smells great."

Jill shook her head as the corner of her mouth lifted. She gathered a spoonful and held it to her mouth but stopped before she took a bite. "Are there crackers?"

Reagan about melted on the spot at the soft way Jill asked the question, with almost a kid-like wistfulness. She held a different package in each hand. "Oyster or saltines?"

"Definitely oyster," Jill replied as she plucked the packet out of Reagan's hand and dumped then stirred them into her soup. She looked toward the empty bag on the coffee table and back up at Reagan. "Didn't you get anything?"

Reagan waved her away. "Nah. I'll eat later."

"Are you sure? We can split this."

She opened the package of saltines. "I'm good with these," she replied as she took a bite.

Jill shrugged and focused on eating her soup while they watched the show. After she finished, she placed the container on the coffee table before grabbing the blanket next to her and wrapping it around herself. Reagan split her attention between the TV and Jill, who seemed to be fighting sleep.

Reagan lifted her arm and rested it along the back of the couch. As she relaxed, she began scratching the top of Jill's head. It elicited quiet hums and Jill snuggled into Reagan's side. Within minutes, she was asleep. Reagan smiled at her and settled in to let Jill enjoy her nap.

Jill woke up to a soft, warm body underneath her, and for the first time in two days, she felt somewhat rested. *Wait. Warm body?* She jerked back and put her arm on the back of the couch to push herself off…Reagan.

"Hey, hey, it's okay," Reagan said in a soothing, quiet voice.

Jill moved to the opposite end of the couch and rubbed the back of her neck. "No, it's not. I'm sorry."

"You have nothing to be sorry for."

"Thank you for staying, but you can go now." She attempted to stand but didn't it make it more than a few inches before falling back into the cushions.

Reagan closed the distance between them and cupped Jill's cheek. "Let me take care of you. Please."

Jill melted into the touch and closed her eyes, savoring the idea that someone would take care of her for once. "You say that like it's easy," she whispered.

"It can be. Just try."

"Okay," Jill said with a nod.

"Let's get you to bed, huh?" Reagan asked with a soft smile.

"Trying to bed me already, Ms. Murphy?"

"Not in your weakened state. When I try, you'll know. Trust me." Reagan basically lifted Jill off the couch and held on to her waist.

"Looking forward to it," she replied as she raised her head to meet Reagan's gaze.

"Me too," Reagan whispered. "But for now, let me help you to bed, okay? You need your rest."

She nodded without a word and swayed as they took their first step.

"Are you okay?"

"I'm good."

They slowly shuffled up the stairs and into her bedroom. She took a quick look at the sorry state of her room. Sheets ruffled, clothes discarded on a chair in the corner. She wanted to apologize but couldn't find the strength.

"Do you need to use the bathroom?"

"Yeah, but I got it," Jill replied gruffly as she shrugged Reagan off.

Reagan chuckled. "Understood."

Jill grabbed a T-shirt and a pair of boxer shorts from her dresser on her way to the bathroom. She grimaced at the bright light and then again when she looked at herself in the mirror. Dark circles under her eyes looked even worse against her paler than normal skin. Her hair looked as if she'd driven in a convertible with the top down. She took out the hair tie and finger-combed her hair into some semblance of order. Even being on her feet for these brief minutes was making her lightheaded, so she took care of business and brushed her teeth quickly. She changed her clothes, happy to be in something fresh.

When she opened the door, she found Reagan standing on the opposite end of the room and looking out the window. She cleared her throat to get her attention.

Reagan turned around. "Oh, hey. All set?"

"Yeah."

She moved forward and reached Jill's side of the bed at the same time as Jill and they both reached for the sheets.

"I can do this myself, Reagan." She looked down at Reagan's hand brushing her own as they gripped the comforter.

"I know you can, but I'm here. So let me help," Reagan said in her ear.

As Reagan stood behind her, all Jill wanted was melt into her warmth. Instead, she whispered, "I'm not good at that."

"I know. Honestly, I'm not the best at it either. We can learn together. Sound good?"

Jill wordlessly nodded and climbed into bed, pulling the sheets up to her shoulders.

Reagan sat on the edge of the bed and brushed Jill's hair behind her ears. "Are you taking tomorrow off?"

"No, I need to get back to the office."

"Don't you think you should give yourself a bit of a break? This might be your body telling you that you need to slow down."

"I can't. There's too much to do."

Reagan sighed. "Can you promise that you'll think about it if you're still feeling crappy in the morning?"

"Maybe."

"I guess that's the best I can ask for."

"Mm-hmm," Jill replied, reveling in Reagan's light strokes on her scalp. "That feels nice." Her eyes fluttered shut until she remembered an earlier conversation. "Did you eat anything? You said you'd eat later, but it's night now," she mumbled.

Reagan let out a quiet chuckle. "I'm okay." Reagan bent down and kissed Jill on the forehead.

Those warm, soft lips were the last thing Jill felt before drifting off to sleep.

CHAPTER THIRTEEN

Reagan sat at her desk, scrolling through bank statements but not registering any of the information. Ever since leaving Jill's apartment, she had wondered if Jill was feeling better. The urge to check in had been strong, but fear had always held her back. She understood that putting herself out there meant risking her heart, whether it was with Jill or someone else, but she had to admit that the risk was heightened with Jill. Something was there and she couldn't try to deny it anymore. On the surface, Jill might not be the ideal girlfriend, but a gut feeling kept telling her to dig deeper.

She thought back to the picture she'd found in Jill's apartment. A happy kid whose eyes didn't have the shadows of pain, not like Jill's eyes had now. Reagan wondered if she could unearth that happiness again. As thoughts whirled in her mind, she sat up and opened a browser. A quick search told her that the Pacers had their home opener that night. Reagan rested her chin in her hand as she stared at the screen. Would she go?

Only one way to find out. She pulled out her phone and called Jill's cell, wanting to bypass Ash.

"Jillian Jacobs."

She sounded distracted. "Hey, Jill, um, it's Reagan."

"Reagan," she breathed.

"Yeah. How are you? Are you feeling better?"

"I am." Jill cleared her throat. "Thanks to you."

Reagan grinned. "Great! Listen, I was just calling to see if you'd want to go to the Pacers game tonight. Home opener."

"A basketball game? Really?" Jill asked with a scoff.

"Well, I might've done a little snooping in your apartment when you fell asleep. I saw that adorable photo of a little girl wearing a Pacers hat and ketchup on her cheek and wondered if that was you."

"Maybe," Jill replied softly.

"So what do you say? I'll even buy you a hot dog."

"You drive a hard bargain there, Ms. Murphy."

"Is that a yes?"

"It's a yes."

She slumped in her seat and slowly released a breath. "How about I meet you at your apartment and we can Uber from there?"

"Sounds great."

"O-okay. Cool. I'll be there at six thirty? Game starts at seven. It means you might have to be a bit of a slacker and cut out of work early."

"Oh, you think you know me, do you?" she asked in a low voice.

"I'd like to."

"Hmm, I'll see you at six thirty."

With that, Reagan realized Jill had hung up. She stared at her phone for a moment before tossing it on her desk. Okay, so maybe she had been a little too much for Jill in that moment. She understood she'd have to take her time, chipping away at her walls piece by piece, probably the right decision considering the current condition of her own heart. But for now, she'd focus on the positive: she had a date.

After a quick pit stop at home to change, Reagan found herself outside Jill's condo. A mixture of nerves and excitement coursed through her body. She took a calming breath before knocking on Jill's door. A moment later Jill appeared in that damn leather jacket.

"Oh, fuck me." Reagan blatantly raked her eyes over Jill from head to toe. Besides the leather jacket, she had on skinny jeans and a low-cut, white top.

"Excuse me?" Jill asked, a grin threatening to break through her serious expression.

Reagan straightened. "What? I didn't say anything." *Shit, that was out loud, wasn't it? Still accurate, though.*

"You definitely did. My my. Such language, Ms. Murphy."

Knowing she'd been caught, Reagan shrugged. "Fine. I won't deny it. You look amazing, Jill. That leather jacket on you..." She cleared her throat. "Let's just say it looks very, very nice. Quite soft and easy to grip if I remember correctly."

A hint of red dusted Jill's cheeks. "Interesting. Maybe you should test that out again later."

"Maybe I will," Reagan whispered as she lightly brushed her lips against Jill's warm cheek. Pulling back, she connected with those dark brown eyes. "Hi."

"Hi," Jill replied with a small smile.

She gestured down the hallway. "Ready to go? Our car should be waiting."

"By all means, lead the way."

The drive to the arena was quick and rather silent, but Reagan snuck glances at Jill every chance she could. The upturned corner of Jill's mouth told her she had caught her every time.

After they went through security, Reagan guided Jill down the concourse to their section. Their seats were in the fifteenth row behind the visitors' bench, seats that had cost Reagan a rather obscene amount of money only a couple hours ago. *Price of last-minute decisions.*

They settled in as the teams warmed up. Jill sat stiffly in the seat and clasped her hands in her lap as she glanced around the arena. Reagan didn't feel all that relaxed either. First date jitters, and even though they had some banter at the condo, she was now fearful she'd say something even more stupid and mess things up.

She tapped Jill on the knee to get her attention. "So when was the last time you were at a game?"

"You know that picture you saw when you were rudely snooping at my place?"

Reagan held up a finger. "Snooping sounds like such a harsh word. Exploring sounds much better and adventurous."

Jill shook her head. "If you say so. Anyway. That was the last time."

Reagan frowned. "How come? You looked like you had a lot of fun."

Jill nodded with a thin smile. "I did. That was until about five minutes after that picture was taken and I spilled my lemonade all over myself and the person next to me. I was never allowed to go again."

"That's not fair. You were just a kid. Accidents happen all the time."

"Yes, well, accidents are not appreciated when they happen in your stepfather's company suite and you spill on one of his biggest clients." Jill shrugged, but Reagan still saw the hint of pain she tried to hide.

"That sucks. But what about now? Don't you have your own clients to woo in a suite?"

"Sure, but that's not what I want to spend my time doing. My boss does that kind of thing. Besides, there's way too much work to do."

"So, you don't make any time for much outside of work, then?"

"Not really, no," Jill replied absently as she watched a couple players shooting threes.

With that, Reagan deflated. "Good to know," she muttered.

After a beat, Jill turned to her with wide eyes. "Shit, that came out wrong." She reached for Reagan's hand and squeezed. "I mean, yes, I put in a lot of hours at the office, and that doesn't leave a lot of free time. But…" She took a breath as if steeling herself for her next words, "but I've never had something, or someone, that was worth freeing up my time." She stroked her thumb across Reagan's knuckles while avoiding eye contact, as if she had been ashamed to admit that.

Reagan turned her hand over and interlocked their fingers. "Are you saying you might've found that?" she asked, tentative and hopeful.

"I'd like to think so."

"Me too." Reagan smiled and squeezed Jill's hand. Jill seemed to relax at that, and she continued stroking Reagan's hand with her thumb.

The announcer began player introductions for the visiting Pistons. The small amount of Detroit fans cheered for their team amongst a fair number of boos from the home crowd. As he announced the starting lineup for the Pacers, Reagan and Jill stood, but neither let go of the other's hand. Reagan let out a yell as the first two players were introduced. She looked over to Jill who just watched with little emotion. She nudged her shoulder and gestured with her free hand to the court as Myles Turner was announced. Jill shook her head then let out the loudest whistle Reagan had ever heard. She winced playfully before squeezing her hand and saying, "That's more like it."

Jill just smiled.

After the introductions, Reagan reluctantly let go of Jill's hand as the National Anthem played. They watched the first few minutes of the game in relative silence. A groan at a missed shot. A small cheer at a great block. The crowd's initial energy made it a little too loud for conversation unless Reagan wanted to shout at her. And she didn't think that would go over very well.

As a TV timeout started, she leaned over and asked, "Want a beer?"

"Sure."

"Any particular kind?"

Jill shrugged. "Surprise me."

Reagan grinned. "My pleasure," she said, kissing Jill's cheek. "Be right back."

She jogged up the steps to the concourse and scanned the area for the closest concession stand—and spotted a souvenir cart. Remembering the picture in Jill's apartment, she decided to make a quick purchase. *After all, she said to surprise her.*

After paying for all the goodies, Reagan balanced the tray of beer and two hot dogs in one hand, while holding a bag to her side. As she approached their row, she was relieved to see that Jill was paying attention to the game and not on her phone. She pounded her fist on her knee as Brogdon missed a three. Reagan grinned at the cuteness and vowed to take Jill to more games in the future.

She shuffled down the row before taking her seat. She handed the tray to Jill, sliding the bag underneath her seat.

"What do you have there?"

"Don't worry about that right now. It's time for dinner," she replied as she took the two beers out of the tray and put them in the cup holders. "Hot dog?" She hoped Jill wouldn't scoff at the idea of eating one. "Sorry, it's not a fancy dinner or anything. I can go get you something else."

"Hand it over, Reagan," Jill replied as she extended her hand. Jill surprised her by unwrapping the hot dog and taking a bite, licking ketchup and mustard off the corner of her mouth.

"Good?"

"Mmm, delicious."

Reagan sat back with a grin and enjoyed her hot dog. Jill seemed to relax beside her as the game continued, finishing her hot dog and washing it down with a large swig of beer. When Reagan finished hers, she grabbed the bag under her seat. "So, you told me to surprise you."

"Okay," Jill said, dragging out the word and narrowing her eyes at Reagan.

She reached into the bag and pulled out a blue and yellow Pacers snapback. Holding it out to Jill, she waited for her reaction.

Jill crossed her arms. "And what do you expect me to do with that?"

"Wear it," Reagan replied as she ripped off the tag and rolled the brim of the hat between her hands before placing it on Jill's head. "There. It fits better this time."

Jill huffed and adjusted the hat, but then her eyes softened. "Thanks, Reagan."

"You're welcome."

Settling in to watch the rest of the second quarter, Reagan rested her hand on top of Jill's thigh. She drew random patterns with her finger, and Jill leaned into her a little more. As the buzzer for halftime sounded, the fans stood to clap before some exited the row.

"Did you need to get up at all? Use the bathroom?"

"No. I'm good." Jill held Reagan's hand loosely in her lap. "Are you still at your par…mom's house?"

Reagan took a deep breath and released it slowly. "You can still say parents. I'll always think of it as my parents' house. And no, I'm not. Moved back to my place about a week and a half ago."

"How is it?"

"Good and bad, I guess," she replied with a sad smile. "It was hard being at home once he was gone. And I know my mom needs time to grieve alone."

"Makes sense."

"I'm glad you could make it tonight," Reagan said, wanting to change the subject to something happier. "Honestly, I wasn't sure you'd say yes."

"What makes you say that?"

"Well, even with seeing that picture at your place, I didn't think this would be your kind of thing."

"You're right. It's not. Maybe you just caught me on a lucky day."

Reagan opened her mouth to ask more, but a tap on her shoulder interrupted their quiet chat. They stood to let two guys get back to their seats. The rest of the game held their attention, and conversation only consisted of random observations of game play. As the final buzzer sounded, Reagan realized Jill had held her hand for the rest of the game. The fact that the Pacers just lost didn't register with her at all.

"Did you have a good time?" Reagan asked as they waited for the Uber.

"I did. Maybe I could be a basketball fan after all."

Reagan smiled widely. "Fandom looks good on you." She flicked the bill of Jill's hat before turning it backward. "But I think it looks better like this."

"Is that so?" she asked with a raised eyebrow.

"Mm-hmm. Because then I can do this," she said, kissing her.

Jill moaned in approval, wrapping her arms around Reagan's waist and tugging her forward so quickly they fell back into a lamppost.

As she grazed her teeth against Reagan's lower lip, Reagan gripped on to her jacket and groaned as she pulled away. "See. Much easier with it backward."

Jill chuckled. "I definitely agree with you." Several pairs of eyes stared at them. She whispered to Reagan, "But as much as I want to continue, I'm not giving strangers a show. That's reserved only for you."

"Right," she replied shakily. An alert chimed, and she pulled out her phone. "He's pulling up."

They turned in time to see a black Elantra stop at the curb. The driver rolled down his window and asked, "Reagan?"

"Yep." She pocketed her phone and opened the back door.

Jill slid in and held out her hand to Reagan as she followed. The driver turned on the radio, leaving them to themselves. Riding along, Jill rested her hand on Reagan's thigh, becoming a little more daring with each passing minute. She slowly moved higher and higher, sneaking a glance every so often to gauge Reagan's interest. Her heated stare and the slight parting of her thighs hinted at exactly what she wanted.

Jill continued her slow strokes as she looked out the window when the song changed. Immediately, the thigh beneath her hand turned to stone. She looked to Reagan, whose face had gone ghostly white, noticeable even in the dark car. The streetlights illuminated her eyes filled with tears.

Panicked, Jill squeezed Reagan's knee. "What's wrong?"

"His song," Reagan choked out before stifling a sob with her hand.

Jill heard the familiar notes of "Lean on Me" and was confused as to what Reagan meant, but within seconds she understood. Her father. "Change the station."

"But this is a great song," the driver replied.

"Change the fucking song. Now," she barked. He obeyed, and Jill wrapped her arm around Reagan. She kissed the crown of her head and whispered that everything would be okay. Reagan stayed relatively quiet, but Jill couldn't ignore the continual shaking of her shoulders.

After the driver pulled up to her building, Jill helped Reagan out of the car and into her condo. Once she closed the door behind them, Jill cupped Reagan's cheek. "Let me get you some water."

Reagan nodded as she moved to a stool. Jill placed the glass in front of her, and Reagan shakily brought it to her mouth and took two small sips.

She pushed a few wayward strands of hair behind her ear. "Feel better?"

"Yeah. Thank you."

"Wanna stay? It's been a long night and I'm worried about you driving home. I have a guest room upstairs." Reagan didn't answer right away and Jill immediately began second-guessing herself. *Am I being too forward? She understands I'm just worried and have no intention of sleeping with her, right?*

Finally, Reagan nodded. "Okay. That'd probably be best."

She led Reagan up the stairs, stopping at the first door on the right. As she pointed into the room, she said, "There's an attached bathroom through that door. Let me go get you something to sleep in." When she tried to turn away, a firm grip on her wrist stopped her. As she met Reagan's eyes, she saw an almost desperate look in them, and fresh tears threatened to spill over.

"I don't wanna be alone tonight," she whispered.

"Okay." She kissed Reagan's forehead and pulled her down the hallway. "Follow me."

Once they were in her bedroom, Jill handed Reagan a T-shirt and a pair of shorts from her dresser and nodded behind her to the bathroom. "Go ahead and get changed. There should be a new toothbrush in the top drawer."

Reagan wordlessly accepted the clothes before heading to the bathroom and shutting the door behind her. Jill stared at the closed door for a moment before grabbing a change of clothes for herself to take into the guest bathroom.

As she finished brushing her teeth, she stared at herself in the mirror. She could never imagine the amount of pain Reagan had endured the past few months. She didn't know what it felt like to have that deep a love for another person. She shook her head, aware of how unsettling that thought was when it came to what she wanted with Reagan. While she wasn't well-practiced in the intricacies of relationships, if that's what Reagan wanted, then she was ready to try. She'd been on her own long enough. Being around Reagan had given her a glimpse into what it would be like to be close to someone—and not just physically. Although that was definitely a perk, she was curious about what Reagan saw in her and what made her ask Jill on a date. But that would have to be a discussion for another night.

Jill returned to her bedroom but didn't see Reagan. The bathroom door was still closed so she knocked twice. "Reagan?" No reply so she knocked again. "You okay?" This time she heard a whimper. *Oh shit*. "I'm coming in."

Reagan was on the floor and curled against the side of the bathtub. Jill immediately dropped to the tile and pulled Reagan into her arms. Reagan gripped her T-shirt so tightly that Jill was afraid it would rip. She buried her face against her chest and wailed. Jill closed her eyes. Reagan had been through so much this year. Was this the first time she had let herself break down? Jill imagined Reagan would try to be strong for those around her. Jill hoped she was being strong for Reagan now. She rocked her in her arms while Reagan continued to cry and murmured, "It's okay. Let it out. You're safe with me."

Eventually, Reagan pulled away and roughly wiped at the remaining tears on her cheeks. She mumbled, "Sorry." She stood, facing away from Jill.

Jill stepped behind her, resting a hand on the small of her back. "You have nothing to be sorry for." She handed Reagan a tissue and rubbed small circles on her back as Reagan blew her nose. "Ready for bed?" Jill whispered.

Reagan nodded and headed for bed.

Jill turned off the lamp, slid in, and pulled the covers up to her shoulders. She lay on her back with her hands at her side, uncertain of the protocol in this situation, especially now that Reagan had calmed down and had seemed slightly embarrassed about what had just happened. Did she offer comfort or was Reagan the type who ignored emotion? *No, that doesn't seem right. She's not like me.*

"I'm sorry for tonight," Reagan whispered in a scratchy voice as she squeezed Jill's hand under the sheets.

Jill heard a sniffle, and then Reagan cleared her throat. With that, Jill went with her gut. She tugged on Reagan's hand, opened her arms and said, "Come here." In no time, Reagan fell into her, wrapping an arm around Jill's waist and resting her head against her shoulder. "You have absolutely nothing to be sorry for. Okay?"

Reagan nodded into her neck, and she felt Reagan's tears on her skin. Jill kissed the top of her head and lightly scratched her fingers up and down her arm. Within minutes, Reagan's breathing evened and she relaxed. Jill let out a slow breath. The fierce need to protect Reagan had felt natural all night. She just hoped she'd always be up to that task, and that Reagan would willingly accept it.

With a last kiss to Reagan's forehead, she pulled her closer and slept.

Reagan woke, turning onto her back and feeling the other side of the bed. Empty. She sighed as she rubbed her face with her hands. Her eyes felt dry and puffy, no doubt from all the crying she'd done. *God, how embarrassing*. She'd really been looking forward to whatever had been about to happen between her and Jill last night. Just thinking about Jill's wandering hand in the car sent delicious tingles through her body. But now, she felt as if everything would come to a screeching halt.

She sat up and twisted from side to side, groaning as she stretched her muscles. Tossing the sheet aside, she stood and looked for her clothes. A smile formed as she found them neatly folded on top of Jill's dresser. She got dressed and went downstairs but stopped when she saw Jill sitting at the island drinking coffee and going over paperwork. She wore sweats and a hoodie, her hair in a haphazard ponytail, and she was wearing her glasses. Reagan melted at the vision in front of her. While she had the urge to wrap Jill in her arms from behind, instead she held back a sigh as she thought about what she needed to do. "Morning."

Jill snapped her head around. "Oh, hey. I didn't wake you, did I?"

"Not at all. Have you been up a while?"

"A couple hours maybe," Jill replied with a shrug.

Reagan looked down at her hands, picking at her thumbnail. "Thanks again for last night. I never imagined I would lose it like that."

"It's okay, Reagan."

"No, I don't think it is. I asked you out and I end up sobbing uncontrollably."

"It's understandable. You just had a tremendous loss. While I don't have much experience with it, I don't think grief has any sort of rule book."

"I guess. But you shouldn't have to deal with it."

"What do you mean?"

"Maybe I'm not ready for something if I can't keep my emotions in check."

"Are you saying you want to end this?" Jill gestured to each of them.

Reagan sighed. "Honestly, no. I like you, Jill. And you seem to have gotten under my skin. But I feel like I've been putting too much of my emotional baggage on you. At the wake and again last night. I know it makes you uncomfortable."

"Do you think I'm not up for it? Supporting you?"

Reagan saw pain flicker in Jill's eyes. "No, that's not it. It's just not fair to you."

Jill pulled Reagan between her legs. "Why don't you let me decide what's fair to me and what isn't?"

"But if it's too much, I'd rather you tell me now than later. I think it'd be easier that way."

"I'm not running away screaming, Reagan. And I don't plan to."

"Are you sure?"

"Yes."

"Will you tell me if it's too much?"

"Yes, ma'am."

"Thank you." Reagan captured Jill's lips in a soft, slow kiss. She pulled back and quirked an eyebrow. "And ma'am, huh? I like that."

"Is that right?"

"Mm-hmm." Jill licked her lips, and it took every ounce of Reagan's strength not to pounce on her. However, rational thoughts prevailed. Standing up straight with her hands on Jill's knees, she took a deep breath and said, "I should get going."

"Oh. Are you sure? There's more coffee if you want to stay."

"I told my mom I'd be over today. We're planning a trip for the week of Thanksgiving. Going to spread my dad's ashes at a cabin we went to every year."

"That sounds nice," Jill replied as she brushed the backs of her fingers against Reagan's cheek.

"It will be. But it's gonna be hard, especially for my mom. We've never been there without him." Jill gently squeezed her hands. Reagan smiled. "It'll be good, though. My mom and I will have time to talk, maybe try to figure out how to find our new normal. But I'll see you on Friday, right? We have our final meeting to go over last-minute details."

Jill unlocked her phone and checked her calendar. "Yep, I have it down for three." She put the phone down and looked at Reagan, biting the corner of her lip and clearing her throat. "What would you say if we changed the time?"

"To when?"

"What about after work? You could come over and we can grab some takeout or something."

"Well, that is a much better idea, Ms. Jacobs," she replied with a kiss.

"I thought so."
"Have a good day. Don't work too hard."
"Yes, ma'am," Jill replied with a grin.
Reagan grinned and waved before walking out the door.

CHAPTER FOURTEEN

Reagan adjusted her bag on her shoulder outside Jill's door. When it opened, Reagan eyed her from head to toe, loving the fact that Jill seemed to have the slightly rumpled, end of the workday wardrobe on. She wore skinny, black dress pants and a white long-sleeve button-up with the sleeves rolled up and the top few buttons undone. Her feet were bare, toenails painted a dark purple. As Jill ushered her into the condo, Reagan placed a soft kiss on her lips.

"Hey, you," she whispered.

"Hi. Glad you could make it."

"How was your day?" Reagan asked as she placed her bag on the island.

Jill took a loose hold of Reagan's fingers in her own. "Busy like always. We have this campaign for a sports drink company that my team has been working hard on. Client seems difficult to please, so every time we think we have it nailed down, they tell us just how wrong we are. Then it's back to square one."

Reagan tapped her finger to her chin. "Hmm. Sounds familiar. I just can't place it," she said with a grin.

"Are you trying to say something about me, Ms. Murphy?"

"You? No. Well, not anymore," she said with a wink. "Your mother…that's a different story."

Jill scoffed. "Tell me about it."

"Wanna get that stuff out of the way? Then I'm all yours."

"Really? All mine, huh?" Jill asked with a lift of her eyebrows.

"For dinner. I'm all yours for dinner."

"Mmm. Tasty."

After replaying her words, Reagan covered her face with her hands. "Shit, that came out all wrong."

Jill chuckled. "I have no problem with how it came out. Looking forward to it, in fact."

"Stop." Reagan playfully shoved her away, pulling a folder from her bag. "Let's get to work."

"Fine. Wine?" Jill asked as she held up a bottle.

"Please."

Jill poured them each a glass and took a seat on the stool next to Reagan.

"First, your mother gave me the final guest list, and she said she didn't have any changes since her last-minute additions from a week ago. Think that's the truth?"

"With my mother? Probably not."

"Perfect," Reagan mumbled. "Well, we'll be prepared in case she surprises us with additional guests. Now, let's move on to timing."

For the next thirty minutes, she went over every detail of the party with Jill. She made a few notes to share with Gwen, but everything seemed in order. Reagan gathered her papers into a neat stack and placed them in her bag. "Okay, I think that's it. If you have questions or adjustments you'd like to make before next Saturday, then let me or Gwen know. Sound good?"

"Yes, thank you. I'm sure I'll be fielding a million questions from my mother during the week. Hopefully she won't have any outrageous last-minute demands. But she's known to have them," Jill said, rubbing the back of her neck. "Ready for some takeout?"

"That sounds great. What are you thinking?"

Jill rummaged through a drawer and held up a few menus. "We've got a diner, Chinese, and Italian. What's your poison?"

"How about Chinese?"

Jill tossed the other two menus back into the drawer and held out the Chinese menu to Reagan. "Let me know what you'd like."

Reagan held Jill's gaze firmly and lifted a shoulder. "Surprise me."

Jill took in a quick breath and bit the corner of her lip. "I will," she whispered, heading back to her phone.

As Reagan listened to Jill's soft voice as she placed their order, she topped off their wine and carried the glasses to the living room.

"It'll be here in thirty minutes," Jill said as she sat down next to Reagan, putting more space between the two of them than Reagan wanted. "So, tell me how you got where you are. Why restaurants?"

Reagan brought a leg onto the couch and rested her arm along the back. "That's easy. All Gwen's idea. We met our freshman year in high school and instantly became best friends. She always loved food and discovering new flavors. In high school, you always dream about what you'll be when you grow up. Gwen knew very early on and she pursued it. Got a job at a restaurant as soon as she could, starting as a server and working her way up to line cook by the end of high school."

Jill tapped her on the knee. "Okay. So how did you get involved?"

Reagan smiled. "Well, I've always loved numbers and logistics, so we made a plan that one day we'd open a restaurant together, Gwen as the chef and me on the business side of things. After she finished culinary school, she moved to Bloomington and found a job at a friend's restaurant. I was still finishing my business degree at IU so we moved in together. And when she wasn't working and I wasn't studying, we spent our free time analyzing restaurants around the country. We looked for any information we could find—how long they took to open, were they successful or did they close, age of the head chef, who bankrolled it—anything and everything. When Gwen wasn't helping with that, she was creating concept ideas and testing out recipes in our tiny galley kitchen. She had some definite fails, but some of the dishes she created are on the menu at The Silo or Wren."

"Can I ask a question that might seem a little rude?" Jill asked, caressing Reagan's knee.

Reagan furrowed her brow, wondering what the question could be that would need that kind of lead-in. "Go ahead."

"How could you afford to open the first one? Opening a restaurant is expensive, right?"

"Heck yes, it is. Thankfully, both Gwen and I have been working since we were fifteen. With my parents' help and some scholarships, college only cost me a few grand a year. I also had a knack for numbers and enjoyed investing. Aside from a few splurges, I saved or invested every dollar I made in high school and college. By the time we had a solid concept and menu put together I had enough saved up to start us out."

"What about Gwen? Didn't she have to contribute anything?"

"Oh, she contributed the most important part—the food and the ideas. We wouldn't be where we are without her amazing skills in the kitchen."

"So, you trusted her that much that you put all your money into her?"

"Of course. She's my best friend. I trust her and will always put my faith in her."

"Oh," Jill replied in a despondent voice, shifting her gaze away.

"What's wrong?"

"I'm fine."

"Don't bullshit me, Jill. You got all quiet."

"It's just..." Jill took a deep breath and leaned her head back against the couch, looking up at the ceiling. "I don't know what that's like. And I don't know if I can do that. I just don't think I'm wired that way. To fully trust someone."

Reagan covered Jill's hand that was still resting on her knee. "Have you ever tried?"

"No. Not really. I mean, Sam knows me better than anyone else in my life. But she doesn't know everything. I guess I'm a little hard to get to know."

"Well, no shit," Reagan said with a wink, hoping to take the sting out of that remark.

Jill chuckled briefly before furrowing her eyebrows and shaking her head. "I think that's the first time I've ever voiced that. I know I can be cold and closed off, but I never wanted to analyze that before. Probably because I was raised not to. What is it about you?" she asked, eyes conveying a hint of innocence and hope.

Reagan smiled softly. "I don't know. Wanna stick around and find out?"

"Yes," Jill whispered.

"Good." Reagan leaned forward to capture her lips. So warm and addicting. That was how she had always thought of Jill's lips. Jill kissed her back, hesitantly at first, as if just speaking her thoughts had been too much and threatened to push her over the edge.

But as soon as Reagan grazed her tongue against Jill's lower lip, Jill granted her access and pulled Reagan onto her lap. She shivered as Jill's fingers dipped underneath the bottom of her shirt. A gentle squeeze propelled Reagan's hips to roll forward, moans escaping from both of them. A knock sounded at the door, and Reagan broke the kiss with a gasp.

"Shit," Jill muttered as she took a deep breath. "That must be the food."

Jill shifted beneath her, but Reagan stopped her with a hand on her chest. "I'll get it."

"No. I will. It's my place and I asked you to come over."

"What I want is for you to stay there. Catch your breath. You're gonna need it later," Reagan whispered in her ear. She hopped off Jill's lap and headed for the door, grabbing cash out of her purse on the way. Holding the bag of food in one hand, she asked, "Chopsticks or forks?"

Jill laughed. "I'm embarrassed to say forks. Could never get the hang of chopsticks. They're in the drawer left of the dishwasher."

"Got 'em." Reagan distributed the food, her mouth watering at the sight and smell of shrimp lo mein. "Ooo, yum. What do you have?"

"Beef and broccoli," Jill said around a mouthfull of food. "Sorry. I don't think I've eaten anything since breakfast."

"No worries. Wanna watch a movie?"

"Sure." Jill put her fork in her container and reached for the remote on the coffee table.

After picking a comedy from her watch list, they sat in silence enjoying their movie and their food. When they were each about halfway done with their containers, they swapped without exchanging a word as if it were the most natural thing in the world. Reagan placed the empty container on the coffee table with Jill following her lead. Reagan moved closer to Jill and within seconds, Jill rested her hand on Reagan's thigh.

As they watched the movie, Reagan's mind drifted to something Jill had said earlier, something about how she was raised. "So, tell me about your family. Gwen was the one with the initial contact with your mother, so I don't really know anything about them aside from meeting your mom at the tasting."

Jill stiffened at the words and removed her hand from Reagan's leg, clasping her hands together in her lap. "Not much to say."

"There should be plenty to say. They're your parents. Do you have any siblings?"

Jill sat up straighter and put some distance between them. Reagan immediately missed Jill's warmth. "First off, it's my mother and stepfather. He's not my father."

"Okay, I'm sorry. How long has he been your stepfather?"

"Since I was born."

Her brow furrowed. "Why don't you like him?"

Jill grabbed her glass of wine and took a big gulp. "My mother got knocked up when she was nineteen by some guy who my grandfather always referred to as 'trash.' My grandfather didn't want anything tarnishing the Prescott name, so he made a deal with the son of his law firm partner, my stepfather. He married my mother in exchange for an immediate partnership in my grandfather's law firm. So, I've had to deal with him since the day I was born." Jill knocked back the rest of her wine before standing and making her way into the kitchen. With jerky movements, she grabbed a bottle of whiskey, poured a splash into a rocks glass and drank it. "Want some?"

Reagan shook her head. *Guess I brought up a touchy subject.*

Jill poured herself two fingers of whiskey before returning to the couch—farther away with her knees pulled up to her chest. She sipped her drink as she blankly stared across the room.

Reagan hadn't meant to bring up something that obviously caused Jill a lot of pain. She debated whether she should press on or just get up and leave. Looking at the expression on Jill's face made the decision for her. "I'm sorry."

"For what?"

"You having a shitty family."

Jill shrugged and took another drink. "It's fine. I survived. Some would even say I thrived."

"You did. You're very successful. There's no arguing that."

"Why do I feel there's something else you want to say, Reagan? If that's the case, then just say it."

Reagan scooted forward a few inches, seeing how close she could get without scaring Jill off. When Jill didn't back away, she moved forward again and lightly took hold of the top of Jill's foot, slowly rubbing her thumb along her ankle. "Is it really thriving if you just hide all of your pain and shut out everyone else around you?"

Jill stiffened but stayed in place. "That's what I was taught. Never show emotion or vulnerability. If you did, you were weak. And the weak didn't succeed." Jill finished her drink but held the empty glass in her hands like it was her lifeline.

Reagan grabbed it from Jill's hands and placed it on the coffee table. She moved closer and rested her hand on top of Jill's knee. "Showing emotion isn't weak. I hope you know that now."

Jill shrugged.

"How did you find out he was your stepfather? Did you ever call him 'Dad'?"

"I did when I was younger and didn't know any better. But I was snooping around his office one Christmas when I was about ten and found what looked to be a contract he signed with my grandfather. There were references to the unborn child. All the dates lined up with my birthday, so I put two and two together and figured I was the unborn child. I didn't fully understand it all, but I brought it to them and asked about it. They didn't even try to deny it. They told me everything."

"But how could they do that? You were just a kid."

"Yeah, well, I was just a bargaining chip." Jill crossed her arms and turned her head away.

Reagan closed her eyes at the pain in Jill's voice and squeezed her knee. "Hey. I'm sorry. That must have been awful and devastating, especially to learn about it as a kid. Jill, would you look at me?" When she turned, her heart broke. Jill's eyes were filled with tears that were ready to fall. "Oh, sweetheart, you're okay."

Biting her lip, Jill whispered, "If it's okay, I'd like to stop talking about me and my family."

"Of course. Come here." Reagan opened her arms, which Jill fell into willingly. She didn't hear any cries or sniffles, but Jill took a few slow, deep breaths. Reagan rested her hand on the back of Jill's neck, gently kneading the tight muscles. Reagan knew how hard it had been for Jill to open up, and she was proud of her.

Jill pulled away and wiped at the corners of her eyes. "Thanks, Reagan."

"You're welcome. You can always talk to me. Okay?"

"Yeah, I know. It might take some time."

"Take as long as you need."

Jill gave her a soft smile then cleared her throat. "Will you tell me about your dad? If it's not too hard, I mean."

"Sure."

Jill patted her thigh. "Put your head in my lap."

Reagan followed her direction and stretched out on the couch, resting her head on Jill's leg. Immediately, Jill ran her fingers through Reagan's hair. "Mmm. That feels wonderful. So, what would you like to know?"

"Everything. Whatever you feel like sharing."

Reagan regaled Jill with several stories about her dad. Some she had experienced firsthand, while others had been told to her over the years. They took her back to happier times before her dad was ever sick. With each story, a peace seemed to come over her, healing a little of her broken heart.

Reagan slowly became aware of something rubbing against her arm. "Huh? What's going on?" she mumbled. She opened her eyes and glanced around the room. The lights were dim but she could see enough to realize she wasn't at home. She was covered with a blanket, something she didn't remember doing. When she rolled onto her back, she felt the warmth from a hand that now rested on her chest. She looked up, and met Jill's amused, brown eyes.

"Hey, you."

"Hey, yourself. How long have I been out?"

Jill turned her wrist, looking at her watch. "A couple hours. It's just after midnight."

Reagan rubbed her face. "I'm sorry. I didn't mean to fall asleep."

"It's okay. You were cute."

"I doubt that. I should get out of your hair." Reagan wanted to sit up but she decided against that once Jill started massaging a line between her breasts. The touch was soothing at first, but once Jill slipped her hand under her shirt and continued the same motions, Reagan's body had a slightly different reaction. "Mmm. You keep doing that and I might not want to leave."

Jill's fingers grazed her nipple through her bra. "You don't have to, you know?"

Reagan stilled her movements and sat up, dislodging Jill's arm. "Don't have to what?"

"You don't have to leave." Jill leaned in, stopping when her mouth was a breath away from Reagan's lips. "Stay. Please."

Reagan closed the distance for a gentle kiss. When she pulled back, she met Jill's gaze and whispered, "Okay."

Jill stood and held out her hand. "Come on. I'll get you something to change into."

Jill pulled her from the couch and they faced each other. "Or I don't have to wear anything at all," Reagan said into Jill's ear before dropping a soft kiss right below it.

Jill swallowed. "I have no objections to that."

"Didn't think you would." Reagan reached under Jill's shirt, trailing her fingers along her sides. "Take me upstairs, Jill."

"Gladly," she replied, pulling Reagan up the stairs and into her bedroom. She stepped around the bed and turned on a lamp.

Reagan pressed against Jill's back, wrapping her arms around her waist. She moved her hair out of the way and placed light kisses along her neck. Jill's skin was warm beneath her lips and smelled faintly of vanilla and sandalwood.

Jill shivered, letting out a low moan as she tilted her head. "Please keep doing that."

Reagan chuckled. "Maybe later. But first I need to see you," she replied as she turned Jill around. She held her face in one hand, brushing her thumb along Jill's bottom lip. "And kiss you."

God, how she wanted to kiss her. But she also wanted to take her time and savor each moment. Reagan stopped right before their lips met, and Jill sucked in a breath. Her patience ran out and she crushed her lips against Jill's, groaning at the hunger with which Jill kissed her back. As Jill wrapped her hands in her hair, Reagan undid the buttons of Jill's shirt. She nibbled her bottom lip and kissed a line from her chin to the base of her throat. Jill sucked in a breath and rolled her hips forward. Reagan skimmed Jill's bare stomach but stopped at the waistband when Jill covered her hands. She pulled back to look into Jill's eyes, afraid she would see regret. "What's wrong?"

"As much as I want this, want you, I need to make sure you're okay."

Jill paused and Reagan's heart sunk. *Please don't tell me to stop*. She wanted Jill so badly. She had been craving her kiss and her touch ever since the night at the bar. And if she was being honest with herself, that craving had started when she first laid eyes on Jill.

"It's been an emotional night, and I don't want to take advantage of you."

Reagan let out a slow breath and relief washed over her. She held Jill's hands and squeezed. "I appreciate the check-in, but I'm good. Way better than good. I've wanted this for a while now."

"God, me too," Jill replied, weaving their fingers together.

"Speaking of check-in…Should we have the safety chat?"

Jill looked at her quizzically until realization seemed to set in. "Oh, right. I'm good. Been tested since my last time. I'm clean."

"Me too. Now, where was I?" Her hands traveled back to Jill's stomach and she traced the taut lines of muscle.

"Fuck me," Jill hissed.

Reagan licked her lips as she slid Jill's shirt off her shoulders, letting it fall to the floor. "Oh, I plan to. Over and over again," she replied, unbuttoning Jill's pants and pushing them over her hips. She stared at Jill in her matching black bra and boy shorts, whispering, "Jesus," as she took in the tone of her legs. Legs she wanted wrapped around her. Before she could make her next move, Jill gripped her hips and pulled her forward.

"You have too many clothes on," Jill said gruffly as she pulled her shirt over her head and undid the button and zipper on her jeans. She held on to Reagan's hips, trying to push her toward the bed.

Reagan gripped Jill's hands. "Ah, ah. This is my show. I want you under me while I explore every last inch of you." Reagan turned her until the back of her legs were up against the bed. After removing the last of Jill's clothes, she tossed her own to the side. Reagan pushed her onto the bed, staring at the beautiful body now on display. A body she needed and wanted to learn. She wanted to know what would make Jill squirm and moan and scream.

So she crawled onto the bed, bending down to capture Jill's lips again. Jill grabbed onto her ass and pulled her into her spread legs. Reagan gasped at the contact. She kissed and licked her way down Jill's neck, taking in the sweet taste of her skin. Sliding her fingers between Jill's folds, she moaned at her wetness. Jill lifted her hips and gasped. She teased Jill's clit, lightly stroking it with two fingers.

"God, Reagan. Please."

"Tell me what you want." Reagan took an erect nipple into her mouth, swirling her tongue around it.

"Inside. Fuck, I need you inside."

Reagan bit down on Jill's nipple and slipped one finger inside at the same time. Jill groaned and threw her head back, reaching out to grip Reagan's forearm.

"More," Jill rasped.

Reagan pushed two fingers in, positioning her thigh behind her hand. She sped up as Jill responded with each thrust, tightly wrapping her legs around Reagan's waist. Jill's breathing quickened and she loudly moaned. She came the instant Reagan brushed her thumb over her clit. Reagan slowly moved her fingers in and out as Jill sunk into the bed.

Before Jill had time to recover, Reagan gently removed her fingers and moved down the bed. She pushed open Jill's legs, kissing along the soft, now wet skin of her inner thighs. As she reached Jill's center, she kissed her lightly before circling her clit with her tongue.

"Oh, fuck," she screamed, holding Reagan's head in place, pushing her closer.

Jill gripped her hair tightly. She wouldn't last much longer. Reagan wrapped her lips around Jill's clit, alternating between sucking gently and flicking her tongue against it. Jill came again with a long, guttural moan. Her ragged breaths and the rolling of her hips slowed.

When the pulsations beneath her lips subsided, Reagan placed a last kiss on Jill's center before resting her head on Jill's stomach. Jill lazily ran her fingers through Reagan's hair. And while her own clit throbbed, she smiled at herself in satisfaction as Jill regained control of her breathing.

"Hey," Jill said, her voice husky.

Reagan lifted her head. "Yeah?"

"I…I…nevermind. No words."

Reagan chuckled and kissed her way along the center of Jill's chest and up her neck, finally placing a long, languid kiss on her lips. When Jill lifted her thigh between her legs, Reagan moaned. She was so close the pressure almost made her come at that very moment.

"Fuck, Reagan. You're so wet," Jill ground out. She placed her hand on Reagan's lower back and pushed her forward. "Ride me."

Wordlessly, Reagan obeyed, grinding herself against Jill's firm thigh. She reached for Jill's free hand, interlacing their fingers and pushing it onto the bed above her head. As she rolled her hips, she covered Jill's mouth with hers, kissing her until they were both breathless. Her pace increased and she pulled back to meet Jill's eyes, their hot breath mingling between them. The sensations threatened to overwhelm her but seeing the desire and tenderness in her eyes centered her.

Soft whimpers escaped her lips. "I'm so close." Within seconds, she came with a shout.

"There it is," Jill whispered into her mouth.

Reagan collapsed on top of her and buried her face in her neck while her hips rolled until the orgasm abated. When her breathing slowed, she pulled back and met Jill's gaze. The vulnerability and openness made her heart clench. She leaned forward for a quick kiss before whispering, "You okay?"

"Yeah," Jill replied. "Much better than okay. You make me come undone so easily."

"Is that a good thing or a bad thing?"

"Probably a bit of both." Jill let out a slow breath. "It's just new, that's all."

"I know," Reagan replied. "But we'll navigate it together, right?"

Jill closed her eyes and nodded. "I'd like that."

Reagan kissed the side of Jill's neck and settled her head against her shoulder. As she tightened her arm around Jill's waist, Reagan felt a sheet cover her naked body and heard a lamp click off. Jill skimmed her fingers along Reagan's bare back. The tender movements being the last thing Reagan was aware of until sleep took over.

CHAPTER FIFTEEN

Jill scrunched her nose, trying to dislodge whatever was causing the tickle. When nothing happened, she opened her eyes to find a mass of dark blond hair in front of her face. She leaned her head back and took a full breath, stretching an arm above her head. She rolled forward again, flattening Reagan's hair with her palm. As she wrapped her arm around her waist, Reagan stirred and melted into Jill's embrace.

She kissed the top of Reagan's bare shoulder. "Morning."

Reagan turned, pushing Jill onto her back and curling into her side. "Mmmm," Reagan mumbled into her chest.

Tired Reagan was adorable. Jill laughed as she kissed the top of her head. "Not a morning person, huh?"

She blinked a few times and wiped at her eyes. "I can't say it's my favorite time of day." Reagan propped her head on her hand, drawing her eyes up and down Jill's body. "Although, if I had this view every morning when I woke up, I think mornings would be my new favorite time of day."

Jill pulled her between her legs. "Is that so?" She lifted her head, brushing small nibbles along the length of Reagan's jaw and down her neck.

Reagan sighed. "God, yes."

"I can do so much more to make morning your favorite time of day."

Jill felt her shudder when she licked the base of her throat. She wanted to touch her everywhere and find each spot that would get that reaction. But when she cupped Reagan's breasts in her hands, Reagan pulled away and pushed herself up.

"What's wrong?"

Reagan glanced down at Jill's bare breasts and licked her lips before raising her gaze. "I can't stay. I'm supposed to meet Carly for coffee in thirty minutes."

"Oh. That's okay," Jill replied, brushing Reagan's hair behind her ears. "Guess I'll just have to show you another time."

"Deal," Reagan said with a smile. "Do you mind if I use your shower?"

"Go ahead."

"Thanks." Reagan kissed her quickly before hopping off the bed and leaving Jill alone.

Jill let out a quiet whimper of disappointment as Reagan retreated into the bathroom. Her exit did little to squash Jill's arousal. As she heard the shower turn on, she slipped her hand between her legs. She was wet and ready, her clit throbbing, and she knew it wouldn't take long for her to come. She rolled her hips into her hand, making slow circles around her clit. Scenes from the night before played over and over in her mind. Reagan's hot breath on her face. The way she gripped her hand. How she sounded when she came. She bit her lip to hold in the moans that threatened to escape. A husky voice from the doorway stole her attention.

"Jill?" Reagan stared at Jill's movements beneath the sheets. Jill watched her eyes widen and she licked her lips. Reagan gripped the doorframe tightly. "Join me," she rasped before disappearing from sight.

Jill threw off the covers and rushed into the other room, sliding the glass door open and stepping into the shower behind Reagan. "What happened to needing to go?" she asked, holding Reagan's hips and pressing into her ass. She let out a sigh at the contact and her nipples hardened against Reagan's back.

Reagan turned and wrapped her arms around Jill's shoulders. "I'll tell her I was having mind-blowing sex. I think she'll forgive me."

"Mind-blowing, huh?" Jill whispered, cupping Reagan's breasts and pinching her nipples until she moaned.

"Oh yeah. But I probably shouldn't be too late, so make it quick."

"My pleasure." Jill moved Reagan out of the spray and up against the wall, the steam and her arousal doing enough to keep her warm. She dropped to her knees, never more thankful than now for her large shower.

After the first swipe of her tongue, Reagan plunged her hands into Jill's hair, the tightness of her grip increasing every time Jill circled her clit. The sharp, quick pain of her hold sent a jolt of arousal to her own core. She wished she could tease her and make this last, but that would have to be for another time. If Reagan wanted to come hard and fast, then Jill would make it happen.

Judging by Reagan's fast breaths and even louder moans, Jill sensed she was about to come and she wasn't far behind herself. Jill slid her hand down her own stomach and between her legs and squeezed her clit between her fingers, groaning at the sensation. The vibration against Reagan's clit made her scream and she came in Jill's mouth. Jill increased the pace of her fingers against her own clit and came a second later. She moved her tongue in time with her fingers as they rode out their orgasms together. Reagan's legs shook against her and she stood quickly, wrapping her arms around Reagan's waist to keep her steady.

Jill buried her face against Reagan's neck as Reagan grabbed her hips and pulled her close. She raised her head to place a soft kiss on Reagan's lips. Its slow deliberateness contrasted with what had just occurred. As she pulled back, Reagan sighed. "Quick enough for you?"

"Yes." Reagan took a deep breath. "Definitely."

"Good," Jill replied with a grin. She turned Reagan until she was under the spray and ran her fingers through her hair. "Now time to get clean."

After taking turns washing each other with a few stray caresses that threatened to ignite another round, they got dressed and made their way downstairs. Reagan grabbed her bag off the counter and slung it over her shoulder.

"Dinner tomorrow?" Reagan asked. Her eyes widened before Jill could answer, and she continued, "Shit. Is that too soon?"

Jill chuckled. Usually she would decline in an instant, but that thought never crossed her mind. "Definitely not too soon. I'm in."

Reagan exhaled and lightly kissed her. "I'll call you tonight." Then with a smile and a wave, she walked out the front door.

Alone, Jill sighed. She expected to feel a powerful urge to end things and move on. *Like she normally would.* But last night confirmed what she'd known since the night in the bar. Reagan was intoxicating and grounding, and she wanted more of her—a new feeling she wanted to explore, and if that meant exploring more of Reagan then she was looking forward to it. A lot.

As Reagan started her car, she texted Carly that she'd be late. She received a reply of "No worries," which was the same reply she would have received even if she was two hours late, instead of her current ten minutes because that's just who Carly was.

When she rushed through the door, she spotted Carly at a booth in the back corner, a mug in front of her, so Reagan stopped at the counter and placed her order.

Sliding into the booth, she said, "I'm so sorry I'm late."

"It's okay. I've been reading," she replied, pointing to the book she'd moved to the side.

"Not surprised by that. How's everything with you?"

Carly stared at her with narrowed eyes, as if she was sizing Reagan up.

"What? Do I have something on my face? My clothes?" She touched her face and looked down at her shirt. Sure, it was the same one she wore yesterday, but Carly wouldn't know that. And she didn't think she had spilled anything on it.

"You look different."

"Different how?" At that moment, a waiter placed Reagan's coffee in front of her. "Thank you," she told him, only to notice that his eyes were on Carly and she was blushing. When he walked away, she asked, "What was that?"

"Nope. Uh-uh. Don't change the subject."

Reagan held up her hands. "Whoa. Wouldn't dream of it."

"Good." Carly folded her hands and leaned in. "Now. What's different? You look…Did you have sex?" she squeaked as she pointed a finger.

Reagan reached across the table and pushed her hand down, looking around to see if anyone was paying attention to them. "Why you gotta be so loud about it?"

"Did you have sex?" Carly whispered.

Taking a sip of her coffee, Reagan delayed her answer. It was fun seeing Carly so worked up. She put the mug on the table and licked her lips. "I may have."

Carly raised her arms in the air. "Yes! I knew it. How was it? Who was it with? Was it Jill? Oh, it has to be Jill. Tell me everything."

Reagan laughed. "Again, you're gonna need to calm down. Let the caffeine kick in first."

"Why? Because you were up all night doing the nasty?"

"You're such a dork. And I love you. But to answer your question, you're damn right I was."

Carly sat back with a groan. "God, you're lucky. It's been so long for me." She looked down with a frown before shaking her head and sitting straight again. "Never mind that. Details. I need details."

"First, yes, it was Jill. Who else would it be?"

"I don't know." Carly shrugged. "You've texted me about her, but you've never said you were exclusive or anything. You could have gone to a bar and hooked up with someone, for all I know."

"And when have I ever done that?"

Carly blinked at her. "First two years of college. Like every weekend. Remember?"

"Okay, hold up. That's a bit of an exaggeration. I only slept with three people during that time. The rest were just harmless make-out sessions. Besides, that was a long time ago. When in recent memory have I acted like that?"

"Fine. Never. So, wait, are you guys exclusive?"

Reagan sipped her coffee. "No. At least we haven't talked about it. We've only been on one actual date. It's not time yet for that chat. Plus, I've told you about her. I think any relationship talk will have to come slowly."

"So, slow to talk. Physical, not so much. Am I getting that right?"

"Basically."

"And..." Carly gestured with her hand, dragging the word out. "How was it?"

Reagan sat back and sighed. "Absolutely breathtaking."

"Wow," Carly whispered.

"Yeah. It just all felt...right. Ya know?"

"I do. But what about everything you told me before? How she can be cold."

"She seems different with me," Reagan replied with a shrug. "I think being cold just keeps people from getting close. I don't think she trusts too easily or has a lot of faith in other people. But I've gotten peeks at her humor and passion and pain. She intrigues me. Plus," she stopped to clear her throat as she played with a sugar packet, "I had, um, a small breakdown after our first date. I couldn't have asked for a better response. She protected me, comforted me. She helped me."

Carly grabbed her hand and squeezed. "Oh no. What happened?"

"I'm okay. Heard 'Lean on Me' in the Uber on the way to her place. Crying ensued. Anyway, she could have just sent me on my way as soon as we got back, but she didn't. The next morning I kinda tried to end things, but she wants to stick around."

"That makes me like her a little more. But what about the client aspect?"

"Not really an issue. Gwen and I talked about it a couple weeks ago, and she thinks I should give Jill a chance. She seems cautiously optimistic about it all. And like she said, Jill won't be our client for much longer."

"Right! When is the party?"

"A week from today."

"Everything ready?"

"Yeah, barring any last-minute changes from Jill's mother. But enough about me. Any possibilities for you?"

She put her elbow on the table and rested her chin in her hand. "Well, there is this woman I keep running into during my walk breaks."

CHAPTER SIXTEEN

On the night of the party, Reagan's job was to help wherever needed and to make sure everything flowed smoothly between the kitchen and the dining room. And to keep Maureen from bothering anyone aside from her. Gwen and her staff had done the majority of the prep either earlier or when they arrived three hours before service was to begin. Now it was just a matter of making sure everything was in its right place.

As Gwen and her sous chef, Jeff, dished up the first course, Reagan had a final meeting with their servers. Most of them had worked for TMG in the past so they didn't need much instruction, but she needed to nail down a few of the finer points of the night. She double-checked that they all knew their assignments and the overall floor plan.

Maureen and Douglas had a large, ornate house with way too much unused space. She couldn't imagine growing up in a place like this and she wondered how Jill felt about it. The front living room opened into the dining room, which thankfully accommodated Maureen's guest list. *Good thing she didn't add any more*.

With a last reminder to come to her if they needed anything, Reagan released the servers so they could attend to any last-minute setup. She turned to check on Gwen but ran straight into Jill instead.

Jill steadied her by gripping her upper arms. "Whoa. You okay?"

"Sorry about that. What's with us and bumping into each other all the time? At the bar. Here."

"I think it worked out pretty well at the bar and since, don't you?" Jill asked, her voice low.

"Verdict's still out," Reagan teased.

Jill whispered in her ear, "I can show you more evidence if you need it. Tonight."

Reagan swallowed and gripped Jill's hand. The heat in her eyes made Reagan want to slip away to one of the many bathrooms in the house and have a little fun. Responsibility won out, and she asked, "My place?"

"Yes."

"I need to get to work and you need to head out there."

Jill groaned. "Do I have to? Got a spare server uniform? It's not like Douglas would even know if I was missing."

"The night will be over before you know it. Then the fun can begin," Reagan replied with a wink.

"Looking forward to it." Jill moved toward the dining room, playfully mimicking banging her head against the doorframe.

Reagan chuckled and waved her away. She turned to see Gwen rolling her eyes and grinning, and she smiled wide. "All set?"

"Yep. Soups are ready to go out. Can you watch the room for course change? Give us a five-minute warning so we can dress the salads."

"I'm on it."

She entered the dining area and stood to the side, her hands behind her back and eyes scanning the room. Watching people eat was boring as hell, but she didn't mind this task as it meant she could sneak glances at Jill and take in how sexy she looked tonight. Reagan had figured she'd be in a dress, but she wore a burgundy suit and vest with a black button-up. Instead of her typical tight bun or ponytail, she had her hair down with loose curls.

Reagan stared so long she almost missed that most of the guests were finishing with their soups. She slipped into the kitchen to signal Gwen, but then resumed her position in the dining room.

When she caught herself staring again, Reagan took a breather in the kitchen, sitting on a stool at the island. "Big house, huh?"

"Oh yeah. Be happy you missed the tour. Maureen likes to brag about the extravagance of it all," Gwen whispered.

"I can imagine."

"Is Jill like that?"

Reagan crossed her arms. "No, she's not. And don't look at me like that."

"Like what?"

"Like you're just waiting for me to see the light or something. That you think I need to come to my senses about Jill or that we're wrong for each other. You honestly don't know her."

Gwen sighed and had the decency to look a little ashamed. "You're right. I'm sorry. I think I'm having a hard time separating all this from who you say she is, especially since she was raised by someone like Maureen." She took a deep breath and let it out. "And I don't know her, so let's change that. Invite her out for drinks with us."

"Really?"

"Yes, really. I'm not trying to be an ass, Reagan. I'm just looking out for you. Gotta make sure she's worthy of you."

Reagan walked around the counter and planted a kiss on Gwen's cheek. "Thank you for that." She looked up to catch a signal from their head server. "Looks like dinner is wrapping up. Time for cake."

Reagan rolled out the cart holding the two-tiered chocolate cake to the front of the room where Maureen and Douglas were waiting. She held back a shudder as she felt Douglas's eyes on her and stepped off to the side.

Maureen held up her hand and used a microphone to grab the attention of the guests. "Thank you for coming tonight to celebrate Douglas. Let's raise our glasses to cheers and sing to this wonderful man."

Reagan noticed a forced smile when she saw one, and the one plastered on Maureen's face screamed fake. As the guests sang "Happy Birthday," Reagan caught Jill's eye and mouthed, "Almost over." She received a faint smile in reply. Clapping and loud whistles broke her connection with Jill, and Reagan rolled the cart back into the kitchen so they could cut the cake.

Dozens of plates were lined up on trays on the counters, topped with pieces from the second cake their pastry chef had made. Reagan's mouth watered at the sight. She made a mental note to check for a leftover piece at the end of the night.

As Gwen and Jeff drizzled chocolate sauce on top of each piece, Reagan sat on a stool and watched their practiced hands as they made each plate presentable. After they finished the last one and the servers took the trays into the dining room, Gwen shook Jeff's hand and then held her hand out to Reagan for a high-five.

"Success?" she asked.

Reagan slapped her hand with a smile. "I think so."

Jeff started cleaning his knives and Gwen sat next to Reagan, taking a swig from a bottle of water. She groaned as she arched her back. "Long day, huh?"

"Yep. But now that this is over, I had an idea."

"You're going to tell me about more work, aren't you? We're not even out of here yet," Gwen whined as she gestured to the dirty kitchen.

Reagan held up her hands. "I know, I know. But I want to do a benefit in memory of my dad."

Gwen's expression went from dread to happiness in an instant. "Shit, that's not work. That'll be an honor. When were you thinking?"

"First Saturday of December, which gives us about a month. It doesn't need to be this huge thing, and I haven't put too much thought into it just yet. But I figured passed hors d'oeuvres, open bar, silent auction. Maybe a cover band? I don't know. Meet on Monday to go over a plan?"

"Sounds good. But for now, let's get this place cleaned up so we can get out of here."

"Deal. You start in here and I'll go check the dining room. See how much we still need to clear." She patted Gwen on the shoulder and walked into the other room. Most people were finished with dessert and had gotten up to refresh their drinks at the bar or circulate amongst the crowd.

Reagan found Jill chatting with a blond woman whose back was to her. She breathed a sigh of relief, knowing that the night was almost over. Soon it would be time to indulge in Jill.

Jill and Sam watched Reagan work the room, but every few seconds Reagan caught Jill's eye.

Sam snapped her fingers in front of Jill. "Who's that?"

Jill's attention pulled back to Sam, who stood in front of her with her arms crossed and a raised eyebrow. "What?"

"Who's the hottie over there that's undressing you with her eyes?"

"She is not." Jill looked back at Reagan and found that Sam was right, and her face flushed. She let out a breath and tore her gaze away. "That's Reagan."

Sam's eyes widened. "Reagan? As in ran-away-from-you-at-the-bar Reagan?"

"The one and the same."

"Shit. She's gorgeous, Jill. Since you seemed to scare her away, mind if I take a run at her?" Sam winked at her before turning her attention toward Reagan.

"You'd better not. And I didn't scare her away. We're kind of dating, actually."

"You're shitting me. How did you manage…crap. Here she comes."

Jill turned with a composed smile as Reagan approached. What she really wanted to do was take her by the hand and leave, but she still needed to make the rounds one last time to appease her mother. "Reagan, hello."

"Ms. Jacobs, I hope you enjoyed the party. Was everything to your liking?" Reagan asked, biting the corner of her bottom lip.

Jill stared at Reagan's mouth until she realized what she was doing and shook her head to clear her thoughts. "It was." She turned and nodded to Sam. "Reagan, I'd like you to meet my friend, Samantha."

Sam shook her hand, holding on longer than Jill would have liked. "Pleasure to meet you, Reagan. Please call me Sam."

"It's nice to meet you. How do you two know each other?"

"We grew up together. Families ran in the same circle," she replied as she gestured to the room. "College roommates too."

Reagan's eyes lit up. "Interesting. So you're who I need to talk to when I want some embarrassing information about this one, huh?" she asked with a nod toward Jill.

"Oh, yes." Sam grabbed her clutch off the table and pulled a card out of it. "Here. Call me sometime. To chat. For a drink. Anything you want."

A light blush dotted Reagan's cheeks. "Thanks, but I think I'm all set on the drinks."

Jill sucked in a quick breath at the charged look Reagan sent her way. She wanted to say something, but Reagan spoke before she could.

"If you'll excuse me. I need to finish clearing everything out of here. Have a good night, ladies." Reagan lightly brushed her fingers against the back of Jill's hand.

She watched Reagan retreat until she was in the kitchen and out of sight. She turned on Sam. "Seriously. What was with the ogling? And the extra-long handshake."

Sam crossed her arms and grinned. "Why, Jill, does this one actually mean something?"

"She does. Okay? Is that what you want to hear?"

"Wow," Sam replied, her grin replaced with a soft smile. "Then I really need to hear all about her sometime. But for now, I think I've had my fill of these people for one night. Mother dearest is coming this way. Call me soon."

Jill nodded as Sam kissed her cheek and left. She took a deep breath as she felt a presence behind her.

"Jillian, there are some people you need to say goodbye to."

She turned, forcing a smile on her face once again as she was led away by her mother. Introductions to the couple didn't register because things like this never did. Most of the guests at the party didn't even care about her stepfather. They just wanted the opportunity to mingle with others who might serve their interests, all while enjoying free food and drinks.

After most of the guests cleared out, Jill decided she'd had enough of playing dutiful daughter and hostess, so she went in search of Reagan. As she pushed open the swinging doors, she watched Gwen direct her staff to pack the last of the supplies from the night. Reagan stood at the large island, looking over some paperwork.

"Hi." Jill gently placed her hand on Reagan's lower back.

"Hey. We're almost done here," Reagan replied with a quick wink.

"Perfect. Gwen, thank you for everything. The food was amazing."

"We're happy to hear that."

Jill nodded at her and turned to Reagan. "Can we chat for a sec?"

"Sure."

She led Reagan through a sliding door and onto the patio where soft white lights were strung along the beams of the pergola.

"What's—"

Jill didn't let her finish because she needed to kiss her. The looks. The promise of what was to come. It had all been too much for her. Reagan was quickly becoming someone she couldn't get enough of and she didn't feel the need to question it anymore.

As she moved to deepen the kiss, the door behind them opened with a loud thud. Jill pulled back and saw her mother standing in the open doorway, a menacing smirk on her face. "Oh, Jillian. The hired help. Really?"

She felt warm all over as rage coursed through her body. "Excuse me. You don't—"

"Looks like you're more like Douglas than I thought," Maureen interrupted with a shake of her head. She turned to Reagan and said, "Sorry, but I imagine you'll be out of her life as soon as she's had her fill. Discarding old playthings is what her father does best. Better watch your wallet around this one, Jillian. These sluts are all the same." She paused for a beat and crossed her arms. "Now, come inside. The last of the guests are leaving and you need to say goodbye." Without waiting for any sort of acknowledgment, she walked into the house.

Jill turned to Reagan with an apology on her lips, but when she saw Reagan's arms wrapped tightly around her torso and how she wouldn't meet Jill's gaze, the words felt inadequate. She couldn't believe her mother. Well, she could. It was just like her to project her own insecurities on someone else.

She took a step forward with her hand outstretched, wanting to comfort Reagan in some way, but Reagan stepped back at her approach. "Reagan—"

"Not a word, huh? You just let me stand here and listen to that. Do you have any idea how that made me feel?"

Her voice was hard and barely above a whisper. The pain in it made Jill's stomach drop. "I'm sorry. After I do this one final task, I'll talk to her. There was no excuse for the words she said. They're not true. At all."

She fought the urge to reach for Reagan again, but even she could read Reagan's body language. And right now it was screaming, "Stay away." Instead, she clenched her fists at her sides and swallowed against the sudden nausea she felt as Reagan continued to avoid her gaze. "She has no right to talk to you like that, and I'll make sure she knows that. Will you wait here for me? I'll be back as soon as possible. Then I can take you home and we can talk."

All Jill received in reply was "Mmm."

She stormed into the house, but forced herself to calm down as she made her way to the front door. Jill needed to put on a polite smile and fake pleasantries for the departing guests. Once her duty was done, she'd let her mother know exactly what was on her mind. It was time for her to realize she couldn't just walk all over people, especially when the person in question meant so much to Jill.

As Jill went inside, Reagan hugged herself a little tighter. Her cheeks still felt hot with embarrassment and she willed herself not to cry. She had never felt so small before. Jill wanted her to stick around so they could talk, but what was there to talk about? Her mother said disgusting things and Jill said absolutely nothing. Her lack of defense was telling and Reagan couldn't stand to be in this house one more moment.

She was about to go back into the house when Gwen stepped outside, her eyes blazing. "What the fuck was that?"

"Let's just forget about it. I just want to go home."

"But Reagan, she shouldn't—"

"Please. I need to get out of here."

Gwen nodded in silence, but Reagan could still see the anger that threatened to bubble over. She knew Gwen would march up to Maureen and give her a piece of her mind if she'd let her. And while that would be entertaining to watch, Reagan needed to go home. She needed to be someplace comforting and not stifling like this house.

After helping Gwen unload supplies and paperwork at the office, Reagan trudged up the stairs to her apartment. The entire day had been draining, emotionally more than physically. She stripped off her clothes as she made her way to the bathroom for a shower. Turning on the water as hot as she could take it, she stood under the spray with her hands pressed against the wall and her head down.

Tears stung her eyes as she repeated Maureen's words over and over. As she let herself process the past hour or so, she found her thoughts shifting slightly. She was upset, not for herself, but for Jill. Sure, the words had stung. No one ever wanted to hear someone say such derisive things about them. But to realize that Maureen was the type of person to say those things about someone close to her daughter was unimaginable. Reagan was also upset with herself. She just left Jill there to deal with Maureen alone. It probably hurt Jill even more to hear her mother talk about someone she cared about. *And I ran off like an asshole.* She admonished herself even more as she pictured Jill's face when she came back to the kitchen and realized Reagan had left.

After toweling off, Reagan put on her softest pair of sweats and a long-sleeve T-shirt. She grabbed a beer and took a long swig. Closing her eyes, she felt the exhaustion of the day wash over her. She'd enjoy one beer and head to bed. Tomorrow she planned to do absolutely nothing, so she'd be refreshed and ready to tackle the planning of her dad's benefit.

She curled up on the couch as she unlocked her phone, mindlessly scrolling through social media. While watching a funny video, she heard a knock at her door. She placed her beer on the side table and waited to see if there'd be another. Sure enough, three quick knocks sounded again.

She pulled open the door to find Jill on the other side, her hands stuffed into the pockets of her coat and her shoulders slumped forward. Reagan gripped the doorframe. "What are you doing here?"

"I thought you were going to stick around until I came back. But you didn't. You left."

"Well, I couldn't stand being in the house of someone who clearly hates me." She crossed her arms and lifted her chin, as if daring Jill to refute that statement.

"I get it." Jill cleared her throat. "I stopped by because I wanted to check on you. I needed to make sure you were okay."

Reagan dropped her arms and sighed. "Want to come in?"

"Thanks." She stood between the living room and dining room, opening her mouth a couple times, but nothing came out.

"Want something to drink?"

The question seemed to shake her from her thoughts. "No, thank you." She clenched her hands in fists at her sides and looked up at Reagan with pain in her eyes. "I am sorry for everything—my mother's words, my silence." She licked her lips as she wrung her hands together. "I'm not her. And I'm certainly not him. I could never apologize enough for the nasty words my mother said to you. Douglas has been screwing around behind her back for years, probably since the day they got married. Lately, it seems like he doesn't even try to keep it a secret. The words she spat at you had absolutely nothing to do with you. Please understand that. You are not some 'plaything' as my mother said. I have never thought of you like that and I never will. I know I haven't always been the relationship type in the past, but this," she gestured between them, "means something to me. You mean something to me, Reagan. I know I can be a bitch sometimes, cold and closed off. You make me want to work on that. And I am trying. I'm not them. I swear."

Reagan cradled Jill's hand in her own. "I know you're not your mother. Or your stepfather. I'm aware of that every time I see you. I'm not gonna lie. Her words hurt. I get that they weren't really about me, but I still felt less than just because of who I am and what I do. The sting of that is just going to take some time to move past. And then for you to just stand there…I thought I meant more to you than that. I thought I was enough for you to finally stand up to her."

Jill stepped closer and squeezed her hands, almost to the point of pain. "I am so, so sorry. I have no excuse except that's just how things have always been between her and me. She tells me everything that I'm doing wrong in my life and I just take it. I know that was the exact opposite of what I should have done, but I guess I was just shocked. Normally she has enough tact to only say things like that in front of me. But I promise you I took care of it. She will never speak to you like that again." She took a deep breath, dropping Reagan's hands and stepping back. "I'm sorry that my family hurt you. I'd take it all away right now if I could. I understand if you don't want to see me again. Um, I'll just get out of here."

As she made a move toward the door, Reagan stopped her with a hand on her wrist. "Jill, I'm not trying to end this, end us. I thought I'd keep you around for a while," she said with a hint of a grin.

"You did, huh?"

"You're growing on me."

Jill chuckled. "Well, that's a ringing endorsement." She cleared her throat and stepped into Reagan's body. "Can I kiss you?"

"I'd be mad if you didn't."

Jill seemed to hesitate before closing the distance and brushing her lips against Reagan's. The kiss was brief but before Jill could move away, Reagan pulled her in for a hug. A sigh escaped her lips as she tightened her hold and cradled Jill's head against her shoulder.

"I'm sorry," Jill mumbled into her neck.

"I know. Me too."

"For what?"

"For your mother. For the love that you obviously missed out on in that house. You deserve better."

Jill let out a shuddering breath and pulled back, discreetly wiping the corner of her eye.

"I'm also sorry for bailing on you. You asked me to stay and I left without a word."

"Reagan, you didn't b—"

Reagan placed a finger to Jill's lips to stop her. "I did. I was hurt and embarrassed. I just couldn't take being in that house anymore. I left you there to deal with your mother on your own."

"It's okay. That type of discussion with her was probably a long time coming. You are a better person than she will ever hope to be and she needed to know that." Jill let out a slow breath. "But I'll get out of your hair. Goodnight, Reagan."

She stopped Jill with a light grip on her forearm. "Stay."

Jill's shoulders dropped and she smiled. "Okay."

They walked hand in hand up the stairs to Reagan's bedroom, only letting go to change out of their clothes. As soon as they got under the covers, Jill opened her arms and Reagan fell into them, resting her head on Jill's shoulder. Reagan sighed at the contact and rubbed small circles between Jill's breasts.

"Thank you for letting me stay," Jill whispered.

"I just needed to feel you. You're my comfort."

"And you're mine."

Reagan lifted her head for a brief kiss. She settled against Jill, wrapping her arm around her waist. The night had been draining for both of them and they were asleep in a matter of seconds.

CHAPTER SEVENTEEN

On Monday morning, Reagan sat in the conference room and looked through the notes she'd made the day before while she waited for Gwen and Beth to join her. She had planned to do nothing yesterday, but the longer she sat around staring at the TV, the more Maureen's words from Saturday night ran through her mind. So, planning the benefit became her distraction.

"Morning!" Beth called.

She carried a tray of coffees and Gwen followed behind. Reagan almost moaned at the sight. "Oh, coffee. Thank you. I forgot to stop on my way in. This is why we keep you around." She grabbed the cup with her initials on it and took a sip, wincing as the piping hot liquid washed over her tongue.

"I think you keep me around so I can remind you that coffee is hot and will burn your mouth if you drink it too soon."

Reagan chuckled. "That too. I took a chance that it had cooled down. Obviously, I was wrong."

"Clearly. So, how was Saturday night? Any issues with the party?" Beth asked as she took a seat across from Reagan.

The question instantly brought back memories from that night and Reagan closed her eyes in response.

"It was fine," Gwen answered as she sat down.

"Fine?"

Reagan sighed. "The party itself went smoothly, no major hiccups aside from a few last-minute guests to accommodate. Which reminds me, I need to send a new invoice out this week. Mrs. Jacobs just had a few choice words for me that I'd rather not get into right now."

Gwen clenched her fists on the table. "But Reagan, she—"

Reagan raised her hand. "We can talk about it later. I want to focus on something that's important to me. And she is not. Okay?"

"Fine." Gwen sighed.

Beth eyed them both. "Well, I obviously missed something and you can catch me up later. But I guess we should move on for now. So is this meeting about the benefit you're planning?"

Reagan let out a breath and turned to the front of her notes. "Yes. I want it to be a benefit but also a celebration of life for my dad. I want to raise money for the Pancreatic Cancer Action Network, but I don't want it to feel like a stuffy fundraiser. I want people to have fun, enjoy some excellent food, and have a chance to win some great items in the silent auction. Think that will work?"

They both nodded in reply.

"Let's see what you've come up with so far," Gwen said.

For the next two hours, Reagan presented the ideas she'd had running through her mind since before her dad had passed. She wanted it to happen at the beginning of December, hoping to catch people when they were in the holiday spirit and a little more generous. However, that meant they only had a few weeks to prepare, but she figured keeping it less formal would make it easier. Gwen and Beth threw out suggestions, and Reagan easily incorporated them into her vision.

As she wrapped up the meeting, she divvied up a list of tasks and scheduled a meeting for the following week. Closing her notebook, she turned to leave the room, but Gwen asked her to stay.

"I'll just go start on some of these," Beth replied, closing the door on her way out.

Gwen leaned her hip against the table and crossed her arms. "It's later, so let's chat."

Reagan sighed and dropped her notebook on the table. "Gwen, it's over and done. I don't really want to think about it anymore."

"I'm sure you don't, but I wanted to check on you. How are you doing?"

"Her words hurt. I can't deny that, but I know they weren't about me."

"Yeah, I kinda got that. Have you talked to Jill?"

"She came over that night and apologized."

"That's something, at least," Gwen muttered. She paused and took a deep breath, as if bracing herself for what she was about to say. "If this gets serious, do you really want to be around people like that?"

Reagan clasped her hands in front of her. "Please stop. Her mother's outburst had nothing to do with me or Jill. She said she talked to her about it, and I think it took a lot for Jill to confront her mother so give her some credit. She means a lot to me, and I hope she'll be around a while. You need to get used to it," she said, pointing at Gwen.

"I'm sorry. I'll try. But I just want what's best for you, Reagan. You're my best friend and business partner and you have always felt like a sister to me. I will always protect you. No matter what."

Reagan hugged her tight. "I know. And I'm thankful for that every day." She stepped back and grabbed her notebook off the table. "You just need to get to know her better."

Gwen groaned. "If I have to."

Reagan threw up her hands. "Just gi—"

"I'm kidding. I look forward to spending time with her as more than a client. Find out why she has you tied up in knots all the time."

"She does not," she replied, feeling her cheeks blush at the innocent fib.

"Well, your face right now and the way you looked at her at the party says it all. I like that look on you. She seems to make you happy. I know that feeling has been in short supply recently."

"Thanks. She does." She cleared her throat and continued, "I'll ask Jill and text you guys some days that might work."

"Perfect." Gwen linked her arm through Reagan's and pulled her out of the office. "Now tell me, she a good kisser?"

Jill shut down her computer and piled up a few loose papers, then picked up her cell to call Reagan.

"Hey, what's up?" Reagan answered, sounding rushed.

"Hey there. I just wanted to see if you'd like to go out to dinner tonight."

"I'm sorry, but I don't think I can. I'd love to see you but I have so much work to do. I'm trying to finalize the invitations for the benefit."

"I understand. Do you need help?"

"No thanks. I've got the template. Just trying to tweak the colors a bit. Then I need to send the order to the printer. And run through the guest list and double-check addresses. And then like a dozen other things."

"Is there anything I can do?" Jill waited for several seconds, receiving nothing but silence from the other end of the line. "Reagan?"

"Huh?"

"I asked if there was anything I can do. You totally zoned out on me," she said with a slight laugh.

Reagan sighed. "Shit. I'm sorry, Jill. I don't think so. I'm stressing out about all of this. I just want it to be perfect."

"I know you do. And it will be. Everyone will see how much thought and care you put into the night. You're bringing a voice to an important cause. The love you have for your father will easily shine through, and people will understand how amazing he was just from what you're doing. Everything will be fine. Just take a deep breath." Jill heard Reagan inhale as she followed the direction.

"Thanks."

"You're welcome."

"Look at you, you big softy. Calming me down with sweet words."

Jill cleared her throat. "I don't know what you're talking about, Ms. Murphy."

Reagan chuckled. "If you say so. But I should get going. I'll talk to you later, okay?"

"Okay. Have a good night."

"You too."

As Jill ended the call, an idea struck. She shoved her laptop and notes into her bag and grabbed her coat. Passing by Ash's desk, she dropped off a packet. "Can you get that up to finance? I'm heading out."

"Already?" Ash asked, eyes wide. "It's only six."

"I have someone…I mean, something to take care of. See you tomorrow."

Ash grinned, then replied in a teasing lilt, "Have a good night then, Ms. Jacobs."

Jill shook her head as she turned away, fighting a grin of her own.

After a quick stop at home to change and then a detour to an Italian restaurant down the street from her condo, she made her way to Reagan's place. As she parked behind the building, she second-guessed her decision. Maybe Reagan wasn't the type of person to want her focus interrupted? Maybe she hated surprises? There were still so many things she needed to learn about Reagan. She didn't want to upset her by being here. If that was the case, she could just drop off the food and leave. She grabbed her bag and the bag of takeout from the passenger seat. *No time like the present.*

When Reagan opened the door, her surprise was obvious. "Hi." She looked Jill up and down and tilted her head. "Did you have the day off?" she asked, pointing to Jill's clothes.

"No. I just stopped home really quick to get into something comfier." She held up the bag of food. "And I stopped for this."

"Yay, food! What is it?"

"Lasagna."

Reagan grabbed the front of her jacket and pulled her in, closing the door behind her. "You really know the way to a girl's heart." She kissed Jill softly. "Thank you," she whispered.

"No need to thank me. I didn't make it." Jill set the bag on the counter and hung her coat and bag on a stool. "On second thought, you should thank me for that. We know this food is safe."

Reagan chuckled. "Come on, you goof. Let's eat on the couch."

Jill settled in, placing the container on the middle cushion. The restaurant was known for its generous portions, so Jill had gotten one meal for them to share. For the next ten minutes, they took turns taking bites of food and telling the other about their day, and Reagan filled her in on the plans for her dad's benefit.

After they'd eaten most of the lasagna, Reagan dropped her fork into the container. With a sigh, she said, "I really appreciate you bringing me dinner, Jill. But I need to do some work. I don't think I'll be great company for the rest of the night."

"I figured." She pointed to her bag by her coat. "I brought some work over too. I thought we could have a working date."

"A working date?"

"Just thought we could spend some time together," Jill murmured.

Reagan moved the container to the coffee table before leaning forward and kissing her. "Softy." Jill blushed. "I'd love for you to stay."

She brushed her lips against Reagan's, cradling her head in her hands. She swiped her tongue along Reagan's lower lip, tasting a sweet hint of sauce.

Reagan whimpered and pulled back. "Okay. None of that on working dates. That's the rule."

"There are rules? No kissing at all?" She stuck out her bottom lip in a mock pout.

Reagan rolled her eyes. "Well, maybe when we take breaks. And there might be something extra as a reward for a job well done at the end of the night."

"Then what are you waiting for? Get your stuff and get cracking."

"On it," Reagan replied as she slapped Jill's thigh.

Jill retrieved her bag and pulled out her laptop while Reagan picked up her own from the coffee table. They sat on either side of the couch, their legs outstretched and intertwined as if this was what they did on a typical night. Maybe it could be—someday—she thought. But she didn't want to get ahead of herself.

Instead, she opened up her laptop and pulled up the budget analysis her head of finance had sent over. Now and then, Reagan flipped her computer around to ask Jill's opinion about font or color choice for the invitations, but the rest of the time they worked in comfortable silence. Once Jill completed her work, she put aside her computer and focused her attention on Reagan. She started by slipping her hand underneath Reagan's pant leg, skimming her fingers along the smooth skin of her lower leg. When Jill kneaded her calf muscles, Reagan sighed and moaned.

Reagan placed her laptop on the floor and leaned her head back against the armrest. "Shit. Do you know how good that feels?"

"I have a pretty good idea, but I'll let you show me another time just to make sure. Want me to keep going?"

"Mm-hmm." After a beat, Reagan opened her eyes and asked, "Would you like to go out for drinks with my friends? Meet them properly and away from business?"

Jill's hands stilled for a second before resuming her caresses. Her initial instinct was to decline. She wasn't good at this stuff. People. Chatting. Knowing it would make Reagan happy, she replied with the only thing she could. "Sounds good."

"Yeah?" Reagan asked with a smile.

"Yeah. I'm not great at things like that, but they're important to you. It'll be good to get to know them." Just saying that made her nerves settle. Reagan's friends were important to her and that probably meant their opinions were just as important. If they hated her, would they pressure Reagan into breaking up with her? She inhaled slowly as Reagan rested a hand on her leg.

"Don't sweat it. They'll love you."

She stroked Reagan's ankle and then her foot, seeming to graze a sensitive spot as Reagan jerked her foot back and sat up. "Ticklish?" she asked with a grin.

"Not one bit."

"Uh-huh. Sure." She looked at her watch, frowning slightly. "It's getting late. I should head out."

Reagan stood and held out her hand. "Nope, you're staying. I think somebody earned a reward," she replied with a wink.

"You or me?" Jill chuckled.

"Yes."

Once they fell into bed, Reagan reached for her and Jill lost herself in Reagan's touch and taste. She fell asleep with a smile on her face and her arm wrapped around the woman who made everything feel right.

CHAPTER EIGHTEEN

Reagan pulled into a parking spot a few blocks away from the bar to meet her friends and Jill—the same bar where Reagan and Jill had shared their first kiss. *Oh, what an interesting night that was.*

As she closed her car door, her phone chimed, a text from Jill.

Harrison pulled me in on something. Sorry, but I'll be a little late.

How long?

Reagan leaned against her car for a moment, her stomach dropping with each minute that passed without a reply. *Crap.* What were her friends gonna think when Jill showed up late? Would they still give her a chance afterward? Well, of course they would. They weren't assholes. *Maybe my nerves are getting to me*. She wanted the night to be perfect and for Jill to get along with her friends. Reagan tried to calm herself with slow breaths. She knew Jill was probably even more nervous than her so she pulled her phone out to text her again.

Sending good vibes that the meeting ends quickly. Can't wait to see you! And remember, my friends will love you.

She made her way down the street, wrapping her arms around herself to protect against the sharp wind. Entering the bar, she ran her hand through her hair and tried to tame the wild fly-aways as she scanned the tables for Gwen and Carly. The feeling of deja vu washed over her as she remembered the night from a couple months back. Seeing their smiles as she spotted them helped wipe away some of her nervousness.

Reagan kissed each of their cheeks before taking one of the empty stools across the table. "Hey, guys. How's it going?"

"Good. Where's Jill?" Carly asked.

"I just got a text from her. She's running late."

"She's not scared of us, is she?" Carly asked.

"Of little ol' you?"

Carly narrowed her eyes. "Is that a short joke?"

"What? Of course not," she replied with a wink. "I would never do something like that."

"Our past suggests otherwise."

Reagan chuckled. "That's true. So tell me about your weeks. Well, not you so much. I see you all the time," she said as she pointed at Gwen. "Carly, you're up."

As Carly started a story about a wand-making class she wanted to try, Reagan's thoughts drifted to Jill and she found it difficult to focus on her friends. Conversation flowed naturally like it always did, and Reagan tried to be stealthy when she checked her watch for the time or her phone for a text just in case she hadn't heard the alert.

But she must not have been stealthy enough because Gwen asked, "Did she bail?"

"What? No. Well, I don't think so. She hasn't replied to my text."

Carly chimed in with her positive attitude. "If she can't make it tonight, we can always reschedule. She's not going anywhere, right?"

"God, I hope not," Reagan replied, wiping her palms on her jeans.

Carly put her elbow on the table and her chin in her hand. "Aww. Look at you. You're all smitten."

"Shut up." Reagan's cheeks warmed and she slipped her hands under her thighs so she wouldn't try to rub it away, as if she could.

"Look, Gwen. She's blushing," Carly said as she elbowed Gwen playfully.

"Oh, that's nothing new." Gwen held up a hand and started counting on her fingers. "It happens when she sees Jill, when she talks about her…" Gwen's attention was pulled away by something over Reagan's shoulder. "And look who's here."

Reagan turned to see Jill rushing across the bar, her hands stuffed in her coat pockets and worry written on her face. Reagan stood and greeted her.

Jill gave Carly and Gwen a small wave and said, "I'm sorry I'm late. My boss called me in for a last-minute meeting." She kissed Reagan briefly before wrapping her in a hug. "I'm so sorry," she whispered into her ear.

"It's fine."

Pulling back, Jill stayed close enough to whisper again. "Fine rarely means fine." She opened her mouth to say more, but Reagan stopped her when she cupped her cheeks in her hands.

"We can talk more about this later. Okay? You're here now and that's all that matters." Reagan kissed her and held her in place a little longer this time.

Jill nodded warily before plastering on a smile that Reagan could tell was forced. She hung her coat on the back of the empty stool. A waitress arrived and quickly took their order. When she left, Jill turned to Gwen with her hand outstretched. "It's nice to see you again, Gwen." She shook her hand quickly and then moved on to Carly. "Hi, I'm Jill. You must be Carly."

She returned Jill's handshake with a grin. "That's right. And I know. We've met."

"We have?" she asked as she sat, resting her hand on Reagan's thigh.

"I work in your IT department."

"Really?"

"Yep."

"I'm sorry. I don't remember meeting you."

Carly shrugged. "No biggie. You saw me, yelled at me, yelled at your assistant, and I left."

"Ah. Well, I'm sorry. I'd like to say you caught me on a bad day, but that sounds like me," Jill replied, frowning.

"Guess that's why they call you the Ogre."

Reagan kicked Carly under the table.

"Ow. What the heck?" Carly bent down to seemingly rub her shin, but straightened with wide eyes. "Oh shoot, I'm sorry. I didn't mean to just blurt it out like that."

Jill chuckled. "It's okay. I've heard that one before. Sometimes, I'd even say it's fitting."

The waitress dropped off their round of drinks. Carly raised her glass of wine to the center of the table. "Cheers, everyone. Welcome to our crazy little group, Jill."

Clinking each glass, Jill replied, "Thanks."

"So, since you didn't recognize Carly, I'm guessing you two don't run into each other at the office at all?" Gwen asked.

"I don't have the need to call IT all that often. I'd like to think I'm pretty tech savvy. I'm sure you can't say the same for some of my colleagues," Jill said with a grin. "How long have you worked at Touchpoint?"

"Only a few months. Replacing your computer was my first assignment."

Jill snapped her fingers and smiled. "Right. I'm remembering that day now. I should get the next round just for that. The computer I had before was awful. So, thank you. Oh, and that bad mood I was in? Blame her for that," Jill said as she gestured to Reagan with her thumb.

"Why me?"

"That was the day we met," Jill said, taking a sip of her gin and tonic.

"It was?" Reagan asked.

"Yep." Jill turned her attention to Carly. "I had just gotten through an excruciating lunch where I was forced to share a table with a stranger. So you can't blame me for the bad mood."

"Hey! Excruciating?" Reagan playfully slapped her arm.

Jill laughed and kissed Reagan's cheek before she whispered, "I think it worked out pretty well for us."

Reagan stared at Jill's lips. "I'd say so." She pressed her lips to Jill's for a moment and sat back in her chair. Gwen and Carly were grinning, and Reagan could see the affection in their eyes. *They like her*. She felt a little giddy at the thought. She always imagined having a partner that could easily be friends with her friends. Tonight was the first step toward that.

"Who's your boss?" Carly asked.

"Harrison Gibbons. He's the VP of marketing. Do you know him?"

Carly groaned. "Unfortunately, yes. He's one of those colleagues you mentioned. I don't think he knows how to use a computer. Also, the first time I went to his office, he took one look at me and asked if 'one of the boys' could help him instead," Carly said as she used air quotes. "He's such a butt."

Jill laughed into her drink, clearing her throat. "A butt?"

"Carly doesn't cuss," Gwen interjected.

"Got it. I haven't, have I? I don't want to offend you," Jill said.

"You're good. Doesn't offend me. I just don't do it," Carly replied with a shrug.

"Makes sense. But to put it in your words, he is a butt. A major one. Hopefully, he'll be retiring in the next year, and I want to take his place."

"And you will," Reagan said, brushing her fingers along Jill's cheek. "I'll be right back. Need to use the restroom." As she slid off her stool, Jill held onto her hand until she couldn't anymore. Reagan mouthed, "It's okay," as she walked away.

"So, what are your intentions with our best friend?" Gwen asked, sitting back in her seat and crossing her arms.

Well, shit. She's going there, isn't she?

Carly slapped Gwen's arm. "Oh, my gosh. What are you gonna do next? Clean a gun in front of her? Make her fill out an application?"

"My dad gave Brett an application," Gwen replied.

"Wait. Did he actually have to fill one out?"

"My dad gave him one the first time they met. Brett just stared at it and then me like a deer in headlights. Luckily, Dad said he was kidding and took Brett into the kitchen for a beer." Gwen rolled her eyes. "So..." Gwen asked, raising her eyebrows.

Jill reached for her glass but realized it was empty. She looked longingly toward the hallway that led to the bathrooms. "Um, well..."

Gwen rested her arms on the table with a teasing smile. "Relax. I'm just kidding."

Jill's shoulders slumped and she let out a nervous chuckle. "Oh, good."

"Don't mind this one. She's always been the protector of us," Carly said, slinging an arm around Gwen's shoulder and pulling her in for a half-hug.

Gwen shrugged and gave Jill a pointed look. "No one messes with my best friends."

Jill took the warning to heart. Gwen didn't say it with much force but Jill knew she meant it. "Understood."

"But I do want to ask you one question," Gwen said, her severe stare softening to a look of interest.

"Go ahead," Jill replied, squaring her shoulders, ready for whatever she had to ask.

"What do you like about Reagan?"

Jill released a slow breath and softly smiled. That was an easy one. "She's smart and funny and determined and absolutely beautiful. But I'm not saying anything that you both don't already know." She twirled her empty glass as she considered her next words. "I know I'm not easy to get to know. I can be closed off and abrupt and abrasive, even in the best of times. You both know that." Gwen and Carly nodded. Jill couldn't read their expressions but she knew she had their attention. "But Reagan...She's the first person to see who I am and wants to know what's behind it. She wants to know me and why I am the way that I am. She makes me feel safe and right and whole. No one I've ever dated has wanted to know me like Reagan does. And I never want to let her go."

Carly looked as if she was on the verge of tears and Gwen cleared her throat and said, "Good answer." She leaned forward again with arms resting on the table. "When was your last relationship?"

Carly opened her mouth to interrupt, but Jill held up a hand to stop her. "It's okay. It was a few years ago, and I was with the guy for a couple months. It just fizzled out. Nothing earth-shattering there."

"Boyfriend?" Gwen asked, her eyebrows lifted.

Jill's hackles raised and she straightened her shoulders. *Great. Here we go*. "Yes, Gwen. I'm bi."

"Me too!" Carly held her hand in the air for a high-five, which Jill tentatively slapped.

"We celebrating something?" Reagan asked as she reclaimed her seat.

"I didn't know your girl was bi," Carly replied.

Reagan opened her mouth to speak, but Gwen got in first. "And by the look on your face, you didn't either."

"That's true. It's not like I know everything about her yet," Reagan replied with a small laugh. She kissed Jill's hand. "But I have zero issues with it."

Jill smiled and squeezed Reagan's hand. She didn't think there would be an issue, but she didn't imagine this was how Reagan would find out.

She opened her mouth to say more, but Carly broke in with a small shout. "I love this song. Let's dance!" She grabbed Gwen's hand and pulled her to the other side of the bar.

"Care to dance?" Reagan asked as she rested her arm along Jill's chair and lightly scratched at the base of her neck.

"Will I get to run after you and make out with you in the hallway?"

"Who knows. The night is young," Reagan replied, slipping off her chair and holding her hand out.

Jill let herself be led to the dance floor where Carly was already turning Gwen in a circle. She wasn't lying when she said she liked this song. Over the course of the next several songs, they danced together in a small circle.

After breaking up in pairs, Jill wrapped her arms around Reagan's shoulders and swayed to the music. She naturally melted into her, smiling when Reagan leaned in for a soft kiss to her neck. They danced and laughed until Reagan checked her watch and gave Jill a look of regret.

"It's getting late. I think I need to head out," Reagan said into Jill's ear.

Jill nodded as Reagan told Gwen and Carly the same thing. They made their way back to the table and Jill and Reagan put on their coats.

"What time do you leave in the morning for Michigan?" Carly asked.

Reagan and her mom were heading to a cabin her family rented every year for the next week. She groaned. "We're leaving at six. Thankfully my mom will drive first."

"Drive safe and text us when you get there," Carly replied, giving Reagan a hug.

When she let go, Jill held out her hand to Carly. "It was nice to meet you. Without yelling this time," she said with a smile.

Carly ignored her hand and pulled her in for a hug. "Likewise. Can't wait to see you again."

"Thanks, Carly."

Gwen eyed her a little more hesitantly but opened her arms. As Jill stepped into them, Gwen whispered in her ear, "Don't hurt her. She's been hurt enough."

"I know. I'll do my best not to," Jill replied as she pulled away.

"Good enough. And I'll try to stop being an ass."

"Good luck with that." Jill fought to keep a straight face.

Gwen chuckled. "Get out of here. Reagan, text us when you get to the cabin."

"Will do."

Jill took hold of Reagan's hand and turned toward the door. As they stepped into the chilly air, Reagan stayed silent, but huddled closer to Jill as they walked.

When they reached Reagan's car, Jill faced her. "I think that went well. Don't you?" She swallowed as she waited for her answer. She thought everything went okay, but Reagan knew her friends. *What if they gave her secret signals to say I'm a bad choice?*

Reagan gave her a wide smile. "It went great. I told you that you all would get along."

Jill let out a breath and relaxed. "Want to come over?"

"I wish I could, but I should really get home. I do have an early morning tomorrow. You know how I love those."

Jill chuckled. "They're your favorite." She took a deep breath and continued, "Are you mad at me?"

Reagan looked at her quizzically. "No. Why would you think that?"

"I was late."

Reagan gave her a soft smile and nodded to her car. "Let's get in. It's too cold to talk outside."

When Reagan unlocked the doors with her key fob, Jill slid into the passenger seat. She started to say something but Reagan stopped her before she could get a word out.

"I'm not mad at you. Not at all," she said, taking Jill's hand. "I'll fully admit that I was a little disappointed that you were late, but things like that happen. I know how important your job is. I get that. I'm sure there will be nights where I might be late to a date because of work. If you thought I was mad, I didn't mean to come across that way. I think I just let my nerves get the best of me." Reagan leaned against the headrest and smiled at Jill. "But my friends like you. How does that feel?"

"Pretty great, actually," she whispered. "I know I don't always make the best first impression." She grinned and winked at Reagan, who chuckled. "But they seem like good people and I look forward getting to know them better."

"Good. Do you know what you should do now?"

Jill narrowed her eyes and asked, "What?"

"Kiss me."

Jill laughed, leaning over the center console. She held Reagan's face in her hand and brushed her thumb over her bottom lip. "As you wish." Jill brushed her lips lightly against Reagan's, savoring the contact. As she pressed closer, she let the warmth of the kiss envelop her and calm the anxiety that had plagued her the entire night. The stress of being late and of meeting her friends didn't matter anymore. Only Reagan mattered, and she relished that.

She pulled back and leaned her forehead against Reagan's. "I should let you get home." Sitting back in her seat, she adjusted her coat and pulled her keys out of her pocket. "Call me when you get to Michigan."

"You'll be the first to know."

Jill smiled and quickly kissed her. "See you when you get back." She exited the car and waved as Reagan pulled away. Walking to her car, a weird feeling settled in her chest and for once, it didn't scare her. She missed Reagan already and knew that would get worse as the week went on. But it also left her feeling hopeful. She never missed anyone. Reagan was changing that.

With a satisfied smile, she headed home.

CHAPTER NINETEEN

As her week in Michigan came to a close, Reagan sat with her mom on the back porch of their cabin overlooking a quiet, clear lake. Wrapped in a large wool blanket, Reagan drank from her mug of tea as she enjoyed the vibrant colors reflecting off the water as the sun set. Despite being bundled up, the crisp air cut through the layers enough to cause occasional shivers. But she couldn't go in, not when it was her last night to revel in the peace around her.

Reagan and her mom had spent the beginning of their week in this very spot, chatting about the past and everything that came with it. The pain, the laughs, the longing for her dad. After spreading her dad's ashes yesterday, they'd also had several conversations about how to navigate their future and what each thought their new normal might look like. Thankfully, they agreed that their future held many trips back to this cabin.

As this was their last night, Reagan was thinking about things that might happen once they headed home. She picked at a fraying piece of wood on the arm of her deck chair. "Do you think you'll sell the house?"

Her mom rocked her chair back and forth. Finally, she let out a breath and looked at Reagan with a bittersweet smile. "No. I don't think I can. It's…It's hard some days. Everything in that house reminds me of him. His slippers in the closet. The last book he was reading on the coffee table. His favorite pint glass in the cupboard." She offered Reagan a sad smile. "No matter where I go, he'll be with me. And for that, I'll always be grateful. We've been in that house since you were five. It holds a lot of memories, and I hope that we will keep adding to those memories in the years to come. Wouldn't mind seeing a grandkid or two playing in the backyard, ya know?" Her mom took a sip from her mug of tea. "Speaking of, how is Jill?"

"Nice segue, Mom," Reagan replied with an eye roll.

"What?" she asked as she placed her hand over her heart and batted her eyelashes several times. "I'm just making conversation. Seeing what's new in your world. Doing my motherly duty, if you will."

"Laying it on pretty thick there, huh?" Reagan shook her head at her mother's antics. "She's great, honestly. Every time we get together, I see more of her."

"I'm sure you do." Her mom grinned.

Reagan tossed her head back with a groan. "You're the worst. I meant seeing who she is as a person."

"Sorry, I'll stop." She raised her hands. "So does that surprise you?"

"Yes and no. Getting her to talk about her feelings is tough. She can shut down if you don't approach it in the right way. But I never imagined she'd center me as much as she has since dad died. She can brighten even my shittiest day with a touch or a word. Relationships are kinda new to her and that might cause its own set of issues. But she's what I want."

Her mom stared at her for a moment. "Sounds like you've got something good there. Something promising."

"I think so. She's been hurt by the people closest to her far too often in the past, and that has definitely made her hesitant to start relationships. I got a small taste of how her mother treats her, and it was awful. Her mother is awful."

"What happened?"

Reagan gave her mom an edited version of the confrontation because no mother wanted to hear that someone had called her daughter a slut. "It all just left me a little shell-shocked. She had absolutely no regard for anyone but herself. I can't imagine what it was like to grow up with a mother like that. And her stepfather. I'm not going to get into that, but I'll just say he's a dick."

"I'd like to wring her neck if I ever see her. Both of them." Her mom took a breath. "Unfortunately, not everyone is lucky enough to grow up in a loving household."

"I'm aware of that. But because of them, I don't think she knows how to express her emotions, especially any type of love. I don't know if it'll ever get to that point, but I'm hopeful," Reagan whispered. "I'm trying to show her she's safe with me. I just hope she knows that."

"I'm sure she does, sweetheart. I can't wait to meet her."

"You'll get to next week. She'll be at the benefit, so please don't embarrass me."

"So, I shouldn't sneak a naked baby picture into the ones I've set aside for the photo wall? Oh! Or maybe that one when you tried to climb over our fence and your shirt got caught on it? You looked so cute dangling there."

"God, no!"

"Party pooper," her mom replied with a sigh. "Are you sure you don't need me to help with anything else for the benefit?"

"I'm sure. Just need the photos. Are they all ready? Can I take them tomorrow when I drop you at the house?"

"Yep. I've got a box on the counter. I'm sorry if I went a little overboard. Sometimes it was just too hard to narrow down which ones were my favorites."

"I get it. I'll take a look and try to use as many as I can."

Her mom looked at her watch. "We have an early start tomorrow, so I'm off to bed. Don't stay up too late. Do you want my blanket?"

"Sure," Reagan replied, spreading it across her lap.

Her mom placed a brief kiss on Regan's forehead. "Don't let anyone else's past dictate how you respond to your present. You have the chance to show her what love is and what it means to be vulnerable with another person. Just be yourself and let her open up when she's ready. It'll be worth it."

"Thanks, Mom. I love you."

"Love you too, honey."

Reagan settled into her chair and wrapped the blankets a little tighter, left alone to ponder her mother's words. She knew her feelings for Jill were growing each day. She wanted to be around her, laugh with her, argue with her, make love to and with her. She wanted everything that came with being in a relationship. But in the back of her mind, she worried that it might be too much for Jill. Maybe too much too soon. The vulnerability Jill had shown her up to this point, though, left her hopeful.

The ringing of her phone pulled Reagan from her thoughts. Looking at the display brought a smile to her face, and she swiped to accept the call. "Hey. I was just thinking about you." She and Jill had texted back and forth a few times throughout the week, but that didn't compare to how it made her feel to speak with her.

"You were, huh? Good thoughts, I hope?" Jill asked.

"Always," Reagan whispered.

"Happy to hear that." Jill cleared her throat. "But how are you? Couldn't always determine your mood through our texts. I've wanted to call, but I didn't know if I should. I didn't want to interrupt your time with your mom."

"You never have to question that, Jill. I like hearing your voice. It settles me."

"I'll make a note of that then."

"You do that. I'm doing okay. It's been an emotional week but definitely something we needed. On Wednesday we took a hike to the top of the hill and spread his ashes."

"I bet that was hard."

"It was. Lots of tears. But I think it's helped and brought some closure for both of us. As much as it could anyway."

"How's your mom?"

"Better. Even though we had time to prepare, it still felt like a shock when…um…once he was gone. I don't know how she stayed so strong through it all. I think the trip has been healing. We've spent a lot of time talking. She's also taken some time for herself and gone hiking or into town for a little shopping. This cabin has always been our favorite spot as a family, and I'm so happy she still wants to come here for future vacations."

"That's great to hear. I'm glad you two spent the time together."

"Me too. I'm lucky to have her." Reagan replayed what she just said and immediately flashed back to the type of person Maureen was. "I wish you had that."

"I know. Me too," Jill whispered. She said nothing else and just as Reagan was about to pull the phone away from her ear to make sure the call hadn't dropped, Jill said, "I miss you."

Reagan's smile grew so big it almost hurt her cheeks. "I miss you too. What have you been up to this week?"

"Mostly just work. Oh, I finally finished season eleven of *Drag Race*."

"Yes! Sorry your favorite didn't win," Reagan replied, and they chatted for a few minutes about the final results. The comforting warmth of Jill's voice had Reagan curling into the chair and she rested her head against the back. She couldn't wait to see her again. Unfortunately, the coming week would be busy with day-to-day work obligations as well as finalizing details for her dad's benefit. That thought alone made her tired, and when she couldn't hold it back anymore, a yawn broke the conversation.

"Shit, it's getting late so I should let you go. Let me know when you're back in town?"

"Definitely." Reagan paused and then whispered, "I can't wait to see you."

"Me too. Sweet dreams, Reagan."

"'Night, Jill." Reagan ended the call and gathered the blankets in her arms. She closed her eyes and breathed in the crisp air. She'd miss this place, but she was excited to head home. It meant she was another day closer to seeing Jill.

Jill paced in her kitchen, trying to think of a way to surprise Reagan and her mom. Reagan had texted her that morning and said they should be home around four. She looked at the clock and realized that time was creeping up on her. She'd already vetoed a couple ideas. A sign seemed too cheesy and way over the top for just a week away. Reagan didn't seem like the flower type, and she had no idea if her mom liked them. Jill figured they'd be exhausted after the long and emotional week. She stopped as the right idea hit her. If they were tired, they probably wouldn't want to cook. *At least, I wouldn't. Although, I never want to.*

She opened her drawer containing the takeout menus and pulled out the one for the Chinese restaurant. Reagan had liked the food when Jill had ordered it the last time. But when she opened her phone to call, she realized she had a major problem. She had no clue where Reagan's mom lived. "Well, fuck," she muttered.

Plopping down on a stool, she rested her chin in her hand and thought about other options. When she thought about who could help, one person came to mind. She opened her phone again and pulled up the website for Wren. She browsed their menu, picking out a salad and entrees she guessed Reagan and her mom would like. *They'd have to like the food from their own restaurant, right?* She hoped so.

A chipper voice answered after the second ring. "Thanks for calling Wren. How may I help you?"

"Hi. Is Gwen there?"

"She is. Do you need to speak with her? I can transfer you."

"No, thank you. Can I place an order for pickup?"

"Sure. What would you like?"

Jill gave her order and received confirmation that it'd be ready in thirty minutes. She breathed a sigh of relief that one part of her plan was in motion. Now, she had to convince Gwen to help her out. If she couldn't, she figured the food she ordered would cover her dinners for the week.

When she walked into Wren, the same chipper voice from the phone greeted her. The woman at the host stand wore a wide smile. "Welcome to Wren."

"Hi. I have an order to pick up for Jill."

"Right." She looked to the table behind her before turning back with an apologetic smile. "Let me go check on it."

"Could you ask Gwen to bring it out?" She cleared her throat. "Please."

"I'll see if she can step away."

Jill nodded as she watched her walk away. She fought the urge to pace again and clasped her hands behind her back instead. A few moments later, the woman returned with Gwen trailing behind her.

Gwen held out the large bag, confusion written across her face. "Hey, Jill. What can I do for you?"

"Thanks," Jill said as she took the bag and held it at her side. "This might sound weird or crazy, but could you give me Mrs. Murphy's address?"

"Why?" Gwen asked, crossing her arms.

Jill nodded to the bag. "This is for them. I thought they'd be too tired from their trip to cook."

Gwen dropped her arms, and the corner of her mouth turned up. "That's really sweet of you." She asked for a pen and pad of paper from the hostess and started scribbling. She handed Jill the slip of paper with the address on it. "You're scoring some major points with me on this. Just so you know."

Jill laughed. "Guess that's good then. Thanks again."

"No problem. Enjoy."

Jill parked on the street in front of Mrs. Murphy's house. Reagan's car wasn't in the driveway, but it was just after four. She got out of the car and grabbed the food from the backseat. When she stepped onto the porch, a wave of uncertainty hit her. Maybe this was a terrible idea. Maybe Reagan would just want to go home for some alone time. It had been a long week already, and she knew her week ahead would be busy. Just as she was about to leave the food on the porch, headlights flashed across her body. *Guess it's too late to bail.*

Once Reagan shut off the car, she and her mom got out with smiles on their faces. Although, the one on Mrs. Murphy's face was smug while the one on Reagan's was more pleased. Jill awkwardly waved to Mrs. Murphy before turning her attention to Reagan. The tenderness in Reagan's eyes washed away the last of Jill's anxiety about coming over.

Mrs. Murphy's voice broke their connection. "Well, who do we have here?"

Jill set the bag on a rocking chair and hurried down the steps, stopping a few feet away from Reagan's mom. She extended her hand. "Hi, Mrs. Murphy. I'm Jill."

"None of that Mrs. Murphy crap. It's Kathy. Now come here." She playfully swatted Jill's hand away and pulled her into a hug.

Jill stood as still as a statue, looking over at Reagan. She begged with her eyes for Reagan to tell her what to do, but Reagan just smiled and shrugged. Jill slowly wrapped her arms around Kathy, who hugged her tighter in response. She couldn't remember the last time her mother had hugged her. *Probably not since I was a kid, if even then*. Physical contact usually consisted of brief, tense cheek kisses. Never anything like this—a hug that made someone feel like they were the only one that mattered at that moment.

"There you go," Kathy whispered in her ear. "It's so nice to finally meet you."

"You too," Jill replied as she melted further into the hug and rested her head on Kathy's shoulder. She took several slow, deep breaths to stop any tears from forming.

Kathy pulled back and held on to her upper arms, staring at Jill for a beat with a grin. "You're coming in, right?"

"If that's okay. I brought dinner."

"That's so sweet. Isn't that sweet, Reagan?"

"Yes, Mother. Very sweet," Reagan replied teasingly as she shut the trunk.

"I'll see you two inside. It's too cold out here."

Reagan slung a duffel bag over her shoulder and rolled a small suitcase behind her as she came to stand in front of Jill. "So sweet of you to bring dinner," she said, her tone mimicking her mother's.

"Stop it," Jill replied, rubbing the back of her neck as she looked toward the house. "She hugged me."

"Oh yeah. It's kind of her thing."

"But why?"

"She likes you."

Jill cocked her head. "But she doesn't know me."

"Well, she knows that I like you so that's good enough for her."

"You like me, huh?"

"Most definitely."

Jill smiled and leaned forward for a tender kiss. She let out a soft sigh as she pulled back, pushing Reagan's hair behind her ear. "Hi."

"Hey. It is very sweet of you to bring dinner," Reagan whispered.

"It's nothing. Here, let me take that bag." Jill reached for the duffel and transferred it to her own shoulder.

"Thanks. Now take me to the food. I'm starving."

"You didn't eat on the drive?" Jill asked as they walked into the house.

"We had some snacks in the car but not nearly enough. It was only about a five-hour drive so we were able to make it home on one tank of gas. My mom's rule is that you're not allowed to stop unless it's for gas or the bathroom. And don't ever think about making those trips separate or else you get a huge amount of side eye and you lose control of the radio."

"Wow. Lots of rules to the Murphy family road trips."

"You have no idea. But maybe you can take one with us someday and find out."

"I'd like that," Jill replied, a light blush dusting her cheeks.

"Great. But since I wasn't allowed to use the bathroom, I really, really need to pee. You can take the food into the kitchen and I'll be right there." Reagan kissed her warm cheek and dashed down the hallway.

Jill took a deep breath before taking the dinner to the kitchen and unpacking the containers.

"Let me get some plates," Kathy said from behind her, making Jill jump a little.

Jill helped transfer salads and the entrees she'd chosen to plates. She didn't know what Kathy would like so she'd chosen three different options—steak, roast chicken, and salmon—hoping at least one of them would work for her. Knowing Reagan and her love of food, Jill knew she'd be happy with any of the three, and Jill would take whatever was left.

She thought that keeping busy with dishing up the food would stall the probable interrogation from Kathy. She'd never met any of her partners' parents before, mainly because she'd never been with one long enough to warrant a meetup. Reagan's mom clearly meant a lot to her, and Jill didn't want to say something stupid that would ruin their new relationship.

Kathy's voice broke her away from her thoughts. "It was sweet of you to do this. I heard you're not really known for that...sweetness."

Okay, ouch, but true. Jill cleared her throat. "That's true. I'd like to think, though, that I have my moments, and I am trying more. Your daughter makes me want to try."

"That's all I ask. And all anyone can really do. You're good for her. Just make sure to let her be good for you too."

"I promise."

"So, what made you choose Wren?"

"Well, I didn't know where you lived so I needed to enlist Gwen's help."

"Very sneaky," Reagan said as she reappeared.

Reagan grazed her hand along Jill's lower back, which earned her a shy smile. "I didn't know what else to do. I wanted it to be a surprise so I couldn't just ask you for the address."

"I'm not complaining." Reagan kissed her. "Guess I need to thank Gwen too."

After settling in the dining room, Reagan opened a bottle of wine and poured each of them a glass. Jill looked around at the food and a sense of panic hit her. "Shit, you're probably tired of eating from your own restaurants." Her eyes widened as she looked at Kathy. "I'm sorry. I didn't mean to say sh…that."

Kathy patted her hand and chuckled. "You certainly don't need to watch your language around me. Reagan's father was known for his colorful language…while he cooked…watched sports…"

"Did any type of furniture assembly," Reagan added with a laugh.

"Lord, that was the worst. I'm so glad you took over that job once you were a teenager. And also never apologize for bringing food from any of their restaurants. If I could afford Gwen, I would have her make all my meals."

With that, Kathy dug into her meal, and Jill turned her attention to Reagan. "And you don't mind either that I stopped at Wren?"

"Not at all. I can't remember the last time I ate there. Or our other two restaurants. It's pretty rare nowadays."

"How come?"

"I'm the numbers gal, remember. I leave the perk of free meals to our employees. And I don't have much time to go from place to place so I do most of my work in the office. Plus, with this fourth restaurant in the works, any sampling Gwen and I do during the day is for that."

"How's that all going?" Kathy asked. "I can't believe I never asked you about it all week."

Reagan spent the next few minutes explaining how far along they were in planning and what came next. Jill sat back, enjoying what a normal family must be like. A parent asking their kid about their lives and caring enough to ask follow-up questions. And when Kathy turned the questions to her, it never felt like the stereotypical interrogation. She asked her about her hobbies and music. Jill found she and Kathy shared a love of Karin Slaughter novels, and Jill promised to find the time to read her latest so she could discuss it with Kathy at a dinner soon.

Before she realized it, they had finished their meals and the wine, and Jill wondered where the time had gone. When she ate dinner at her mother's house, she counted down the seconds until she could leave. With Reagan and her mom, it was the complete opposite. She felt at ease here. She felt at home.

Kathy stood first, taking her plate and glass into the kitchen. Jill and Reagan followed her, but not before Reagan surprised her with a lingering kiss.

"Mmm. What was that for?"

"For being you and doing all this."

"I should do it more often then."

"I wouldn't complain," Reagan replied with a wink. She took Jill's plate out of her hand and stacked it in the sink.

Kathy wiped her hands on a towel and nodded to a box on the counter. "Don't forget to take those pictures when you go."

Jill peeked into the open box. "Pictures?"

"Shit," Reagan said under her breath.

Jill raised an eyebrow. "What?"

Kathy hung the towel on the oven door handle and reached for the box, flipping through a stack of photos she picked up. "Reagan asked me to put some pictures together for the benefit next week. Want to see some?"

"Oh no," Reagan grumbled, covering her eyes with her hand. "Mom, I think it's getting a little late. We should be going."

Jill recognized the look on Reagan's face—embarrassment. As tempting as it was to see pictures of Reagan when she was younger, Jill decided she'd rather stay in her girlfriend's good graces. "Your stunning daughter is right. But how about another time?"

"Stunning, huh?" Kathy asked with a raised eyebrow. "A little heavy on the flattery, don't you think? Bringing us dinner was bound to get you laid already. Don't need to do anything more."

"Oh, Christ," Reagan muttered.

Jill's cheeks reddened, and she looked between the two women with wide eyes. "Um, but I really do have an early day at work tomorrow. Plus, I'll see these at the benefit."

"The good ones aren't in that box…yet," Kathy replied with a grin.

"How about you show me those next time?"

"Next time?" Kathy asked.

Jill held up her hands. "Not that I'm trying to invite myself over here again."

Kathy pulled her in for a hug. "I'm just teasing. You're welcome back anytime."

"Thanks, Kathy."

"Now, you two go have some fun."

Reagan kissed her mom on the cheek and gave her a hug. When they left, she groaned. "I'm sorry for her. She's not great at holding her tongue."

Jill chuckled. "She's a riot. But was she right?"

"About what?"

"Did bringing dinner over mean I'm getting laid tonight?"

"Follow me home and see."

CHAPTER TWENTY

As Jill followed Reagan to her place, they caught every single red light. When they were stopped by the third one, Jill pulled next to Reagan and put on her best pout, throwing her hands up in the air. Reagan threw her head back and laughed. Was she enjoying her impatience or was she struggling just as much? Either way she was dying to show Reagan just how much she wanted her.

She pulled into the spot next to Reagan, who had already gotten out of her car and was hurrying up the stairs. Jill licked her lips as she followed behind, warring with the fact that she needed to be closer to Reagan while also enjoying the view she had of Reagan's ass. The need to be near her won out as Jill stopped behind her and wrapped her arms around her waist, nibbling Reagan's neck as she tried to unlock her door.

"Keep that up and we'll never get inside. And we really need to because it is way too cold out here."

"I know plenty of ways I can warm you up," she whispered, unbuttoning Reagan's jeans.

Before she could slip her hand inside, Reagan cheered and pushed open the door. "Finally!"

Jill kicked the door closed and pushed Reagan up against it. She stripped off their coats, letting them fall to the floor. She crushed their lips together and smiled when a bite to Reagan's lower lip resulted in a hiss and then a groan. She walked her toward the bedroom. She immediately missed the full body contact and couldn't make it more than a few feet before she pressed Reagan into a wall, grabbing her ass and pressing slow, wet kisses along her neck. When she reached the base of her throat, she was thwarted by Reagan's sweater—momentarily. She yanked it over her head and threw it on the floor, as if the sweater had offended her.

Pressing their lips together, she turned Reagan toward her bedroom again until she remembered that meant going upstairs. She reluctantly broke their kiss in order to make it upstairs safely. She took advantage of the break to unbutton her own shirt and slide it off.

At the foot of the bed, they discarded their T-shirts and bras. Jill wrapped an arm around Reagan's waist. The first touch of bare skin to bare skin flipped something in Jill's consciousness and she paused, holding Reagan against her. She didn't want to rush. She wanted to savor every taste. She wanted to bask in every gasp her touch would elicit.

Reagan pulled back, breathing heavily and furrowing her eyebrows. "What's wrong?"

Jill licked her lips as she studied Reagan's face. "At first, I wanted to fuck you hard and fast." Reagan whimpered and her eyes fluttered closed. "But now, I want to make love to you slowly and indulge in every part of you."

"You can have me anyway you want. Just have me," she rasped.

Jill lightly held onto Reagan's hips as she kissed her, unhurried and almost lazy. Each stroke of her tongue matched the slow brush of her fingertips up and down Reagan's sides. As she pressed kisses down her neck and across her shoulder, she unzipped her jeans, reveling in the way Reagan continually rolled her hips forward as she tried to make Jill go faster. She slid her hands inside and cupped her ass before removing her jeans.

When she trailed her fingers up the backs of her legs, Reagan shivered against her touch, gripping Jill's shoulder. She peppered kisses along her inner thighs and Reagan let out her first gasp. Oh, how she loved that sound. She closed her eyes as her nose brushed against the front of Reagan's underwear and her mouth watered. Before she could get distracted, she stood and gently pushed Reagan back until she sat on the bed.

Reagan undid Jill's jeans as she pressed soft kisses to her stomach. Jill moaned and let her head drop back and she pushed her hand through Reagan's hair. Her lips were so soft and warm and when she flicked her tongue just above her waistband, Jill rolled her hips forward and let out a strangled, "Yes." She stepped out of her jeans and kicked them to the side.

Jill held Reagan's face in her hands and lightly brushed her thumbs along her cheeks. The lamps from the first floor provided just enough light to make out Reagan's features. She didn't want to miss a single expression of pleasure tonight. She wanted to see all of her. "You are so beautiful."

She turned her head and kissed Jill's palm. "Thank you," she whispered.

Jill's hands went to the waistband of her underwear and Reagan lifted her hips as she slid them off. "Move up the bed."

Reagan moved back until she could lie down and rest her head on a pillow. Jill shoved her own underwear down and kicked it off, kneeling on the bed and settling between Reagan's legs. She lightly caressed Reagan's arms and intertwined their fingers, pushing Reagan's hands above her head.

Jill held Reagan's gaze as she ground her hips. Reagan's mouth parted and she sucked in a breath. She bent down, stopping until her mouth was an inch away from Reagan's. Each time Reagan lifted her head to close the distance, Jill retreated, teasing her. She swiped her tongue along Reagan's bottom lip before pressing their lips together. Reagan tried to increase the pace, but Jill pulled away. "Slow. Remember?"

"I don't know if I can take it. I need you so badly, Jill." Reagan rolled her hips and fought against Jill's grip. "I need more."

Jill smiled against her neck as she let go of Reagan's hands and trailed her fingers down the center of her chest. Reagan writhing underneath her sent a shock of arousal straight to her core and she was struggling to maintain control of the situation. She felt the slickness between her own thighs and squeezed them together to relieve some of the pressure. Because right now she wanted more of Reagan. Jill cupped Reagan's breasts, brushing her thumbs across her nipples until they became stiff peaks. She took one in her mouth and lazily circled it with her tongue. Reagan buried both of her hands in Jill's hair, pulling her as close as possible.

Reagan's little murmurs of pleasure spurred her on and she continued lower as she alternated between kisses and gentle bites along her stomach. When she reached her hip bone, Reagan squirmed and let out a noise that was half giggle and half moan. Jill growled low in her throat as she bit down and then soothed the spot with a swipe of her tongue.

As she got closer to Reagan's center, her familiar scent washed over Jill and she spread Reagan's legs farther apart. She traced a line from her knee and along her inner thigh with soft kisses.

Reagan's grip on her hair tightened as she repeatedly whispered, "Please."

God, she needed to taste her, needed to hear her call out her name. Jill flicked her tongue against Reagan's clit. Reagan bucked her hips so forcefully that Jill had to grab onto her hips and hold her down. She explored Regan's center with her tongue, taking note about which areas gave her the most pleasure.

As she swirled her tongue around her clit, Jill teased Reagan's entrance with one finger, gathering her wetness and trailing it along her folds.

Reagan let out a frustrated groan. "Jill, stop teasing me."

Jill chuckled and Reagan moaned at the added vibration. She slid two fingers inside, bottoming out as she sucked at her clit. Reagan's answering scream went straight to her own clit. She reached between her own thighs and stroked her center, wanting a hint of relief.

But it wasn't the same as having Reagan touch her. Sure, she could give herself an orgasm, but she wanted Reagan's soft fingers stroking and pinching her clit as she came. As she felt Reagan pulse beneath her tongue and clench around her fingers, she knew she would come within seconds. But Jill didn't want her to, not without her. She wanted them to share that moment.

Jill slowed her fingers and moved up Reagan's body. Her head was thrown back and her eyes were shut tight. "Reagan, look at me."

Reagan lifted her head met Jill's gaze, her eyes slowly coming in to focus. "Are you okay?" she asked, reaching out to rest her hand on the center of Jill's chest.

"I…I need you. I need you to touch me. I want us to come together. Please." Desperation dripped from Jill's voice and within seconds, Reagan's fingers were stroking her clit. She rolled her hips forward for more contact as she groaned. "Yes, right there."

Jill entered her again, and Reagan arched off the bed, giving Jill ample opportunity to take an erect nipple into her mouth. She bit down and Reagan screamed, "Fuck!"

Reagan matched her stroke for stroke and it took every ounce of willpower for Jill not to come right then and there. She lifted her head and rested her forehead against Reagan's, keeping eye contact as their pace and breathing increased. She felt completely exposed by Reagan's intense gaze, and for once, it didn't make her want to run away.

"Almost," Jill whispered as she let out a throaty groan.

With a final thrust, Jill fell over the edge, not only from Reagan's touch, but from the way she screamed Jill's name and held her close with a tight grip on her neck as she came. She groaned as the climax washed over her and light flashed in front of her eyes. It took all of her strength to keep her eyes open and maintain the connection they shared.

Jill closed the distance and brushed her lips against Reagan's, their rapid breaths mingling between them. "You're incredible," she murmured against her lips before kissing her again.

As the pulses around her fingers stopped, Jill slowly withdrew her fingers and Reagan sucked in a breath. "I could say the same thing about you. Where did all that come from?"

She shrugged. "I just needed you. All of you."

"I'm not complaining," Reagan replied with a chuckle.

Jill gently rolled off Reagan and settled on her side with her head propped in her hand. She stared at Reagan, relishing the sleepy contentment on her face as she pulled the sheet up to cover their bodies. She loved when Reagan got like this, and she loved that she could do this to her. Jill stiffened for a moment. Love? No way. Not yet. *I don't do love*. Well, maybe she could. Reagan was certainly showing her it was possible. But what if she hurt Reagan? She closed her eyes at the sharp pain that thought brought to her.

She must have stayed silent for too long because Reagan cupped her cheek and asked, "You okay?"

Jill licked her lips as she processed the speeding thoughts going through her mind. "I, um…" Even if she did love her, she couldn't tell her that yet. It was too soon and Reagan could still realize that Jill wasn't the one for her. She cleared her throat. "Do you have any plans in the morning?"

Reagan looked toward the ceiling as she took a second. "I don't think so. Why?"

"I was wondering if I could take you somewhere."

"Sure," she replied with a smile.

"Don't want to ask where?"

"I trust you," Reagan said, as if it was the easiest statement to make.

Jill's heart clenched and tears stung her eyes. She didn't think she could explain at the moment how much that phrase meant to her. So instead of trying to, she wrapped her arm around Reagan's waist and pulled her against her, burying her face in the crook of her neck.

Her voice was hoarse when she said, "Thank you."

Reagan squeezed her hand and pulled it between her breasts. Jill fell asleep to the rhythm of Reagan's heartbeat beneath her fingers.

The next morning, after Reagan indulged herself in another round with Jill, they were on their way in Jill's car to the still undisclosed location. Only the clothes Jill set out gave her small hints. As Reagan showered, Jill had rummaged through her closet and tossed a flannel button-up, thick socks, and a pair of hiking boots onto the bed. She'd been told her jeans from the day before would be okay as long as she didn't mind them getting dirty. She never pictured Jill doing any activity that might stain her clothes, so she was certainly intrigued.

Most of their car ride was spent in relative silence except for the low volume of the radio. Reagan kept a gentle grip on Jill's thigh, enjoying that her light scratches along Jill's inner thigh led her to shift her legs a little farther apart.

They pulled into a gravel parking lot in front of a large, white building with a dark green roof. "Happy Tails Animal Shelter. Why'd you bring me here?"

Jill took a deep breath and intertwined their fingers, staring at their joined hands. Was she nervous? Did she want to adopt a puppy together or something? Reagan panicked for an instant, but the more she thought about it, the less it scared her.

"I volunteer here."

Well, that wasn't what she expected. "Really? Since when?"

"The past couple years." She gave a small shrug. "I've been donating money longer than that. One year, they sent out a mass email asking for volunteers because they had a shortage after many of the summer volunteers went back to college. So, I figured, why not?"

"That's very sweet of you," Reagan replied, squeezing Jill's knee.

"Don't give me too much credit. I still don't stop by enough. Some months it's more money than volunteering."

"Well, I'm sure they're still grateful for the money. Every bit helps, right?"

"Of course. Ready to do some work?"

Reagan smiled wide. "Definitely."

Jill led her inside. "You'll have to fill out some paperwork and unfortunately you won't be able to handle the animals just yet. But maybe, if you like it here, you could come back?"

Reagan's heart tugged at the hope in Jill's voice. She was sharing something precious with her and she would never turn down a chance to learn more about her. "I'm sure I'll love it, and already I can't wait to come back."

When they reached the reception area, Jill knocked on the counter and a woman around their age looked up from her clipboard. "Jill. I didn't expect to see you today." She grinned as she glanced at Reagan. "Who do you have here?"

Jill lightly pressed her hand to Reagan's lower back and bit her lower lip for a moment. "This is Reagan. She's, um, my girlfriend."

Reagan couldn't hold back her smile if she tried. Her cheeks warmed as she held Jill's gaze.

"Don't hurt yourself there, Jill," she said with a chuckle. "I'm Stacey, the intake coordinator here. It's nice to meet you. She dragged you with her, huh?"

"Something like that."

"Well, before you do anything, I need you to fill out some paperwork. Can't volunteer here without it, and because you're brand new, you can't handle any of the dogs yourself yet."

"Jill told me already. I understand."

"Great. Fill these out and then I'll let you know how you can help."

Reagan filled out the necessary forms and they were given the tasks of unloading food and cleaning out some of the cages. After hanging up their coats in a locker, Jill led her to the loading area in the back and they started the first job.

At first, they worked in comfortable silence, naturally maneuvering around each other. But coming here had Reagan curious. "Is this typically what you do when you come here?"

"Pretty much. Unload supplies, laundry, clean around the facility. I could work more at the front desk or facilitate the adoption appointments if I wanted. But that's not really my thing." Jill shrugged.

"How come?"

"I'd rather not deal with people. I do that enough at work. Coming here means I can lose myself in whatever task they need me to do. Gives me time to think, I guess."

"That makes sense. Is it ever hard to work here? I mean, there have to be some abuse cases, right?"

Jill nodded and frowned. "Unfortunately, yes. Cases of dog fighting, neglect. Some days I just want to go home and punch something. Or cry."

Reagan brushed her fingers along Jill's forearm. "That must be so tough. How do you do it?"

"I just try to remind myself that they'll find a good home more often than not. And this place is a chance of hope for them. Stacey and the rest of the workers make it their mission to provide a safe environment until the animals can find their forever home."

"Seems like they do amazing work here."

"Oh, definitely," Jill replied with a smile.

After stacking the final cans of cat food on the shelf, Reagan crossed her arms and leaned against the doorway, licking her lips as she watched Jill pull the last of the bags of food off the truck and into the storage room.

She stopped and looked at Reagan with a raised eyebrow. "What?"

"No offense, but I just haven't seen you do anything very physical since we met. Just enjoying the view, that's all." Her cheeks warmed at the admission.

Jill closed the distance between them and held on to Reagan's hips. "Last night wasn't physical enough for you? Or this morning?"

Reagan felt her cheeks heat further and she looked around, hoping no one heard that. "That was plenty physical," she murmured. "This is just different, I guess. You're just so buttoned-up all the time and wearing your fancy dress clothes. Don't get me wrong, those are sexy as hell. But it's also nice to see you a bit more laid-back. I just love seeing new sides to you."

"You do, huh?"

"Yeah. I like seeing what's important to you."

"You're important to me."

"I was kind of hoping so," she replied with a grin. "Calling me your girlfriend and everything."

Jill bit her lip. "Yeah, sorry about that. Was that okay?"

"More than okay." She tilted her head for a quick kiss. "So what's next?"

"Follow me."

For the next hour, they made their way through two aisles of dog cages, cleaning out the empty ones and replacing the bedding in the occupied ones. Reagan's heart clenched each time Jill had to go in with a dog. She bent down and talked softly to each one, making sure they were comfortable before she swapped the bedding.

It wasn't that it was surprising to see Jill like this, because it wasn't. Reagan was seeing the sweet and patient side of Jill more and more lately. But she still felt an odd mix of emotions. On the one hand, she was incredibly honored that Jill was trusting her enough with this new view into her world, but on the other hand, she was sorry that no one else got to see this side of her and appreciate it, especially her family. Not that they'd even know how to appreciate something this precious.

Once Jill finished the last cage, she excused herself to talk to Stacey. While she was gone, Reagan took her time reading the info sheets hanging on the front of the cages. It was interesting and heartbreaking to see the circumstances that brought all of these dogs to the shelter.

Reagan turned as the door opened behind her. Jill held a blue leash in one hand and their jackets in the other. "I always finish my time here by walking at least one dog. Stacey said we can have Max today."

They stopped in front of a cage that held a two-year-old beagle named Max. His brown ears flopped up and down as he hurried to the door to meet Jill. She whispered to him and introduced herself before opening the door and attaching the leash to his collar. After putting on their coats, they walked out the back door.

Reagan spent a few minutes looking around the large property. Several other people were walking dogs of their own. She was thankful it was a sunny day, the warmth of the sun covering up the chill in the air. Jill seemed content in her role of dog walker, giving praise to Max when he listened to her commands.

"Have you ever thought about getting a dog?"

Jill shook her head and frowned. "I don't have time. I'm too selfish."

Reagan brushed her fingers along the back of Jill's hand. "Well, I think you've proven you can make time for things you care about."

Her cheeks reddened and she rubbed the back of her neck. "That's still a work in progress."

"I've appreciated your efforts so far." Reagan winked.

"My *efforts*, huh? Well that's good to know. I'll have to make sure to keep working at them, though."

"Of course, don't want to get lazy," she replied, her voice low.

Jill chuckled and continued walking, keeping Max at her side.

"So why animals?"

Jill furrowed her brow. "What do you mean?"

"You could donate money and your time to any cause. Why animals?"

She didn't answer for a moment, and they stayed quiet as they continued along the path. Maybe she'd never thought about it before. Maybe this was just the first place that popped up on her radar when she went searching for a charity.

Jill licked her lips and murmured, "Their love is unconditional."

She closed her eyes at hearing the hint of pain in Jill's voice. It made sense if she thought about it. So much of the love in her life was conditional, if anyone could call it love at all. Her heart ached for Jill and the family she had to endure.

"I get it."

"I thought you might." Jill smiled softly and held her gaze. "It's why I brought you here."

"Thank you," she whispered.

"You're welcome."

They finished the walk without another word because it didn't feel like any more words needed to be said. Jill had taken a big step by asking Reagan to come today and that wasn't lost on her. It felt as if their relationship was taking a turn toward something serious, something real. She'd felt it last night when Jill had slowly taken her, and she felt it even more now after having the privilege to learn more about Jill. She needed to make sure she never took little moments like this for granted.

When they arrived back at Reagan's, they sat quietly in the car for a moment before either one of them made a move or a sound. Jill kept her car running which felt like a signal that their time was done for the day.

A few strands of hair had escaped from Jill's ponytail, and Reagan pushed them behind her ear, trailing her finger along her jaw before dropping her hand. "Thank you for taking me today. I had a great time."

"Yeah?"

"Of course. Would you like to come in? Maybe order some takeout and watch a movie?"

Jill's brow furrowed and she bit her lip as if contemplating the right thing to say. "I think I better go home. I should probably get some work done. Today…well, today was, um…"

Realization dawned on Reagan. Today had been a big step for Jill and she was probably feeling out of sorts. It wasn't every day that she let someone in as much as she had with Reagan. "It was a lot?"

Jill let out a long sigh. "Yeah, it was. I'm sorry, I—"

Reagan covered Jill's hand with hers. "You have nothing to apologize for. I totally get it. Just so you know, this week is going to be really busy with all the last-minute things I need to get done for the benefit, so I don't know how available I'll be."

"It's okay. If you're ever in need of another working date, I'm in," she replied with a wink.

"I might take you up on that." Reagan leaned across the console for a kiss. Her eyelids fluttered open as she pulled away. "I'll see you at the benefit."

"Yes, you will."

Reagan exited the car and walked up the stairs, giving a little wave once she was on her balcony.

As she unlocked her door, Jill called up from the street. "Hey, Reagan?"

She turned around and rested her arms on the railing. "What's wrong?"

"Does the offer still stand?"

Reagan smiled. So she didn't want to go home, after all. *She wants to spend more time with me*. The thought made her stomach do a little backflip. "Of course. Come on up."

Jill shut her car door and hurried up the stairs. She wrapped her arms around Reagan's waist with a smile. "So, what's for lunch?"

CHAPTER TWENTY-ONE

Reagan felt like a nervous ball of energy. She knew everything was ready for the evening, but she was still frazzled. Tonight meant everything to her. She just hoped all her efforts from the past several weeks would pay off. Almost a hundred people had RSVP'd and most of the invitees who couldn't come sent donations along with their responses, so she should already consider the night a win.

Reagan entered the space they purchased for their fourth restaurant. The sale had closed at the end of September, and she and Gwen had been remodeling it ever since.

The kitchen remodel was complete, but the rest of the building was a blank slate. They had refinished the hardwood floors and had mock-ups of what they wanted the space to look like. For now, they'd had to rent all the tables and chairs from a rental company. She wanted the evening to be fun, so she had set up cornhole boards in the back corner along with signs about how to play. The front of the room held the photo wall she'd put together and an information table where guests could drop off donations and also pick up pamphlets for volunteer opportunities with several local cancer outreach programs.

Her phone dinged in her back pocket, and it was a text from Jill. She had texted her earlier in the day during a minor breakdown that the night was going to be a disaster. Her panic had increased when Jill hadn't gotten back to her right away. Seeing her name on the screen sent instant relief to her nerves.

Sorry I was in a mtg. Tonight will be amazing because you are amazing.

Reagan took a deep breath and smiled as another message came through.

You've poured your heart and soul into this and everyone will see that. I'm so proud of you and can't wait to see you tonight.

Thanks :) Reagan texted back. *See you soon!*

Reagan pocketed her phone, feeling more composed than she had ten minutes ago. Seeing that setup was moving along, she went into the kitchen to check on Gwen. "Need anything?" she asked.

Gwen drew a line on the sheet of paper she had taped to her workstation, capped her pen, and stood in front of Reagan. She gripped Reagan's shoulders, shaking her playfully. "For the hundredth time, I've got things covered back here. We chose a simple buffet meal for a reason. I've got this. Why don't you go home and get ready?" Gwen glanced at her watch. "By the time you do that and get back here, you'll only have a half hour to obsess over all the details."

"That's probably a good idea," Reagan mumbled.

"Everything will be okay."

"Jill said that too."

"Maybe you should listen to your girlfriend then."

Reagan grinned. "Maybe I should. Just don't tell her I said that. Okay, I'm heading home. Call me if you think of anything you need."

"Just go."

"I'm going." Reagan held up her hands and left.

Within ten minutes, she was home and stripping off her clothes as she took the stairs up to her loft. She showered quickly and dried her hair, pulling the wavy locks into a messy bun at the nape of her neck. She leaned forward to get closer to the mirror as she applied a small amount of eyeliner, the only makeup she usually wore. After putting on a bra and a pair of boyshorts, a slight wave of panic hit her as she stood in front of her closet. She had been so busy lately that she hadn't put any thought into what she wanted to wear.

She stated on the invite that the dress code for the night would be dressy casual. She also asked people to wear purple if they could, as that was the color for pancreatic cancer awareness. She pulled out the only three purple options she owned—a dress, a button-up, and a blazer.

It had been a while since she'd last worn a dress. She didn't hate them, but she also didn't love them. The thought of wearing heels all night made the decision for her and she put the dress back in the closet. She tapped her lips with her finger as she stared at the last two choices. As the host of the event, she supposed she should dress as nice as she could. *Blazer it is, then.*

When she put the purple button-up back, she exchanged it for a white and navy checked one, and grabbed a pair of dark blue jeans, a gray sweater, and her favorite pair of black dress shoes from Tomboy Toes. She got dressed and checked herself in the mirror. She had left the collar of her shirt unbuttoned and adjusted it so it sat on top of the sweater just right. Next, she cuffed her jeans a couple times for a little extra flair.

She closed her eyes, taking a few deep breaths. It was time to honor her dad, and she prayed that everything went smoothly tonight.

Jill tried to wrap up some last-minute calls as Friday came to a close. She had actually planned to leave on time for once so she could get to the benefit early and help Reagan with anything she needed. As soon as she hung up her phone after a call with their lead designer, the phone rang again. Catching the extension on the readout, she mumbled, "Fuck." She thought about ignoring it, but Harrison would just call her cell phone if she didn't answer. She held in a groan as she picked up the receiver. "Hi, Harrison."

"Jillian," he bellowed. "Listen, I was supposed to have dinner with the Apex Aviation executives in a half hour. I need you to go in my place. Tell them how amazing we are and we'll give them top-notch service and all that. We need this account."

"I'm sorry, Harrison, but I can't. I was just about to leave the office for a prior engagement I need to attend. Why can't you?"

Now his tone had gone from jovial and conciliatory to brusque and threatening. "You will do this, Jillian. It doesn't concern you why I can't go. Refusals of requests aren't looked at too kindly when promotion time comes around. My recommendation of who should replace me when I retire carries the most weight. Just think about that."

Jill clenched her jaw. *What a fucking low blow*. "Where?" she ground out.

Harrison gave her the restaurant, the address, and the names of the three people she'd be meeting with. "Do whatever you need to do to convince them to sign with us. Don't screw this up." And with that, he hung up.

Jill squeezed the receiver in her hand and tapped it on her forehead. Suddenly, she slammed it into the cradle and shouted, "God fucking damn it. Ash, get in here." She went to her closet and grabbed her checkbook out of her bag. As she wrote out the check, she tried to block out the hurt she was about to cause Reagan. She hoped a generous donation would lessen the blow when she didn't show up.

Ash stood in front of her desk with their hands behind their back, looking hesitant.

She stuffed the check into an envelope with a note which she held out to Ash along with a bouquet of purple lilies she had picked up a few hours earlier. "Give these to Reagan when you go to the benefit tonight."

"No," Ash replied, making no move to take the items. "Give them to her yourself. There is no reason for you to skip the—"

"Stop talking." She didn't want to hear the rest of what Ash had to say. Their words would probably be the same ones running through her head. This wasn't a good reason, but she didn't have a choice. She would just need to get Reagan to understand.

"Jill, you're going to crush her."

"Just give them to her. I'll try to come by after this dinner meeting."

Ash snatched the envelope out of her hand but took the flowers with more care. Jill heard them mutter "bullshit" under their breath as they walked out of the office.

Once Ash closed—slammed—the door, Jill held her head in her hands. Fear, frustration, and anger threatened to overwhelm her. She had been working so hard over the years to get where she was in the company. And she was so close to her goal of taking over once Harrison retired. If she took over his position, she would be able to dictate the amount of hours she worked. Sure, there would still be long nights at the office, but she'd have more freedom, which meant more time for Reagan. While it might hurt now, it would benefit them in the future. She just needed Reagan to see that.

And if she was going to have a productive meeting with these potential clients, she needed to ignore the sense of dread in the pit of her stomach.

After the second raffle drawing of the night, Reagan took her time making the rounds with the guests. While there were a good number of people she didn't know, most were people that she was at least acquainted with or who had known her dad. Everyone seemed to be enjoying themselves, and after checking in with Gwen, she was satisfied the kitchen staff didn't need anything.

When she returned to the main room, she found Sam and Ash standing by the bar. She smiled as she took in Ash, looking dapper in a purple bow tie and suspenders combo. They stood with their hands behind their back, and Sam stood just behind them. "Hey, you two. It's great to see you again. Glad you could make it. Did you come with Jill?" she asked, looking around for her, but understanding hit her as she took in the stricken look on Ash's face and the anger radiating from Sam. "She's not here, is she?"

"I'm sorry, Reagan. No, she's not. She sent me with these," they replied, holding out flowers and an envelope. "Boss called her to take a meeting. She said she'd try to stop by afterward, though."

Reagan took the items from Ash and opened the envelope. Inside was a personal check for ten thousand dollars, and a handwritten note that said, "I'm sorry. — J." Tears burned, but she refused to let them fall. She closed her eyes to gather her composure before plastering a forced smile on her face.

"Thank you for delivering this, Ash." She nodded at Ash and Sam. "Please enjoy yourself tonight. There are plenty of great items up for auction. If you'll excuse me." Not waiting for a reply, she turned in the direction of the kitchen and threw the flowers into the first trash can she passed. As her emotions bubbled to the surface, she bypassed the kitchen and headed straight into the office.

She closed the door and leaned against it, taking deep, slow breaths to try and stop the tears from falling. But no matter what she tried, she couldn't hold them back. She stumbled to a club chair in front of the desk and plopped down. She stifled a sob with the back of her hand as understanding hit her. Jill had chosen her job over one of the most important nights for Reagan. She finally knew where she stood. Jill would always pick work. She'd never be the priority.

That realization hit her like a freight train, stealing her breath for a moment. She jumped when she heard the door open.

Gwen's eyes landed on her and she said, "Hey, there you are. Your mom was looking for you. She wants…What's wrong? Are you crying?"

Reagan didn't have the strength to tell Gwen the truth, to let her know that she felt abandoned. Instead, she wiped the tears away with the back of her hand and tried to smile, which probably looked more like a grimace. "I'm okay. Emotional night, ya know?"

"Sure," Gwen replied, looking concerned and not at all convinced. "Your mom is near the bar. She wanted to introduce you to someone."

"Tell her I'll be right out."

Gwen nodded. "Are you sure you're okay?"

"I'm good. Just want to freshen up a bit."

Gwen closed the door without another word, and Reagan plucked a few tissues out of the box on the desk. She carefully wiped at her eyes so she wouldn't smear her eyeliner. She needed to find the strength to make it through the rest of the night. Then she'd break down once she was alone.

She found a mirror in the top drawer of the desk and checked her reflection. She definitely didn't look happy, but only a few people in attendance would really notice. Thankfully, they wouldn't say anything in the crowd. She'd just have to try not to get cornered by her mother or her friends.

Reagan slowly walked down the hallway, giving herself a little extra time to pull herself together. She found her mom waving to her from the bar. She forced a smile as her mom introduced her to an old high school friend of her dad's. She nodded in all the right places, laughed when she was supposed to, but she didn't register a word he said.

She spent the rest of the evening on autopilot, finding the energy for more raffle drawings and a speech at the end of the night to thank everyone for coming and their generous donations. She was grateful she had prepared well for it, otherwise she knew she would have bombed. Guests started trickling out once her speech ended. Several people made a point to tell her how wonderful the night was. The praise was great to hear, but it never rivaled the unending thought running through her mind. *I wasn't important enough to her.*

Once the last guests had left, Gwen and Reagan stood in the empty space in silence. Reagan was tired. Tired from the planning. Tired of the socializing. Tired that she couldn't depend on the one person she wanted.

She cleared her throat as she stared out the front windows. "You okay with calling it a night? I just want to get home. I can come in tomorrow and clean up."

"Don't worry about it. I'll take care of it."

"Thanks," she rasped.

"Did she have a good reason?" Gwen asked, her voice hard.

Did she? Jill knew the importance of the night. She'd seen Reagan's stress from planning and her breakdowns from grief. Reagan couldn't think of a single excuse that would make everything all right. She turned away as tears filled her eyes. "I don't think so."

CHAPTER TWENTY-TWO

The sight of Jill's car hit Reagan like a punch to the gut. She pulled into her parking spot and shut off her car, staring past the steering wheel as she tried to gather her thoughts. She leaned against the headrest and took a few breaths, tamping down the anger that threatened to bubble over. She grabbed her bag from the passenger seat and threw it over her shoulder as she got out. When she made it to the top of the stairs, she found Jill sitting in one of her deck chairs.

She slowly rose and stuffed her hands into the pocket of her coat. "Reagan—"

"Don't." Reagan stopped her in a clipped tone as she unlocked her door and stepped inside. She really wanted to slam the door in Jill's face, but she gripped the knob instead as she held it open.

"Can I come in?" Jill asked in a low rasp.

Reagan clenched her jaw, fighting the urge to let Jill say what she had to say right in the doorway. But she couldn't be that heartless. "Fine. It's freezing out." She turned on a lamp by the couch and tossed her bag on the island. After taking off her coat and hanging it on a stool, she held on to the edge of the counter as she closed her eyes and counted to ten, hoping to calm herself.

Jill stepped inside and closed the door. "I'm so sorry. You know I wanted to be there more than anything. I—"

"If that were true, you would have been there."

"I had every intention of being there. I was so close to leaving for the day, and then fucking Harrison came at me with this bullshit dinner meeting!"

Reagan turned and crossed her arms. "Why didn't you just tell him no?"

"I couldn't."

"Why not? Would he have fired you?"

Jill opened her mouth to speak but closed it just as quickly.

"That's what I thought."

"It was a mistake. I see that now. He threatened to withhold my promotion, and I just felt so powerless. I've worked so hard to get where I am, and the flashing thought that it would be all for nothing scared me."

Reagan pinched the bridge of her nose. She deserved better and Jill needed to know that. "Look. I know how important your job is, Jill. You're gunning for this promotion, and I support that. And I knew there would be times where work would need to take priority. But tonight…Tonight I wanted to be the priority. Tonight was important to me. Then for you to throw money at me, like that would make it all better…" Reagan paused and took a shuddering breath. "It made everything ten times worse. You, of all people, should know that throwing money at an issue never fixes it."

Tears filled Jill's eyes. "I wasn't trying to throw money at you. That wasn't my intention."

"It wasn't? Then what was it, Jill? Because that's exactly what it felt like! Did you even think for one second about how it would feel to receive that? A ton of cash and a fucking lame-ass apology delivered by your assistant? I felt like I wasn't worth your time or attention. You treated me exactly the way your mother and stepfather treat people."

Jill's eyes flashed and she clenched her fists at her sides. "But you're still going to cash that check, aren't you?" Jill asked, her words as icy as the steps outside.

"You're damn right I am. Just because you wrote it to make yourself feel better, doesn't mean it's not going to a good cause. If it could keep one more dad around a little longer for his kids, then it'll be worth it. Even if you're not." Reagan bit her bottom lip to keep it from quivering.

"Wow," Jill whispered, her shoulders sagging. Her nostrils flared with sharp inhales and she audibly swallowed.

"We both knew this," Reagan gestured between them, "was a long shot. Let's just end it now before we get any deeper."

"You can't mean that." Jill took a step forward, reaching for Reagan, but Reagan stepped back and held up her hand.

"You should leave."

Jill stared at her, her eyes searching for something. Reagan stood her ground and stared right back. She was too angry to offer comfort. Too hurt.

Jill wiped away the lone tear that had fallen and walked out the front door.

Reagan had expected Jill to slam the door on her way out. Instead, it closed with a quiet click, and with it came finality. Her deep anger was replaced by unbelievable sadness. Her stomach dropped, and she clutched it as she tried to control her breathing, willing herself not to get sick. In a daze, she stumbled over to the couch.

She reached for a pillow and held it to her chest. One tear fell and then two. And before she could gain control of herself, her body shook with sobs. She fell onto her side and placed the pillow under her head. As she curled her legs onto the couch, she pulled the blanket off the back and wrapped herself in it.

The thoughts flooding her mind moved a mile a minute. One second it was like she was reliving the moment she realized Jill wasn't coming to the benefit, and her anger spiked. The next she had to stop herself from finding her phone and calling Jill to come back. Her mind replayed the pain of the night over and over until she fell into a fitful sleep.

Jill walked through her door and tossed her keys on the counter. She let her coat drop to the floor. She had driven home in a daze, which had probably been a terrible idea, but thankfully she made it home in one piece. She thought about grabbing a bottle of whiskey and drinking straight from the bottle, but it held no appeal. At least not yet. She needed comfort first. Then she could try to forget.

She walked upstairs to her bedroom, stripping off her clothes and folding them neatly into a dry-cleaning bag. Focusing on this task was the only way to hold herself together. She let out a sigh as she pulled on her thickest socks, softest sweats, and an old T-shirt. When she went into the bathroom to wash her face, she left the light off. She couldn't stand to look at herself right now.

"How could I be so stupid?" She'd known sending the check and flowers in her place had been a dumb idea, yet she had still done it. She'd thought she could get Reagan to understand, but that had been an epic failure.

She went downstairs and stopped in the kitchen, pouring herself a generous glass of wine instead of whiskey. She wanted comforting smoothness instead of the burn of the whiskey. Her heart burned enough at the thought of what had just happened.

She took her glass into the living room, curled up in the corner of the couch, and turned on a random episode of *Drag Race*, wanting some distraction, but she immediately turned it off. She now associated the show with Reagan, and watching it would only bring back memories of their time together.

Instead, she took a sip of wine and tried to see her space through Reagan's eyes. She must have thought it was cold and drab with no personal touches. So different from Reagan's apartment that had pictures of family and friends everywhere. Now, as she looked around, she had never felt more alone.

Reagan was probably right. She wasn't worth it. Why would anyone want to be with someone who couldn't open up? Couldn't be vulnerable. Couldn't see past their own ambition. When Reagan had compared her to her mother and stepfather, that had hurt most of all. But it was the truth. That was exactly how she had treated Reagan and the whole night. *Guess it was only a matter of time before I became just like them.* She had probably always been destined to become like them. After all, growing up without love didn't bode well for knowing how to love others. Now that she understood this was who she was, it was time to stop running from the truth.

Maybe it would be easier to continue living the life she did before Reagan. Keep her focus on work. Never let anyone get close. She was better off accepting her lonely existence. No one would get hurt that way, except maybe her. *And I deserve it.*

CHAPTER TWENTY-THREE

Jill's back hurt from being hunched over her desk for the past couple hours. She straightened in her chair, glancing at Ash, who had been in her office taking notes for her as she worked. They looked bored as they scribbled on the side of their notepad.

Jill shuffled through a pile of papers, slamming her hand on the desk when she couldn't find what she wanted. "Where's the fucking schedule from design? Get Rebecca on the phone now. It should have been on my desk two days ago."

"She's not in this week."

"Are you fucking kidding me? Get me her cell number. She's going to put us behind if she doesn't get her shit together." When Ash didn't move, Jill threw her hands in the air. "What the hell are you waiting for?"

"It's almost seven o'clock on Christmas Eve, Jill. Have some compassion."

"Ash, if you don't get out of my office right now and get me her number, I will make sure you never step foot in this building again. Got it?"

Ash stood and tossed the notepad onto the chair, clenching their fists at their side before turning for the door. Instead of leaving, Ash quietly closed it and went to stand in front of Jill's desk again. "Fire me if you want, but I'm going to say something first. You hate this time of year, I get that. I know you like to bury yourself in work because you can't stand spending time with your family during the holidays, but think of everyone else. I'm not even saying this for my benefit. Think of your employees who have families or friends they want to spend time with." Ash paused and took a deep breath. "Look, I know things have been rough since things ended with Reagan."

"Watch it."

"No, someone needs to say this. You're working way too much. Your temper is through the roof. Almost everyone who comes in contact with you is considering quitting. Jill, you are killing yourself here. If you want to do that to yourself, then fine. Go ahead and do it. But don't be so self-absorbed that you bring everyone else down with you. You're punishing yourself, and everyone around you for ruining things with Reagan. You can't tell me you're not acting this way because of her. You either need to find a way to patch things up with Reagan or move on."

"Leave, Ash." Her voice caught as she continued, "Please."

They shook their head, turned and left. Jill covered her mouth with her hand to quiet a sob. Ash was right. Ash was always right. They had tried to tell her she would crush Reagan by not showing up to the benefit, and she did. They were right again that she had been punishing herself every day since that night. And with that came punishing the people around her.

She just wanted to feel better and she missed Reagan so much. Jill didn't know how much she had been missing until Reagan came into her life. She had nothing to look forward to after work. She didn't receive random text messages during the day that brought a smile. There were no more surprise dinners. No one to talk to. No one to open herself up to. She missed Reagan's touch and her warmth. She missed her.

Jill wiped the tears from her eyes and picked up her phone. She unlocked it and pulled up her texts with Reagan. They hadn't spoken a word for almost three weeks. Jill hadn't meant to count the days since the night of the benefit, but every day without Reagan was a day of pain. Before she could second-guess her actions, she typed out three words and sent them. She started typing more, but didn't want to go too far, so she deleted them.

She stared at the phone, willing a reply to come, but it never did.

As her mom turned on a playlist of Christmas music, a knock at the front door pulled Reagan away from mashing potatoes. She opened it to Carly, Gwen, and Brett, and each of them held an item of food and a gift. Her friends had come over at some point during Christmas week each year since they graduated high school. It had started out as a way to make sure they got together during school breaks since they'd all gone to separate schools. Now it was a tradition they couldn't give up, although it was rare that their celebration happened on Christmas Eve. Reagan figured her friends didn't want her and her mom to be alone this year.

"Come on in," Reagan said as she hugged everyone and ushered them inside the house. She watched as they naturally settled into the roles they'd created for themselves over the years. Gwen wasn't allowed to cook for them so she and her husband, Brett, were in charge of bringing the wine. Carly brought a tray of cookies and a platter of raw veggies because she always felt like she needed to have a balance between the two. Reagan and her mom were responsible for cooking dinner, which consisted of beef tenderloin and garlic mashed potatoes.

Reagan resumed mashing and added a little salt after tasting a small spoonful. When Gwen tried to sneak her own spoon in the pot, Reagan swatted her away. "Stop it. You know better than that."

"Hey. I'm the expert here. I think I should have a say—"

"A say in what?" Reagan's mom asked as she walked into the kitchen and enveloped Gwen in a hug.

"I just need to make sure Reagan's potatoes are as good as yours, Kathy."

"Suck-up," she said, playfully pushing her away. "All right. Hop to it, folks. Let's set out the food."

Everyone chipped in to move the spread to the dining room table. They ate and drank and laughed for over an hour, and Reagan enjoyed every second. Throughout the meal, her gaze flicked to her dad's empty chair, but Gwen and Carly always seemed to notice and brought her back in to the conversation.

Once everyone had their fill with the food, Reagan volunteered to clear the table. She put the dishes on the counter when she heard her phone chime from her back pocket. The banner notification told her it was a text from Jill.

I miss you.

She turned around and leaned against the counter so her back was to the dining room. Why was she hearing from her now? Was she just lonely? Three dots appeared on the screen but disappeared only seconds later. What else did she want to say? She stared at the phone, wanting those dots to flash across the screen again.

Reagan jumped when Carly touched her arm. "Whoa. You okay?" Carly asked.

"Yeah. I'm fine."

"Are you sure? You look a little antsy."

Reagan glanced to her mom and friends who were still chatting and drinking wine. Satisfied they were occupied, Reagan pulled Carly into the hallway. "I got a text from Jill. She told me she misses me."

"Aww," Carly replied with a sweet smile before shaking her head and holding up a hand. "Sorry, wait. Which reaction do you want? Do you still want me to hate her?"

"I never wanted you to hate her. I just…What does she want?"

"You can ask her and find out."

Reagan stared at the phone in her hand, her brow furrowed. "No. Not yet. I need some more time."

"Take all the time you need then." Carly took a deep breath and let it out. "I don't know if I should tell you this, but the rumor mill says she's being a terror at work."

"How so?"

Carly shrugged. "I only know what I hear, but supposedly she's working all the time, yelling at people. More than she had been, at least. People are wondering what happened since she'd been better for a while. I try to stay out of it."

"Oh." Reagan chewed the inside of her bottom lip. Was it because of the breakup? Or was it because that's who Jill really was?

"Reagan, Carly," Gwen called from the other room. "It's time for presents."

"Be right there," Carly replied.

Reagan grabbed hold of Carly's wrist. "Please don't say anything to them. I really don't want to get into it tonight."

"No problem. But I'm here whenever you need me. Okay?"

"I know. Thanks."

Carly patted her arm and Reagan followed her into the living room where the others were seated around the room, a small pile of presents on the coffee table.

Reagan pushed the thought of Jill out of her mind. At least for now. She knew Jill would be waiting for her in her dreams. Like she did every night.

When Jill woke up the next morning, she was exhausted and completely wrung out. After leaving work last night, she had come home to her condo and wallowed in her unending loneliness. Even a couple glasses of wine and some chill music had done nothing to squash the ache in her chest when she'd realized that Reagan wasn't going to text her back. No matter how many times she had checked her texts, she had never gotten a reply, and she had fallen asleep with the phone in her hand.

She threw off her covers and padded over to the window, opening the curtains to take in the quiet streets below, only a handful of people milling about. *Right, it's Christmas.* Holidays were difficult for her as they reminded her of how alone she was, especially this year. Typically, she'd attend her family's formal dinner out of obligation, but she hadn't heard from or talked to her mother since the night of Douglas's party and she wasn't about to start now.

Thinking about spending the day holed up in her condo filled her with dread. It was in the quiet moments that she missed Reagan the most. Her mind would go into overdrive and she'd replay everything that had happened from the very first day they met. The unpleasant memories overshadowed the happy ones, leaving her in a perpetually shitty mood.

She needed to do something, get moving and keep her mind occupied. Normally, work would fill that role, but for the first time she didn't want it to. Work had dominated her life and ultimately it was responsible for this situation. No, she needed something more fulfilling.

Furry faces flashed in her mind, and after a change of clothes and a cup of coffee, she found herself pulling into the parking lot of Happy Tails. She parked next to Stacey's truck and hoped she'd let her in. Stacey didn't answer with the first series of knocks so she waited a minute and tried again.

Stacey opened the door with a furrowed brow. "Jill, what are you doing here?"

Jill rubbed the back of her neck with her hand. "I was wondering if I could help out today?"

Stacey waved Jill inside and reached behind the front desk for a clipboard. "Not a Christmas fan?"

"Something like that," Jill mumbled.

"Well, join the club. Here's the list of everything I wanted to get done today. It'll be nice to have someone else chip in."

Jill took the clipboard and scanned the list. "I'll take the first three tasks for now."

Stacey made a note on the paper. "You know where everything is, but if you need something, just let me know."

"Thanks." Jill cleared her throat and wrung her hands for a moment before asking, "Did Haley get adopted?"

"Haley? Which one? We've had a couple recently."

"Black and white pit lab mix. I walked her a few months ago."

Stacey nodded and went to her computer. After a minute, she said, "Yeah, on September thirtieth."

Her heart dropped a bit and she held back a sigh. *Add Haley to the list of things I've lost.* "Oh, okay. That's great," she replied, trying to sound cheerful. "She was a good one. Well, I'll get started then."

Jill stored her phone and car keys in an empty locker. She went straight to the laundry, starting a load of towels before grabbing a bucket and window cleaner to take care of every window and mirror in the place. Even though the job didn't require much thought, she lost herself in the motion of her hands instead of letting her mind wander to all her problems.

Four hours later, three loads of towels were washed, the windows were spotless, and the food inventory was done. "Anything else you need?" she asked Stacey.

"Nope. I finished the rest while you were working."

Jill frowned. That meant she'd have to go back home and she didn't want to just yet. "Is it okay if I take one of the dogs for a walk?"

Stacey studied her for a beat and Jill wanted to squirm under the scrutiny. "Cage six. He'll be good for you."

"Okay," Jill replied, dragging the word out. *How would he be good for me?*

When she entered the dog wing, she grabbed a leash off a hook and stopped in front of cage six. Inside, a tan dog with pointy ears perked up and strutted to the front of the cage, alternating between sitting and half-jumping with his tail wagging constantly. She looked at the form attached to the door. *Rufus.* Four-year-old terrier-pit mix.

"Well, hey there, Rufus. Want to go for a walk?" He answered with two quick jumps. "Guess that's a yes."

She opened the door and knelt down, making sure to introduce herself properly, but Rufus didn't seem to like following the rules of a first meeting and gave her sloppy kisses on her cheek. She pulled away and roughly wiped at the wet spots with the sleeve of her sweatshirt. "Yuck. Okay, none of that." She stood and hooked the leash to his collar. "Let's go."

Right out the gate, Jill realized this would not be a calm walk like it had been with Haley. Rufus pulled Jill down the entire hallway until he stopped at the backdoor, tail wagging furiously. "Sit," she said firmly. She nodded as he barely sat, his tail wagging so much his entire backside moved with him.

When she opened the door, he darted in front of her, zigzagging along the path as he sniffed everything within reach. It took all her strength to keep him under control. She tried to correct him a few times, and he listened briefly and stayed near her side—until another leaf blew. She shook her head at his exuberance and just let him enjoy himself.

She took in a deep breath of the crisp winter air. They hadn't had snow yet so the ground was just drab, brown grass with leftover dead leaves. The day was gloomy with overcast skies and it fit her mood perfectly.

They neared a picnic table at the back of the property, a popular spot for employees and volunteers to take breaks. She sat on top of the table with her feet on the bench, and looked around to see if Stacey was anywhere in sight. Satisfied that she wasn't, Jill patted the space next to her. "Come on up." Rufus joined her, tongue out and panting slightly.

She scratched the top of his head and he leaned into her touch. "You're just a lovable little guy, aren't ya? I think you'll find a home in no time. Just like Haley. I'm glad she was adopted. I mean, selfishly, it would have been nice to see her today, but she's better off in her forever home."

Jill stared off into the wooded area behind the yard and pampered Rufus with head and body scratches. "You know, I was upset about a girl when I met Haley. Kinda like now," she whispered. Rufus lifted his head and rubbed his wet nose along her neck. "Don't worry, it's the same girl. Her name's Reagan."

Just saying her name brought a lump to Jill's throat and she struggled to swallow against it. "I screwed up, Rufus, and she's gone now. I picked a job over her on such an important night. And I don't even love the job. Not that that even matters. I should never have picked the job over her. Nothing is more important than her." Tears stung her eyes and she willed them away but it was no use. As they fell freely, she tried to keep telling her story. "I was a big idiot and lost the first woman who wanted to figure me out. I told her I missed her and haven't heard a word. She's done with me and it's the worst pain I've ever felt."

Rufus put his head into Jill's chest and nudged it against her chin. He sat still as she wrapped her arms around his neck and cried. She cried for Reagan. She cried for him and all the other animals that needed a home. And she cried for herself, for knowing that she was responsible for pushing Reagan away. For ruining the one constant in her life that had made her feel whole.

The cold seeping into her bones brought her out of her moment. It wasn't fair to Rufus to keep him out here for so long. She slid off the table and Rufus jumped down after her. On their walk back, he settled down as if sensing calm was what she needed.

She unhooked the leash and let him back in to his cage. As he sat, she knelt down and took his face in her hands. "Thanks for listening. Sorry I cried all over you. A little payback for your kisses." She kissed the crown of his head. "You'll find your home soon. I just know it. Bye, buddy." Jill closed the door and waved to him before heading down the aisle.

She found Stacey doing some paperwork behind the front desk. "I'm heading out."

Stacey sat back in her chair, twirling her pen on the desk. "Took your time out there, huh?"

Jill avoided her gaze, no doubt her eyes were red and puffy. "Yeah. Sorry about that. I'll see you next time." She continued on her way toward the front door.

"Hey, Jill?"

Jill stopped and turned around.

"Things will get better. Whatever it is. It'll get better. It just takes time."

She nodded and left quickly. Tears burned her eyes as she got in her car. She rested her forehead against the steering wheel as the sobs overtook her once again. Stacey was wrong, though. Reagan didn't want her and she was all alone. How could that ever get better?

CHAPTER TWENTY-FOUR

A knock on her front door drew Jill's attention away from the marketing schedule she had been editing for the past hour. With a sigh, she opened the door and found Sam on the other side, holding a bottle of wine. "What are you doing here?"

"It's New Year's Eve."

"I know that. And I feel like I need to repeat my question. What are you doing here? I figured you'd be out at a club tonight."

"Not this time. They're starting to feel a little overrated. Besides, I'd rather spend some time with my best friend."

Jill scoffed, moving to reclaim her stool so she could get back to work. "You're better off going to the club. I need to work so I probably won't be great company."

"Why the hell are you working?"

"What else is there to do?" Jill asked as she made a note to get another mock-up of a magazine ad.

"I don't know. Go out and celebrate? Have a movie marathon? Get shit-faced drunk if you so choose?" Sam took off her coat and draped it across the stair railing.

Jill shrugged. "None of that holds much appeal, I guess."

"Are you okay?"

She heard the sincerity in Sam's voice, but she pretended to look through some papers, afraid she'd lose it again. "I'm fine."

"Bullshit."

She looked up at the stern tone of Sam's reply. "I am. Why wouldn't I be?"

Sam threw up her hands and paced. "I don't know. Maybe because you haven't been out for a drink with me in over a month and haven't replied to any of my texts. Or maybe because I know that you're working at least seventy hours a week. Or maybe because your heart is shattered."

"Oh, please." Jill shook her head and made more notes. One of those statements finally registered and she stopped writing and looked up at Sam. "Wait. How the hell do you know that I've been working seventy-hour weeks?"

Sam stopped pacing and crossed her arms. "Because you're running your poor assistant ragged. They haven't had a full weekend off since you and Reagan broke up."

"How would you know? And why would their weekends off concern you, Sam?" Jill glared at her friend. She didn't like where this was going. *Is she really trying to get with Ash?*

"Never mind that. I just know from someone, let's call them a mutual friend, that you aren't treating yourself very well. And we…I'm concerned."

"Friend my ass," Jill mumbled.

"What?"

"Nothing." Jill got up and retrieved the bottle of wine. "I'm fine. Just leave it alone." She opened the wine quickly and poured herself a glass, but before she could take a sip, Sam snatched it and put it out of reach. Jill threw her hands up. "Hey. What's the point of bringing wine over if I can't drink it?"

"You aren't fine. I know our friendship hasn't been the deepest over the years, but I care about you. Hell, I even love you, for crying out loud."

Jill snorted and leaned against the island, but she didn't offer the same sentiment to Sam even though it was true. Sam had been the only close friend she'd had in her entire life, but she still had a hard time telling her she loved her. *That's sad. No wonder I suck at relationships.*

"We're the same, you and me. Keeping everyone at arm's length, never letting anyone in, even each other sometimes. But Jill, don't you miss it?"

"Miss what?"

"Letting her in."

Jill swallowed against the lump in her throat, tears pricking her eyes. "Yes," she whispered.

"Then do something about it. Talk to her. Get her back."

"No. It's too late. She's better off without me. Like you said, I don't let anyone in. It's better that way."

Sam sighed. "You know you're not as standoffish and cold as you want people to think you are, right?"

"What do you mean?"

"All the money, not to mention the time, you spend on all those forgotten dogs and cats at the shelter. That just proves you have a kind heart and can open it to others. Just let someone in who's a little less furry this time."

Jill ignored the joke and furrowed her brow. "How do you know about that?"

Sam shook her head. "For someone so smart, you can be really stupid."

"I've proven that time and time again, but why am I this time?"

"I'm your accountant, you nut. I know about all your charitable donations."

"Okay. But how do you know about the time?" Jill raised her eyebrows and crossed her arms before nodding. "Ah. That blabbermouth of an assistant I have that I'm supposedly running ragged. I can't believe they—"

"It's not their fault. It just came up."

"How much time have you been spending with Ash?"

"That's not important."

"Oh, I think it's very important."

"You're right, it is, but not right now. We're talking about you."

Jill pinched the bridge of her nose and pointed at Sam. "Fine. But we will talk about this. Got it?"

"I got it."

Jill headed into the living room, collapsing on the couch and holding her head in her hands. "What am I gonna do, Sam?" she asked, her voice cracking.

Sam sat next to her, rubbing her hand in slow circles on Jill's back. "What do you want to do?"

"I miss her. So much that it hurts sometimes. Nothing has felt right since I fucked everything up."

"So then tell her that."

"It's not that simple."

"It can be."

"No. I hurt her so badly. I can't get the way she looked at me that night out of my head. The pain in her eyes, the disappointment in her voice. I did that to her. I caused that. Me. She didn't deserve that. And I don't deserve her. She's so much better off without me."

Sam sat on the coffee table in front of Jill and took her hands. "Stop torturing yourself. You deserve happiness too."

"But—"

"I'm not finished."

"Sorry," Jill muttered.

"You have spent your entire life feeling unloved by those who should love you the most. I know it's easier to push everyone away, but just stop and go talk to her. Yes, you did something incredibly shitty. Own up to it. Fight for her."

"What if she just doesn't want me?"

Sam shrugged. "I guess that's a risk you'll have to take. But I've seen the way she looks at you. I have a good feeling she's missing you as much as you're missing her. You won't know until you talk to her. So get off your ass and do it."

"I don't know."

Sam softly sighed. "Just think about it, okay?"

She nodded.

"Do you want to watch a movie? Or would you rather be alone?"

"I think alone might be best. I need to sort through some things. Try to make sense of the thoughts racing through my mind right now."

"Okay. Tell any of the negative ones to fuck off."

Jill laughed. "I'll try."

Sam kissed her on the cheek. "Call me if you need me."

"I will."

Sam stood and put on her coat as she walked to the door.

Jill called out, "Hey, Sammy?"

Sam turned around. "Yeah?"

"Thank you."

"You're welcome," she said, quietly shutting the door behind her.

Jill relaxed into the couch, wiping the last of the tears from her cheeks. She replayed the conversation she had with Sam over and over. It was hard to admit that she had ever been or would ever be worthy of Reagan's love. Not after what she'd done.

She had promised Sam she would think about talking to Reagan, but at the moment she didn't have the strength to figure out what that entailed. Instead, she did what she did best—buried herself in work.

She grabbed a stack of mail from a side table as she passed by. She couldn't remember when she had last gone through it, and judging by the tall stack, it had been a while. She flipped through each piece and divided it between piles to look at later, recycle, or open immediately. When she came across an envelope that had "SECOND NOTICE" written in red on the outside, she dropped the rest of the stack onto the counter. Her breath caught in her throat as she saw the familiar initials of TMG in the top left corner.

"What the hell?" she muttered. She ripped open the envelope and unfolded the piece of paper, which had a sticky note attached to it.

I left your mother a copy of this the night of the party and sent an additional reminder. I've received no reply. Please pay upon receipt.

No signature but she easily recognized Reagan's handwriting. She skimmed her finger along the words as if she could feel Reagan's presence through the note.

What should I do? She could pay it and forget about it. Send a check in and be done with it. But the last time she sent a check in for something, it ruined the best thing in her life. Taking the bill to her mother didn't hold much appeal either, but it was probably the best option.

Jill glanced at her watch, noting it was a little before nine p.m. Not too late to stop by her mother's house, especially if she was entertaining. "Time to get this over with."

Reagan sat on her mom's couch as they indulged in their New Year's Eve tradition of watching *Return to Me*. They had watched it as a family one year when she was a teenager, and for a reason Reagan couldn't remember, they watched it every year since before the ball dropped at midnight in Times Square. When they started it tonight, she was afraid it would be too much for her or her mom, and they'd end up shutting it off and crying. But it never happened. The jokes in the movie hit a little differently this year with her dad gone, but anytime the four older guys popped on the screen, she imagined her dad sitting next to her and chuckling, and it brought a bittersweet smile to her face.

As the credits rolled, she grabbed the empty popcorn and candy bowls, but her mom stopped her with a hand on her arm. "I got this. Want another beer?"

"Yes, please."

She unlocked her phone for what had to be the fifth time in the last hour to look at the text message she'd received from Jill on Christmas Eve.

I miss you.

Those three words had been etched on her mind since she'd received them. She'd opened her phone dozens of times since, wanting to reply, but she always stopped herself. She didn't want to admit how much power those words had over her. Part of her wanted to stay angry at Jill, but the rest of her wanted to text her, call her, go see her. *Maybe I should send her a repl…*

Her mom sat next to her. "You're going to burn a hole in that phone."

She dropped the phone onto the couch. "What?"

"I've caught you staring at that message three times tonight. It's from Jill, isn't it?"

"Yeah. She sent it on Christmas Eve."

"What did she say? Did you answer?"

She sighed as she took the bottle of beer that her mom held out for her. "She told me she misses me. And no. I haven't said anything."

"Why not?"

"I don't know what to say. Or if I even want to say anything at all."

"Do you miss her?"

She stared at the bottle and began peeling off the label. "I don't want to, but I do," she whispered.

"Why don't you want to?"

"Because I want to be angry with her. Missing the benefit showed me what was important to her. And it wasn't me. Then with the check…I felt like she was buying me off. Shoving it in my face that she could throw around her money as if it would make everything better. It felt awful. She hurt me."

"I know she did, sweetheart."

She turned at the placating tone in her mom's voice. "Why do I feel like there's a 'but' in there somewhere?"

"She made a rather generous donation that night, too."

"Because she felt guilty."

"Maybe so. But I'm still going to tell her thank you if I ever see her again."

Reagan almost choked on the sip of beer she was taking. "What? Why?"

"Now don't look at me like that. If I see her, I will still give her a piece of my mind for hurting you. But that was the biggest single donation we got that night. It's going to a good cause."

"I know," Reagan grumbled.

Her mom put her beer on the coffee table and turned to Reagan, bringing a leg up onto the couch. "I've never told you this before, but your dad skipped our engagement party."

"He did?" Reagan asked, eyes wide. "What happened?"

"It wasn't a big thing, just family and a few friends were coming over for a cookout. We had a fight that morning."

"About what?"

"It was so stupid," her mom said with a laugh. "We couldn't agree on a paint color for the living room. We had moved into that first house like two weeks before. Damn, we yelled at each other for probably a good five or ten minutes before he stormed off. When people started showing up for the party and he still hadn't come back, I asked everyone to leave."

"No way. Then what?"

"Well, he showed up about a half hour after everyone left. I was busy cleaning up all the food that no one ate. He placed a paint can of the color I wanted on the counter and pulled me in for a hug, crying and apologizing over and over. We spent the rest of the night talking, nibbling on all that food…and each other."

Reagan was too stunned to even comment on that last part. "Why did he run out? I can't picture Dad doing something like that."

"He got scared. With the stress of the new house and the engagement, he had a minor freak-out and needed a break."

"Did that make you question wanting to be with him?"

"For a minute, maybe. But I knew that if he had walked back in that door and told me he still wanted to be with me, I would be all in. He's who I wanted." Her bottom lip quivered as she tried to smile.

"Oh, Mom." Reagan put her beer down and wrapped her in a tight hug. She cradled the back of her head and gently rocked her while she cried. She couldn't imagine the pain her mom had been going through for most of the year. If she could take it all away, she would in an instant.

Her mom pulled away, grabbed a tissue from the side table to wipe her eyes and blow her nose. "I'm sorry. I just miss him."

"I know you do. My shoulder is always available for a good cry. You don't need to be so strong all the time, you know."

"Thanks, sweetie. There's a reason you're my favorite daughter."

"I'm your only daughter and only child, Mother."

"And therefore, my favorite."

She rolled her eyes, grabbed her beer and took a few sips as her mom changed to a channel broadcasting the celebration in New York. She watched the revelers cheer and wave at the camera. But within minutes, her mind drifted and she thought about what she'd just learned. Over the years, her parents had argued too many times to count, but she'd never have called any of it fighting. They never stayed angry with each other for more than a few minutes. So hearing that her dad had stormed out was shocking. "Did you ever worry that Dad would run away again?"

"God no, never. People make mistakes all the time. It's what they do and how you respond to them that matters. If people admit when they're wrong, then hopefully that can start the path to forgiveness. And each person needs to decide which mistakes they are willing to forgive. Something I forgive might be something you never would, and vice versa."

"So, you're saying I should forgive Jill?"

"I didn't say that. I can't tell you what to do, honey. You'll know in your heart whether or not you want to reply to her and ultimately forgive her. If you need more time, that's fine. Or if you need her to be out of your life, that's fine too. You just need to do what's right for you."

"Thanks, Mom."

"You're welcome." She rested her head on Reagan's shoulder. "Now, think I'll be awake at midnight?"

She looked at her watch. "Seeing as you still have an hour, I'm gonna say it's highly unlikely. Especially since that was your third beer. I give you ten minutes before you fall asleep."

"Pssh. I can beat that. I just need to sit up then." She shifted her position and wrapped a blanket around her torso.

To her mom's credit, she lasted almost forty-five minutes before she slouched to the side and fell asleep against the arm of the couch. Reagan gently lifted her legs onto the couch and adjusted the blanket. She slid down the couch so her mom could stretch her legs in her sleep if needed.

She stared blankly at the TV as she recalled her mom's advice. *Do what's right for me.* She hadn't felt right for most of the year. First, with her dad's illness and passing, and now, with the aftermath of the breakup. But she couldn't deny that the times she had felt right were mostly when she was around Jill.

She closed her eyes and thought back to their fight at her place. Besides being angry with Jill, she was also upset with herself. The things she said to Jill—accusing her of being like her mother and telling her she wasn't worth it—still made her sick to her stomach. She had probably hurt Jill as much as Jill had hurt her.

The countdown had started in New York, and she reached for her phone. She unlocked it as the ball dropped, again staring at Jill's text. Those three words had the power to overwhelm her if she let them. She scoffed at herself. *Who am I kidding? They already have.* She couldn't lie to herself anymore. She missed Jill terribly. She had wanted to brush off the text as soon as she had gotten it, blame it on Jill just being lonely around the holidays. But she knew deep down that it was more than that. Jill never expressed her feelings easily, so she imagined that sending that text had been difficult for her.

Reagan watched as people celebrated in the streets of New York. With a new year came new beginnings, and Reagan just needed to decide if she wanted Jill to be part of those beginnings or not.

Nadine opened the front door with raised eyebrows. "Ms. Jacobs. We weren't expecting you."

"Is my mother home?"

"Yes. Please come in." Nadine stepped aside and waved her in.

"Thanks."

"Can I get you anything?"

"No, thank you. I won't be staying long."

"Very well. I'll show you to the den."

"It's okay. You can retire for the night."

"But—"

Jill held up her hand. "It's getting late. If my mother puts up a fuss, I'll tell her it was my idea."

Nadine continued to eye Jill with suspicion. "If you're sure?"

"I am. Have a good night. Oh, and Happy New Year."

"Thank you, Ms. Jacobs. You too. Goodnight."

Jill found her mother sitting in a leather chair, one leg crossed over the other and a tumbler of whiskey in her right hand. She softly cleared her throat. "Hello, Mother."

Her mother turned so quickly she splashed whiskey over the side of her glass but didn't seem to care. "My darling daughter," she slurred.

Jill held in a sigh. She didn't expect to find her mother drunk. Drinking, yes. Drunk, no. Her mother didn't like anyone to see her drunk, even if it was at home. She'd always told her it was unseemly. So even though her mother drank often, she usually kept herself in check. "Is everything okay?"

"Oh, just great," she replied before taking a long sip. "What brings you by this evening?"

"TMG sent me the final invoice for Douglas's party. It's a second notice and R…they said they tried to send it to you, but you haven't paid it," Jill said, placing the sheet of paper on the table to the side of her mother's chair.

"Yes, of course. I will pay it tomorrow. Now, join me in a drink."

"I'd rather not. I need to head back home."

"Get yourself a drink and sit with me," her mother stated firmly.

Holding back a groan, Jill poured herself a small amount of whiskey. She sat in the chair next to her mother and took a sip. Her mother's gaze flicked to the invoice and then landed on Jill.

"How is your little girlfriend?"

Jill clenched her jaw and leaned forward. "First of all, she's not my little anything. She is a grown, well-respected, and highly successful woman. I still cannot believe the vitriol you threw at her the night of the party. She had been nothing but nice to you and accommodated all of your crazy requirements for that fucking party. You looked at her like she was trash. Second—"

"You remind me of your father."

"Stepfather, for the last fucking time. And I am nothing like him. If you keep saying shit like that, I'm leaving." She started to rise.

"I meant your real father." Her mother drank the rest of her whiskey and held the empty glass in her hands, staring at it as if she didn't know what it was.

"What?" Jill whispered.

"You have that fire in your eyes. The unwavering conviction in your voice. I've seen it before in regards to your work. But this..." She gestured up and down. "...this is the first time I'm seeing it when you're fighting for someone you love."

"I don't—"

"You do love her. I can tell."

"How?"

"You looked at her the way Greg used to look at me. And I used to look at him."

"Greg." Jill's bravado faded and she slumped back in her chair. "That was his name?"

"Yes."

"You've never told me that before," Jill whispered. "Why? Why couldn't you have told me about him more?"

"It was agreed upon." Her mother looked away, ashamed. "In the contract."

"The fucking contract. You signed away my right to have a proper family. How could you? Did you know that I still remember every second of that day I found out? I can still hear the indifference in your voice as you laid out everything as if it were all a neat little package. You hurt me and I was just a kid. And for what? You didn't want to lose access to the family money, is that it?"

"Your grandfather—"

"My grandfather was a chauvinistic asshole, and you married someone just like him. Was all that money worth it? Tell me. Was it worth trading for this life of luxury?"

"No," her mother whispered, regret shadowing her features. "It was never worth it."

Confused, Jill slumped into her seat. "Then, why? Why did you put me through everything you did?"

Her mother stared into the fireplace as if trying to find the answer in its dying embers. "I was young, only nineteen when I got pregnant with you."

"Yeah, I know. I figured out the math when I was a kid. That's no—"

"Please. Let me finish."

Her mother turned her head, and Jill's eyes widened at the shimmer of tears in her eyes. Jill nodded.

"Greg was my first love. My only love. He worked at a car repair shop, and one day I had a flat tire just down the road from it. Since it was the time before cell phones, I couldn't call anyone. So I walked a few blocks to the shop and he was the first person I saw." A wistful smile overtook her features briefly. "His hands and coveralls were smeared with grease. He stupidly made a move to shake my hand, as if I would get that grease all over my hands."

"Of course not."

They shared a small chuckle.

"Anyway, he walked me back to the car and went about putting on the spare tire. He fished a Snickers bar out of his pocket and gave it to me. I was rarely allowed candy when I was younger, so I relished it. I ate while he worked, and conversation just seemed to flow naturally between us. He put the spare on quickly and drove us to the shop. Once he finished, he didn't charge me and asked me on a date."

"What did you say?"

"No, of course. My father's voice was in my ear with words of scorn. Much like the ones I said to Ms. Murphy." She shook her head. "But there was something there. I couldn't ignore it."

"Something special."

"Yes," her mother replied quietly. "About a week after that, I brought him a Snickers bar to repay him. I must have done that every week for about a month. That led to secret dates and to more," she said with a wave of her hand. "And it led to you."

"What happened then?"

"Well, when I told my father I was pregnant, he forbade me from seeing Greg again. Since he hadn't heard from me, he kept coming around, but my father put an end to it. I'm not sure how. I assume he threatened him." Her mother sighed. "Then he made the contract for Douglas. We got married a month later. And that's how we've ended up here."

"What happened to Greg?" Jill cleared her throat. "To my father?"

"He died in a car accident when you were one."

"Oh." Jill looked down with a furrowed brow. "Did he know about me?"

"No."

She shook her head and turned away. *Can I mourn someone I never had?* She wondered if it would have made a difference if he had lived longer. Would she have been able to know him? Would he have sought her out? Would he have shown her the love she never had or felt? Her heart began to race and her breathing quickened.

Her mother's shaky voice interrupted her spiraling thoughts. "I'm sorry, Jillian."

Jill nodded but she remained silent. The apology felt heavy on her heart. It had been something she'd wanted to hear her entire life, but now she didn't know if it even changed anything. She had been robbed of a father, one who seemed like he would have loved her if his love for her mother was any indication. She felt cheated, and it made her sick to her stomach. "Can I ask you something?"

"Anything."

"Why do you stay here? With Douglas? You obviously don't love him."

"No, I don't. But I don't have anything else. I might as well stick with what I've done to myself."

"Don't you want more?"

"No. My 'more' has been gone a long time." She closed her eyes and shook her head. She walked to the drink cart and poured herself another glass. She held it in her hands and moved closer to the fireplace, staring down at it once more. Without turning toward Jill, she said, "Be better than me, Jillian. Fight for your *more*. For your something special. Don't give up like I did."

Jill sat still, not wanting to break the strange mood that had come over the room. All the words entering her brain felt inadequate. Never had her mother poured out her heart like that. Probably to anyone. Maybe only Greg. Then she lost him because she chose money and family pride over love. That wasn't any better than Jill choosing work over Reagan. But Jill had something her mother never did—a second chance. She promised herself she wouldn't waste it.

"I won't," she blurted, her resolve strengthening.

Her mother murmured an acknowledgment but remained facing the fireplace. She straightened as she emptied her glass in one long gulp. "Have a good night, Jillian."

And with that, the mask her mother usually wore returned. Jill placed her glass on the coffee table. With one last look at her mother's stony form, she left.

CHAPTER TWENTY-FIVE

When her alarm went off at six in the morning, Jill wanted to throw her phone across the room, but that would only lead to more problems than she already had, so she resisted that urge. She rubbed at her eyes, feeling the puffiness beneath her fingertips. She'd had yesterday off, New Year's Day, and had spent most of it moping around her condo and thinking about everything her mom had told her the night before.

It had been a surprise for her mother to speak so openly about her biological father. It pained Jill to know that her mother had lost the love of her life, and she couldn't help but feel sorry that her mother had felt stuck with Douglas and had punished herself ever since. Jill didn't want to be like that. She needed to learn from her mother's mistakes as well as her own. After understanding how freeing it felt to be cared for by Reagan and to be open with her, she didn't want to go back to her cold existence and only live for what was next at work. She wanted to live for Reagan. Live for herself.

After her third glass of wine last night, she'd decided that today would be the day she'd go all in. She'd talk to Reagan and apologize for being such a shitty person. If she didn't take her back, then at least Jill would know she tried. She couldn't go another day without trying.

Since Reagan had never answered her text from Christmas, Jill doubted that she'd answer any other texts or calls from her now, which meant she needed to get someone to help her. Her first thought was to ask Carly, or even Kathy, as they were the ones who never seemed to have much hesitation about her being in Reagan's life. But that didn't feel like the right move. If she was going to do this, she needed to convince the one person who never really warmed to her from the start. She needed to talk to Gwen.

Jill parked in front of Wren, begging the universe that Gwen would be there. She knew it would be a risk showing up here this early. If she wasn't here, then she'd have to call her, but she'd rather talk to her in person.

She tried to open the front door but it was locked. She peeked through the windows but initially didn't see anyone until a movement near the back caught her eye. She knocked on the window and waved.

A young guy with a charcoal gray apron opened the door. "I'm sorry, but we're closed. We don't open until eleven."

"I know. I need to talk to Gwen."

"I'm sorry, but I said we're—"

"Wait, you worked the Jacobs party a couple months ago, right? That was for my stepfather." The guy looked vaguely familiar, but her memory of that night was filled with Reagan and the shit show of her mother's, not Gwen's employees. She figured it'd be worth a shot to ask, though. It would at least let him know she was a client and not some crazy stalker.

"Ah, right. Follow me." He led her to the back of the restaurant and pointed down the hallway toward the open door at the end. "She's in there."

"Thanks." She took a few calming breaths before she knocked on the open door. "Hey, Gwen."

Gwen looked up from her desk and glared at Jill. Placing her palms on the desk, she stood up slowly. "Jill. What the hell are you doing here?"

"I need your help."

"If you've come to secure our services again, then I will politely ask you to get the fuck out of here."

Jill held up her hands. "No, I didn't come here for that. I need your help with Reagan. I need to talk to her."

"She's the last person in the world I should help you with. I fucking told you not to hurt her and you did. Horribly. Why should I help you?"

She stepped into the room and tentatively sat in the chair in front of Gwen's desk. Her eyes burned and tears threatened to fall. "I know I don't deserve it. Or deserve her. I made a terrible mistake. I see that now. Fuck, I saw it then too. I was just too blinded by success and the chance for promotion that I let the best thing that has ever happened to me slip away. My world has been upside down since she left. She's the only person who wanted to know me, the real me. And I messed it up. I miss her so much, Gwen."

Gwen stayed silent for a moment. "You need to tell her that."

"I know. I want to so badly. That's why I need your help."

"Why? What do I have to do with any of this?"

"I-I don't think she ever wants to hear from me again. I texted her at Christmas but never got a reply. I thought maybe you could help by getting her in the same room with me. Please."

"How do you expect me to do that?"

"I don't know. Maybe say you need her to meet you at Gale's? And then I can be there waiting for her."

"Why Gale's?"

"That's where we met," Jill replied with a slight upturn of her lips.

"Hmm. Okay, kinda romantic." Her soft expression turned again to a frown as she crossed her arms and stared down at Jill. "So you want me to lie to my best friend?"

"That's one way to look at it." Jill's shoulders sagged as she acknowledged that consequence.

Gwen raised her eyebrows, staring pointedly back at her.

"You know what? This was a stupid idea. I'm sorry to bother you." Jill wiped a tear from the corner of her eye and headed for the door.

"Wait."

Jill turned and held her breath. Gwen seemed to mull over what she wanted to say. "I'll make sure she's there." Gwen looked at her watch and said, "Be there at eleven thirty."

Jill let out a slow breath, the tightness in her chest that she'd felt for the past month easing slightly. "Oh, thank you." She had the strange urge to hug Gwen but figured that'd be a little too much, especially when Gwen looked menacing with her arms crossed and a wary smile on her face that was more like a scowl.

"Don't make me regret it."

"I won't." She turned to leave but stopped. "Can I ask you something?"

"Another favor?" Gwen asked, sounding annoyed.

"No. Um, why did you agree to help me?"

"You made her happy. I was always afraid that losing her dad would break her, but it didn't. And that's largely because of you."

"You think so?"

"I do. You eased her pain. Brought hope and light back into her life. And then you made a boneheaded move that broke her. Bring that light back to her."

"I'll try. I promise. Thanks, Gwen."

Gwen nodded and returned to her desk, and Jill took the hint to leave. She drove to her office with a sense of relief. Her plan was falling into place. Now she just needed to get through a morning of work and then she'd finally get her chance to apologize to Reagan.

But when she walked down the hallway to her office, it was hard to ignore how no one made eye contact and shifted their direction to avoid passing by her. *Maybe because you've been an asshole to each of them.* As she reached her outer office door, she realized the biggest coworker she had hurt would be right behind it.

She'd made so many mistakes over the past few weeks. She'd taken her anger out on every person she came into contact with during the day and that was so unfair. If she was going to be a better person for Reagan, she needed to do the same thing with the other people in her life who she cared about. She took a deep breath and walked through the door.

"Morning, Ms. Jacobs," Ash said curtly, glancing at her briefly before continuing to type up something on their computer. "It would have been nice to know you were going to be late. I've already had to field three calls and make up an excuse for your absence."

Jill cleared her throat. "Ash, I'd like to apologize to you. I've been such an asshole, and I took it out on everyone else, but you most of all. I'm sorry for threatening your job."

"More than once," Ash said. They turned in their chair and folded their hands on the desk.

"Right. More than once. That was unprofessional of me and I really didn't mean it. You're the best assistant I've ever had. And honestly, I'd be so overwhelmed without your help. If you ever feel the need to find someplace better or just get away from me, I'll understand and I will write you a glowing recommendation. Just say the word."

Ash stared at her long enough that Jill had to resist the urge to squirm or run into her office. Finally, they stood and waved her off. "Don't go falling on your sword. I've handled your outbursts for so long already. Why not a few more?"

Jill let out a slight chuckle. "I'd say these were a little worse than normal. I am sorry, Ash."

"I know. You've been having a rough few weeks and that sucks, but you basically did what Harrison did to you to everyone else. It wasn't cool."

"I promise never to do it again."

"Good enough." Ash put their hands in their front pockets and gave Jill a slight grin. "You're gonna fight for her, aren't you?"

"Why do you think that?"

"Well, you're not one to apologize easily. You must have had a come to Jesus moment in the last couple of days."

Jill let out her first genuine laugh in weeks. "That's true. And I am going to try, as long as she'll listen to me first. That's the big question right now. But I need to get some work done. Could you bring me a cup of coffee when you get a chance, please?"

"Wow. A please without prompting. I should mark this down as a historical moment."

"Oh, shut up." She hung her jacket and bag in her closet before sitting at her desk and turning on her computer. She had to deal with one conference call and a few minor tasks before she could leave to meet Reagan at Gale's.

She was grateful she didn't need to lead the conference call because she definitely couldn't focus on it. As her lead designer droned on, her thoughts drifted to what she would say to Reagan. She had tried to plan out a small speech last night, but she didn't want it to sound rehearsed or robotic. She needed to tell Reagan what was in her heart and the only way to do that was to say whatever came to her in the moment.

Once the call was over and she crossed off two items from her to-do list, she put on her coat and walked out of her office. "I'm heading out to talk to Reagan. Wish me—"

"Ah, Jillian." She stopped midsentence as Harrison walked through the door. "The CEO of Apex Aviation is in town and I told him you'd take him to lunch to go over the progress of the campaign. Meet him at noon at St. Elmo."

"No."

"Excuse me?"

"I already have a meeting to attend so I can't make it. For once, do some work and take him yourself."

His face reddened and he pointed at her, his finger only inches from her face. "Watch your tone."

"No, Harrison, I won't. You throw things at me time and time again, and usually at the last-minute. All because you don't want to do them. I've had enough. If I lose your endorsement for the promotion, then so be it."

"You might lose more than that. Do you want to lose your job?" he asked, giving her a smug smile.

"Harrison, you won't fire me. That would mean you'd have to do all the work yourself and we both know that will never happen. Now, I need to leave or I'm going to be late. You can brief me on your meeting later."

Jill didn't wait for a reply. Instead, she walked around him and out of the office. She hurried to her car and drove off, panicking that she might be late. That wouldn't be the way to start her apology. She ignored the fact that she could be out of a job by the time she returned to the office. Frankly, she didn't care anymore. Seeing the regret her mother had about her father had stirred something inside her. She never wanted to live with that kind of regret for the rest of her life. And she knew that if she didn't try again with Reagan, that would be exactly what would happen. She needed to fight for her "something more" and she couldn't let anything, or anyone, stand in her way.

CHAPTER TWENTY-SIX

As soon as Reagan ended a call with a supplier, her phone rang again. She sighed loudly, thankful she was alone in her office. She'd been on call after call all morning long, and a headache bloomed above her right eye from the incessant ringing. Looking at the screen brought a smile to her face.

Swiping to accept the call, she said, "Thank god it's you. I was ready to throw my phone across the room."

"Bad day, huh?" Gwen asked with a chuckle.

Reagan groaned and rested her head against the back of the chair. "I've talked to eight different suppliers and I've only been in the office for an hour. Who comes back into the office for only the last day of the week after a holiday? I knew I should have taken the rest of the week off," she grumbled.

"I still don't know why you didn't. But listen, I've got the perfect way for you to break up your day."

Reagan sat up. "I'm listening."

"Damien wants to try out some new recipes for his late-night bar menu and asked for my opinion. Told him I'd bring you along to talk about how they'd work, you know, numbers-wise."

Reagan's stomach rumbled at the mere mention of food, making her realize that aside from a mug of her mom's turkey broth last night, she hadn't eaten since yesterday afternoon. "You don't have to ask me twice. I'm in. Are you coming to the office first? What time do you want to head over to Gale's?"

"Um, I'll have to meet you there. So, be there at eleven thirty, okay?"

"I'll see you then." Reagan ended the call and tossed her phone on the desk. She scrolled through her email, hoping it would be distraction enough for the next couple of hours.

When Reagan opened the door to Gale's Tavern, she waited as two guys in front of her were given a table. As they walked away, she stepped up to the host stand and saw a familiar face. "Hey, Amy."

"Oh, hey. Just one today?" she asked as she reached behind her for a menu.

"No. I'm actually supposed to meet—"

"Table for two, please."

Reagan lost the ability to speak when she heard the voice that had haunted her dreams for the past month. She turned and found Jill standing only a few feet away. Jill held her hands behind her back, and her eyes bore into Reagan. They held so much emotion, but the one that stood out was overwhelming uncertainty and that was something she rarely attributed to Jill.

Reagan still couldn't find her voice. Her gaze flicked back to Amy who looked at them with anticipation, wanting one of them to make a decision. She turned back to Jill whose eyebrows were raised, also waiting for her answer. Reagan needed answers, too. But more than that, she needed Jill. Reagan nodded to Amy. "Table for two."

"Right this way," Amy said.

Reagan followed and she felt Jill right behind her. Just being close to her was affecting her. Her body hummed with the familiar pleasure that being near Jill always brought. She wanted to hold on to the anger that had consumed her since the night of the benefit, but she found it wasn't as strong as it used to be. In fact, it was practically nonexistent, at least on the inside. Outwardly, she didn't want Jill to know how much she had affected her, not until she knew why she was here. She needed to keep her guard up. She couldn't take being hurt anymore.

Amy led them to the same table she and Jill had shared on that fateful day of their first meeting. Both sat down as Amy retreated wordlessly to the front. Now it was just the two of them, staring at each other in silence. Since this seemed to be Jill's show, she'd wait her out until Jill said what she came to say.

Jill toyed with the silverware in front of her, flipping it around and then straightening it again. Now that she had Reagan in front of her, her mind had gone blank. What she really wanted to do was to wrap her in a hug. She wanted to feel her touch, her warmth. She wanted her and missed her. *What if I screw this up? What if I lay out all my feelings and it doesn't change anything?* She felt the familiar burn of tears at the corners of her eyes but she willed them away. She couldn't break down, not yet at least. She cleared her throat, trying to keep her voice even. "It's really good to see you."

"What are you doing here? I'm supposed to be meeting Gwen," Reagan asked, arms crossed and looking a little pissed.

"Um, well, you're actually not. I asked her to get you here."

"Why?"

"I needed to talk to you, Reagan. I need to apologize." Reagan stayed silent for a moment which made Jill nervous, and she resisted the urge to fiddle with the silverware again.

"I'm listening."

The softness to Reagan's voice hit Jill in her core, and she wondered if Reagan was missing her too. The thought brought a fresh round of tears and she didn't care if any fell. She needed to show her emotions. Reagan needed to see that she could. She took a deep breath and leaned forward, folding her arms on the table. "I am so sorry that I missed the benefit. I knew how important that night was to you, and I know how important your dad was and the hole it created in your heart when he passed. It was idiotic of me to think that sending all that money with Ash was a good idea. It…it was a really shitty thing to do. I'm so used to being surrounded by people that solve their problems with money that I lost my head for a moment. And then when Harrison threatened my promotion, I panicked. I figured no matter what I chose, it would be wrong. But that's not the case. I should have always chosen you. I always want to and will always choose you. If you'll let me."

Reagan slightly cocked her head to the side as if studying Jill. "Why now? What's changed?"

"Believe it or not, I talked with my mother a couple nights ago."

"Really? What did the lovely Maureen have to say?"

"She told me about my father. My biological father."

"Holy shit. What about him?" Reagan sat up and extended her arms on the table as if she wanted to reach for Jill, but she pulled them back just as quickly and rested them in her lap.

Jill recounted the entire conversation she'd had with her mother on New Year's Eve. When she got to the point in the story where she heard about her dad dying without knowing who she was, Reagan reached out and brushed her thumb over her knuckles. Jill finished the story and took a sip of water, trying to calm herself.

"Wow. That's a lot to take in," Reagan replied, squeezing Jill's hand. "How are you feeling about all that?"

"I'm not sure. I don't really know how I should feel. Everything with my dad…" Jill shook her head. "I think that will take a while to process."

"Do you think you'll ever want to learn more about him? Get in touch with his family? Anything like that?"

"I…I don't know. The thought has definitely crossed my mind, but I don't think I'm ready to think about what that might open up."

"Maybe we could figure it out someday? Together?"

"Really?" Jill whispered.

"Yeah. I've been missing you so much. I shouldn't even admit how many times I pulled up your last text just to look at it."

"How many?" Jill asked, trying to hold back a grin.

"Let's just say I lost count after a hundred." Reagan chuckled but then said seriously, "I'm sorry for everything I said that night. I know your job is important to you. I was never trying to diminish that. But you hurt me so badly and so easily. I felt like I was being bought off. That you were trying to use your money to sweep away the pain you obviously knew you'd cause."

Jill hung her head for a moment, letting the accusation settle, before meeting Reagan's gaze again. "You're right. That was never my intention, and I'm so sorry I did that to you." She took a breath and let it out slowly. "But, we might not have to worry about the whole job thing once I get back into the office."

"Why?"

"I kind of told Harrison to fuck off and do his own work before I came here. In more polite terms. He wasn't ruining anything else between us anymore."

"Wow. I'm really not trying to make you pick me over work."

"I know you're not. I probably should have done something like that a long time ago. I was just trying to do everything I can to get the promotion. He knew that and he took advantage of it. But it's just not as important anymore. You are."

"Thank you," Reagan whispered. "I still need to apologize to you. I think we both said and did things that night that we wish we could take back. At least, I know I did. You're not like your mother or your stepfather. You have proven that to me so many times, but especially right now. I could never imagine either of them doing this—laying out all of their feelings for another person."

"You're right. That whole bizarre conversation with my mother made me realize something."

"What's that?"

"That I need to hold on to what is special to me. She lost the love of her life when she let others get in the way. I can't let that happen to us and I can't repeat their mistakes. Over the past few weeks, I saw what it might be like without you in my life, and

I was miserable. You opened my eyes to what it truly means to love another person. And yes, that is absolutely terrifying, but you are everything to me, Reagan. You challenge me, support me, and you see me. You make me want to be better for myself and for others." Jill stopped to take a breath. "That night, you told me I wasn't worth it."

"Jill, I'm sor—"

Jill held up a hand. "No, you don't need to apologize for that. You were right. I don't think I was then, and I wasn't as all in as you needed me to be. But I want you to know that I am now. I will prove to you that I am worth it. I didn't know what it would be like to lose you. And now that I know, I never want that to happen again."

"I don't either. You calm me like no one else ever has, which I've desperately needed this past year. I've felt so adrift since I ended things. It was a horrible mistake and I'm sorry for everything." Reagan sniffed and dabbed her eyes and nose with her napkin.

"So, you want to try again?" Jill whispered.

"I do. More than anything."

Jill smiled widely as the tears fell. She squeezed Reagan's hand and brought it to her mouth, placing a soft kiss on her knuckles. The rapid beating of her heart slowed as she stared at the woman in front of her. The grumbling of Jill's stomach pulled her out of the trance she found herself in. She cleared her throat. "Since I got you here under the pretense that you'd be getting food, and I know how important food is to you, did you want to order some lunch?" *Please say no. Please say no.*

Reagan intertwined her fingers with Jill's. "Hell no. I really, really need to kiss you. And while I have no problem kissing you here, it's what will happen afterward that I think will be highly inappropriate for a public place."

"Thank god. Let's get out of here." Jill took a couple twenties out of her pocket and tossed them on the table. Even though they hadn't ordered anything, they had taken up a table close to lunchtime and she didn't want to be rude. *Guess I can learn new things after all.*

They walked outside hand in hand, and Jill steered them to her car parked a couple blocks away. But after a few steps, she pulled Reagan down a side street and gently pressed her back against a brick wall with an arm wrapped around her waist. She mapped Reagan's features with her eyes. Her warm smile, the hint of freckles on the bridge of her nose, and the hazel eyes that held a mixture of emotions. Hope, wariness, passion, and maybe even love. She cupped Reagan's face, caressing her bottom lip with her thumb. She leaned in slowly, savoring the way Reagan's breath hitched as she moved closer.

"Please," Reagan whispered as she reached up and tightly wrapped her fingers around Jill's wrist.

Jill brought her lips to Reagan's, whimpering at the initial contact. She had missed this so much. With Reagan, kissing her felt as important as breathing, something she needed to live.

The kiss was slow and unhurried, as if Jill needed to familiarize herself with the taste and feel of Reagan's lips. She tasted the sweetness of Reagan mixed with the saltiness of tears that had run down both their faces. Her body melted against Reagan because the contact of their lips wasn't enough. She needed more.

Reagan pulled back before she could deepen the kiss, leaning her forehead against Jill's. "Do you need to head back to the office?"

"Nope. Just let me do one thing really quick." She pulled out her phone and sent a text to Ash.

Not coming back to the office. See you tomorrow.

Within seconds, Ash had replied with a GIF of Phoebe and Rachel from *Friends* clapping and jumping. Jill chuckled and showed it to Reagan. "I think they're a little excited for us."

"Clearly. Now take me home. I think we need to get reacquainted properly."

EPILOGUE

Reagan sat in the passenger seat as Jill drove to the soft opening of TMG's fourth restaurant. With a grin, she turned to look in the backseat where her mom was blindfolded. She hoped anyone who pulled up next to them didn't think they were kidnapping someone. Once she and Gwen had agreed on a name for the restaurant, Reagan had kept it a secret from her mom, a task that had proven to be rather difficult over the past couple of months. Reagan had stopped herself several times when updating her mom on the progress of the renovations. But the day was finally here, and she couldn't wait for the big reveal in just a few minutes.

Her mom sighed as they turned a corner and she bumped into the door. "This feels completely unnecessary."

Reagan reached back and squeezed her mom's knee. "I told you, I have a surprise for you. Now hush. We're almost there."

"I know how to keep my eyes closed."

"I'm sure you do, but I know you, and you would never keep them closed like I asked."

"Fair point."

Jill chuckled and shook her head. "You'll love it, Kathy."

"She knows?"

"Of course she does. I had to share it with someone. Plus, it'd be hard to blindfold the driver. Safety hazard and all that."

"You could have shared it with your own mother," she grumbled.

"Nah. That's no fun. You can take it off in a few minutes, so find some patience back there."

Her mom mumbled something under her breath, but Reagan couldn't make out what it was. She looked over at Jill and gave her an exaggerated eye roll to which Jill replied with a quiet laugh.

As Jill parked in front of the restaurant, Reagan took a deep breath and looked at the scene just beyond her window. Carly, Gwen, Brett, and a handful of friends waited outside the restaurant with wide smiles. "Ready, Mom?"

"Please get me out of this car."

"Okay, okay." Reagan squeezed Jill's hand and got out. She opened her mom's door and reached in to grab her hand, helping her out of the car and making sure she didn't trip over the curb. She positioned her mom and stood to the side. "On the count of three, you can take off the blindfold. One, two, three."

With that, her mom took it off and stared up at the big white letters against the brick building that said *Conor's*. She brought her hands to her mouth and gasped. "You named it after him?"

Reagan put her arm around her mom's shoulders. "We did. Do you like it?"

Her mom brought her in for a hug and whispered in her ear, "Thank you."

"I love you, Mom."

"I love you too. He'd be so proud of you."

Reagan nodded against her mom's shoulders, trying to hold back her tears. When her mom let go, she turned to Jill and wrapped her in a tight hug. Reagan watched as her mom whispered in Jill's ear before pulling back with a grin.

"Kathy," Jill exclaimed, swatting her arm before putting her hands behind her back.

Her mom walked off with a wink and went after Gwen next.

"What'd she say?" Reagan asked, narrowing her eyes at the slight blush on Jill's cheeks.

"First, she thanked me for making you so happy," Jill replied.

"Uh-huh. What else?"

Jill pulled a hand from behind her back and dangled the blindfold in front of Reagan. "Then she handed me this and told me to make good use of it."

"Oh my god," Reagan groaned as she buried her face against Jill's shoulder. "Maybe we should have taped her mouth shut too."

Jill chuckled and held Reagan away from her, pushing a lock of hair behind her ear. "I heard your mom. She's right—your dad would be so proud of you. And I am too, Reagan. I know none of this has been easy, but you never shied away from any of it. I consider myself lucky to have been by your side through it all. I love you so much."

"I love you too," Reagan replied, leaning forward for a gentle kiss.

"Now, I believe someone promised me I'd get some food today."

"So bossy," Reagan said as she plucked the blindfold from Jill's hand and put it in her back pocket.

"What are you going to do with that?"

Reagan grinned and whispered in her ear, "Stick around and maybe you'll find out tonight."

Bella Books, Inc.

Women. Books. Even Better Together.

P.O. Box 10543
Tallahassee, FL 32302

Phone: 800-729-4992
www.bellabooks.com